MARY BALOGH

NICOLA CORNICK

COURTNEY MILAN

THE HEART *of* CHRISTMAS

HQN™

Recycling programs
for this product may
not exist in your area.

ISBN-13: 978-0-373-77427-2

THE HEART OF CHRISTMAS

Copyright © 2009 by Harlequin Books S.A.

The publisher acknowledges the copyright holders of the individual works as follows:

A HANDFUL OF GOLD
Copyright © 1998 by Mary Balogh

THE SEASON FOR SUITORS
Copyright © 2005 by Nicola Cornick

THIS WICKED GIFT
Copyright © 2009 by Courtney Milan

This edition published by arrangement with Harlequin Books S.A.

® and TM are trademarks of the publisher. Trademarks indicated with ® are registered in the United States Patent and Trademark Office, the Canadian Trade Marks Office and in other countries.

www.HQNBooks.com

Printed in U.S.A.

CONTENTS

A HANDFUL OF GOLD
Mary Balogh

CHAPTER ONE

THE GENTLEMAN sprawled before the dying fire in the sitting room of his London lodgings was looking somewhat the worse for a night's wear. His gray knee breeches and white stockings were of the finest silk, but the latter were wrinkled and he had long before kicked off his shoes. His long-tailed evening coat, which had molded his frame like a second skin when he had donned it earlier in the evening, had now been discarded and tossed carelessly onto another chair.

His finely embroidered waistcoat was unbuttoned. His neck cloth, on the arrangement of which his valet had spent longer than half an hour of loving artistry, had been pulled open and hung unsymmetrically against his left shoulder. His dark hair, expertly cut to look fashionably disheveled, now looked unfashionably untidy from having had his fingers pass through it one too many times. His eyes were half-closed—and somewhat bloodshot. An empty glass dangled from one hand over the arm of the chair.

Julian Dare, Viscount Folingsby, was indisputably foxed.

He was also scowling. Drinking to excess was not among his usual vices. Gaming was. So was womanizing. And so was reckless living. But not drinking. He had always been careful to exclude from habit anything that might prove to also be addictive. He had every intention of one day "settling down," as his father phrased it, of being done with his "wild oats," another of the Earl of Grantham's clichés. It would be just too inconvenient to have to deal with an addiction when the time came. Gambling was not an addiction with him. Neither were women. Though he was exceedingly fond of both.

He yawned and wondered what time it was. Daylight had not yet dawned, a small comfort when this was December and daylight did not deign to show itself until well on into the morning. Certainly it was well past midnight. *Well* past. He had left his sister's soirée before midnight, but since then he had been to White's club and to one or two—was it one or two?—card parties at which the play had been deep and the drinking deeper.

He should get himself up from his chair and go to bed, but he did not have the energy. He should ring for his valet, then, and have the man drag him off to bed. But he did not have even the energy to get up and ring the bell. Doubtless he would not sleep anyway. He knew from experience that when he was three sheets to the wind, an approximately vertical position was preferable to a horizontal one.

Why the devil had he drunk so deep?

But drunkenness had not brought oblivion. He remembered very well why. That heiress. Miss Plunkett. No, *Lady* Sarah Plunkett. What a name! And unfortunately the chit had the face and disposition to match it. She was going to be at Conway for Christmas with her mama and papa. Emma, his youngest sister, had mentioned the fact in the letter that had reached him this morning—no, yesterday morning. He had put two and two together without further ado and had come up with the inevitable total of four. But he had not needed to use any arithmetical or deductive skills.

His father's letter, which he had read next, had been far more explicit. Not only were the Plunkett chit and the Plunkett parents to join their family gathering for Christmas, but also Julian would oblige his father by paying court to the girl and fixing his interest with her. He was nine-and-twenty years old, after all, and had shown no sign of choosing anyone for himself. His father had been extremely patient with him. But it was high time he finished with his wild oats and settled down. As the only son among five sisters, three of them still unmarried and therefore still unsettled, it was his duty....

Viscount Folingsby passed the fingers of his free hand through his hair again, unconsciously restoring it almost to simple dishevelment, and eyed the brandy decanter a short distance away. An impossible distance away.

He was not going to do it—marry the girl, that was.

It was as simple as that. No one could make him, not even his stern but annoyingly affectionate father. Not even his fond mama and doting sisters. He grimaced. Why had he been blessed with a singularly close and loving family? And why had his mother produced nothing but daughters after the initial triumph of his birth as heir to an earldom and vast properties and fortune—almost every last half penny of which was entailed and would pass to a rather distant cousin if he failed to produce at least one heir of his own?

His lordship eyed the brandy decanter again with some determination, but he could not somehow force resolution downward far enough to set his legs in motion.

There had been another letter in the morning's post. From Bertie. Bertrand Hollander had been his close friend and coconspirator all through school and university. They were still close even though Bertie spent most of his time now overseeing his estates in the north of England. But Bertie had a hunting box in Norfolkshire and a mistress in Yorkshire and intended to introduce the two to each other over Christmas. He was avoiding his own family with the excuse that he was going to go shooting with friends over the holiday. He intended instead to spend a week with his Debbie away from prying eyes and the need for propriety. He wanted Julian to join him there with his own mistress.

Julian did not currently have a resident mistress. He had dismissed the last one several months before on the grounds that evenings spent in her company had become even more predictable and every bit as tedious as evenings spent at the insipid weekly balls at Almack's. Since then he had had a mutually satisfactory arrangement with a widow of his acquaintance. But she was a respectable woman of good ton, hardly the sort he might invite to spend a cozy week of sin in Norfolkshire with Bertie and his Debbie.

Damn! He was more foxed than he knew, Julian thought suddenly. He had gone somewhere tonight even before attending Elinor's soirée. He had gone to the opera. Not that he was particularly fond of music—not opera at least. He had gone to see the subject of the newest male gossip at White's. There was a new dancer of considerable charms, so it was said. But in the few weeks since she had made her first onstage appearance, she had not also made her first appearance in any of the beds of those who had attempted to entice her there. She was either waiting for the highest bidder or she was waiting for someone she fancied or she was a virtuous woman.

Julian, his father's summons and Bertie's invitation fresh in his mind, had gone to the opera to see what the fuss was all about.

The fuss was all about long, shapely legs, a slender, lithe body and long titian hair. Not red, nothing so vulgar. Titian. And emerald eyes. Not that he had been able to see their color from the box he had occupied during the performance. But he had seen it through his quizzing glass as he had stood in the doorway of the greenroom afterward.

Miss Blanche Heyward had been surrounded by a court of appropriately languishing admirers. His lordship had looked her over unhurriedly through his glass and inclined his head to her when her eyes had met his across the room. And then he had joined the even larger crowd of gentlemen gathered about Hannah Dove, the singer who sang like her name, or so one of her court had assured her. For which piece of gross flattery he had been rewarded with a gracious smile and a hand to kiss.

Julian had left the greenroom after a few minutes and taken himself off to his married sister's drawing room.

It might be interesting to try his own hand at assaulting the citadel of dubious virtue that was Blanche Heyward. It might be even more interesting to carry her off to Bertie's for Christmas and a weeklong hot affair. If he went to Conway, all he would have was the usual crowded, noisy, enjoyable Christmas, and the Plunkett chit. If he went to Norfolkshire…

Well, the mind boggled.

What he *could* do, he decided, was make her decision his, too. He would ask her. If she said yes, then he would go to Norfolkshire. For a final fling. As a swan song to freedom and wild oats and all the rest of it. In the spring, when the season brought the fashionable world to town, the Plunkett girl among them, he would do his duty. He would have her big with child by *next* Christmas. The very thought had him holding his aching head with the hand that had been holding his glass a minute before. What the devil had he done with it? Dropped it? Had there been any brandy left in it? Couldn't have been or he would have drunk it instead of sitting here conspiring how he might reach the decanter, on legs that refused to obey his brain.

If she said no—Blanche, that was, not the heiress— then he would go down to Conway and embrace his fate. That way he would probably have a child *in the nursery* by next Christmas.

Julian lowered his hand from his head to his throat with the intention of loosening his neck cloth. But someone had already done it for him.

Dammit, but she was gorgeous. Not the heiress. Who the devil was gorgeous, then? Someone he had met at Elinor's?

There was a quiet scratching at the sitting room door, and it opened to reveal the cautious, respectful face of his lordship's valet.

"About time," Julian told him. "Someone took all the bones out of my legs when I was not looking. Deuced inconvenient."

"Yes, my lord," his man said, coming purposefully toward him. "You will be wishing someone took them from your head before many more hours have passed. Come along then, sir. Put your arm about my neck."

"Deuced impertinence," his lordship muttered. "Remind me to dismiss you when I am sober."

"Yes, my lord," the valet said cheerfully.

SEVERAL HOURS before Viscount Folingsby found himself sprawled before the fire in his sitting room with boneless legs and aching head, Miss Verity Ewing let herself into a darkened house on an unfashionable street in London, using her latchkey and a considerable amount of stealth. She had no wish to waken anyone. She would tiptoe upstairs without lighting a candle, she decided, careful to avoid the eighth stair, which creaked. She would undress in the darkness and hope not to disturb Chastity. Her sister was, unfortunately, a light sleeper.

But luck was against her. Before she could so much as set foot on the bottom stair, the door to the downstairs living room opened and a shaft of candlelight beamed out into the hall.

"Verity?"

"Yes, Mama." Verity sighed inwardly even as she put a cheerful smile on her face. "You ought not to have waited up."

"I could not sleep," her mother told her as Verity followed her into the sitting room. She set down the candle and pulled her shawl more closely about her shoulders. There was no fire burning in the hearth. "You know I worry until you come home."

"Lady Coleman was invited to a late supper after the opera," Verity explained, "and wanted me to accompany her."

"It was very inconsiderate of her, I am sure," Mrs. Ewing said rather plaintively. "It is thoughtless to keep a gentleman's daughter out late almost every night of the week and send her home in a hackney cab instead of in her ladyship's own carriage."

"It is kind of her even to hire the hackney," Verity said. "But it is chilly and you are cold." She did not need to ask why there was no fire. A fire after ten o'clock at night was an impossible extravagance in their household. "Let us go up to bed. How was Chastity this evening?"

"She did not cough above three or four times all evening," Mrs. Ewing said. "And not once did she have a prolonged bout. The new medicine seems really to be working."

"I hoped it would." Verity smiled and picked up the candle. "Come, Mama."

But she could not entirely avoid the usual questions about the opera, what Lady Coleman had worn, who else had made up their party, who had invited them for supper, what they had eaten, what topics of conversation had been pursued. Verity answered as briefly as she could, though she did, for her mother's sake, give a detailed description of the costly and fashionable gown her employer had worn.

"All I can say," Mrs. Ewing said in a hushed voice as they stood outside the door of her bedchamber, "is that Lady Coleman is a strange sort of lady, Verity. Most ladies hire companions to live in and run and fetch for them during the day when time hangs heavy on their hands. They do not allow them to live at home, and they do not require their services mostly during the evenings when they go out into society."

"How fortunate I am to have discovered such a lady, then," Verity said, "and to have won her approval. I could not bear to have to live in and see you and Chastity only on half days off. Lady Coleman is a widow, Mama, and needs company for respectability when she goes out. I could scarcely ask for more pleasant employment. It pays reasonably well, too, and will get better. Only this evening Lady Coleman declared that she is pleased with me and is considering raising my salary quite substantially."

But her mother did not look as pleased as Verity had hoped. She shook her head as she took the candle. "Ah, my love," she said, "I never thought to see the day when a daughter of mine would have to seek employment. The Reverend Ewing, your papa, left us little, it is true, but we might have scraped by quite comfortably if it had not been for Chastity's illness. And if General Sir Hector Ewing were not unfortunately in Vienna for the peace talks, he would have helped us, I am certain. You and Chastity are his own brother's children, after all."

"Pray do not vex yourself, Mama." Verity kissed her mother's cheek. "We are together, the three of us, and Chastity is recovering her health after seeing a reputable physician and being prescribed the right medicine. Really, those are the only things that matter. Good night."

A minute later she had reached her own room and

had entered it and closed the door. She stood for a moment against it, her eyes closed, her hands gripping the knob behind her back. But there was no sound apart from quiet, even breathing from her sister's bed. Verity undressed quickly and quietly, shivering in the frigid cold. After she had climbed into bed, she lay on her side, her knees drawn up, and pulled the covers up over her ears. Her teeth were chattering, though not just with the cold.

It was a dangerous game she played.

Except that it was no game.

How soon would it be, she wondered, before Mama discovered that there was no Lady Coleman, that there was no genteel and easy employment? Fortunately they had moved to London from the country so recently and under such straitened circumstances that they had few friends and none at all who moved in fashionable circles. They had moved because Chastity's chill, contracted last winter not long after their father's death, had stubbornly refused to go away. It had become painfully clear to them that they might well lose her if they did not consult a physician more knowledgeable than the local doctor. They had feared she had consumption, but the London physician had said no, that she merely had a weak chest and might hope to recover her full health with the correct medicines and diet.

But his fees and the medicines had been exorbitantly expensive and the need for his services was not yet at an end. The rent of even so unfashionable a house as theirs was high. And the bills for coal, candles, food and other sundries seemed always to be piling in.

Verity had searched and searched for genteel employment, assuring her mother that it would be only temporary, until her uncle returned to England and was apprised of their plight. Verity placed little faith in the wealthy uncle who had had nothing to do with them during her father's life. Her grandfather had held aloof from his youngest son after the latter had refused an advantageous match and had married instead Verity's mother, the daughter of a gentleman of no particular fortune or consequence.

In Verity's opinion, the care of her mother and sister fell squarely on her own shoulders and always would. And so when she had been unable to find employment as a governess or companion or even as a shop assistant or seamstress or housemaid, she had taken up the unlikely offer of an audition as an opera dancer. She was quite fit, after all, and she had always adored dancing, both in a ballroom and in the privacy of a shrubbery or empty room at the rectory. To her intense surprise she had been offered the job.

Performing on a public stage in any capacity—as an actress, singer or dancer—was not genteel employment for a lady. Indeed, Verity had been well aware even before accepting the employment that, in the popular mind, dancers and actresses were synonymous with whores.

But what choice had she?

And so had begun her double life, her secret life. By day, except when she was at rehearsals, she was Verity Ewing, impoverished daughter of a gently born clergyman, niece of the influential General Sir Hector Ewing. By night she was Blanche Heyward, opera dancer, someone who was ogled by half the fashionable gentlemen in town, many of whom attended the opera for no other purpose.

But it was a dangerous game. At any time she might be recognized by someone she knew, though no one from her neighborhood in the country was in the habit of staying in London and sampling its entertainments. More important, perhaps, she was making it impossible to mingle with polite society in the future if the general should ever decide to help them. But she did not anticipate that particular problem.

There were more immediate problems to deal with.

But what she earned as a dancer was just not enough.

Verity huddled deeper beneath the bedcovers and set her hands between her thighs for greater warmth.

"Verity?" a sleepy voice asked.

Verity pushed back the covers from her face again. "Yes, love," she said softly, "I am home."

"I must have fallen asleep," Chastity said. "I always worry so until you are home. I *wish* you did not have to go out alone at night."

"But if I did not," Verity said, "I would not be able to tell you about all the splendid parties and theater performances I attend. I shall describe the opera to you in the morning or, more to the point, the people who were in the audience. Go back to sleep now." She kept her voice warm and cheerful.

"Verity," Chastity said, "you must not think that I am not grateful, that I do not know the sacrifice you are making for my sake. One day I will make it all up to you. I *promise*."

Verity blinked back tears from her eyes. "Oh yes, you will, love," she said. "In the springtime you are going to dance among the primroses and daffodils, unseasonable roses in your cheeks. Then you will have repaid me double—no, ten times over—for the little I am able to do now. Go to sleep, you goose."

"Good night." Chastity yawned hugely and only a minute or two later was breathing deeply and evenly again.

There was one way in which a dancer might augment her income. Indeed she was almost expected to do so. Verity hid her head beneath the covers once more and tried not to develop the thought. But it had been nagging at her for a week or more. And she had said those words to Mama earlier, almost as if she were preparing the way. *Lady Coleman declared that she is pleased with me and is considering raising my salary quite substantially.*

She had acquired quite a regular court of admirers in the greenroom following each performance. Two of the gentlemen had already made blatant offers to her. One had mentioned a sum that she had found quite dizzying. She had told herself repeatedly that she was not even tempted. Nor was she. But it was not a matter of temptation. It was a matter for cold decision.

The only possible reason she would do such a thing was her mother's and Chastity's security. A great deal more money was going to have to be found if Chass was to continue to have the treatment she needed. It was a matter of her virtue in exchange for Chastity's life, then.

Phrased that way, there was really no decision to make.

And then she thought of the advent of temptation that had presented itself to her just that evening in the form of the gentleman who had stood in the doorway of the greenroom, looking at her insolently through his quizzing glass for a minute or so before joining the crowd of gentlemen gathered about Hannah Dove. His actions had suggested that he was not after all interested in her, Verity—or rather in Blanche—and yet she had been left with the strange notion that he had watched her all the time he was in the greenroom.

He was Viscount Folingsby, a notorious rake, another dancer had told her later. Verity would likely have guessed it anyway. Apart from being almost incredibly handsome—tall, well formed, very dark, with eyes that were both penetrating and slumberous—there was an air of self-assurance and arrogance about him that proclaimed him to be a man accustomed to having his own way. There was also something almost unbearably sensual about him. A rake, yes. Without a doubt.

Yet she had been horribly tempted for that minute. If he had approached her, if he had made her an offer...

Thank heaven he had not done either.

But soon, *very* soon, she was going to have to consider and accept someone's offer. There! Finally she was calling a spade a spade. She was going to have to become someone's mistress. No, that was calling a spade a utensil. She was going to have to become someone's *whore*.

For a dizzying minute the room spun about her, closed eyes notwithstanding.

For Chastity, she told herself determinedly. For Chastity's life.

CHAPTER TWO

JULIAN VISITED the greenroom at the opera house two evenings after his previous appearance there. There were a few men talking with Blanche Heyward. Hannah Dove was invisible amidst her court of admirers. His lordship joined them and chatted amiably for a while. It was not part of his plan to appear overeager. Several minutes passed before he strolled over to make his bow to the titian-haired dancer.

"Miss Heyward," he said languidly, holding her eyes with his own, "your servant. May I commend you on your performance this evening?"

"Thank you, my lord." Her voice was low, melodic. Seductive, and deliberately schooled to sound that way, he guessed. Her eyes looked candidly—and shrewdly?—back into his. He did not for a moment believe she was a virtuous woman. Or that what little virtue she had was not for hire.

"I have just been commending Miss Heyward on her talent and grace, Folingsby," Netherford said. "Damme, but if she were in a ballroom, she would put every other lady to shame. No gentleman would wish to dance with anyone but her, eh? Eh?" He dug one elbow into his lordship's ribs.

There were appreciative titters from the other gentlemen gathered about her.

"Dear me," his lordship murmured. "I wonder if Miss Heyward would wish to court such—ah, fame."

"Or such notoriety," she said with a fleeting smile.

"Damme," Netherford continued, "but one would love to watch you waltz, Miss Heyward. Trouble is, every other man present would want to stand and watch, too, and there would be no one to dance with all the other chits." There was a general gust of laughter at his words.

Julian raised his quizzing glass to his eye and caught a suggestion of scorn in the dancer's smile.

"Thank you, sir," she said. "You are flatteringly kind. But I am weary, gentlemen. It has been a long evening."

And thus bluntly she dismissed her court. They went meekly, after making their bows and bidding her good-night—three of them out the door, one to join the crowd still clustered about Hannah Dove. Julian remained.

Blanche Heyward looked up at him inquiringly. "My lord?" she said, a suggestion of a challenge in her voice.

"Sometimes I find," he said, dropping his glass and clasping his hands at his back, "that weariness can be treated as effectively with a quiet and leisurely meal as with sleep. Would you care to join me for supper?"

She opened her mouth to refuse—he read the intent in her expression—hesitated, and closed her mouth again.

"For supper, my lord?" She raised her eyebrows.

"I have reserved a private parlor in a tavern not far from here," he told her. "I would as soon have company as eat alone." And yet, he told her with his nonchalant expression and the language of his body, he would almost as soon eat alone. It mattered little to him whether she accepted or not.

She broke eye contact with him and looked down at her hands. She was clearly working up a refusal again. Equally clearly she was tempted. Or—and he rather suspected that this was the true interpretation of her behavior—she was as practiced as he in sending the message she wished to send. A reluctance and a certain indifference, in this case. But a fixed intention, nevertheless, of accepting in the end. He made it easier for her, or rather he took the game back into his own hands.

"Miss Heyward." He leaned slightly toward her and lowered his voice. "I am inviting you to supper, not to bed."

Her eyes snapped back to his and he read in them the startled knowledge that she had been bested. She half smiled.

"Thank you, my lord," she said. "I *am* rather hungry. Will you wait while I fetch my cloak?"

He gave a slight inclination of his head, and she stood up. He was surprised by her height now that he was standing close to her. He was a tall man and dwarfed most women. She was scarcely more than half a head shorter than he.

Well, he thought with satisfaction, the first move had been made and he had emerged the winner. She had agreed only to supper, it was true, but if he could not turn that minor triumph into a week of pleasure in Norfolkshire, then he deserved the fate awaiting him at Conway in the form of the ferret-faced Lady Sarah Plunkett.

He did not expect to lose the game.

And he did not believe, moreover, that she intended he should.

It was a square, spacious room with timbered ceiling and large fireplace, in which a cheerful fire crackled. In the center of the room was one table set for two, with fine china and crystal laid out on a crisply starched white cloth. Two long candles burned in pewter holders.

Viscount Folingsby must have been confident, Verity concluded, that she would say yes. He took her cloak in silence. Without looking at him, she crossed the room to the fire and held out her hands to the blaze. She felt more nervous than she had ever felt before, she believed, even counting her audition and her first onstage performance. Or perhaps it was a different kind of nervousness.

"It is a cold night," he said.

"Yes." Not that there had been much chance to notice the chill. A sumptuous private carriage had brought them the short distance from the theater. They had not spoken during the journey.

She did not believe it was an invitation just to supper.

But she still did not know what her answer would be to the inevitable question. Perhaps it was understood in the demimonde that when one accepted such an invitation as this, one was committing oneself to giving thanks in the obvious way.

Could it possibly be that before this night was over she would have taken the irrevocable step? What would it *feel* like? she wondered suddenly. And how would she feel in the morning?

"Green suits you," Lord Folingsby said, and Verity despised the way she jerked with alarm to find that he was close behind her. "Not all women have the wisdom and taste to choose clothes that suit their coloring."

She was wearing her dark green silk, which she had always liked though it was woefully outmoded and almost shabby. But its simple high-waisted, straight-sleeved design gave it a sort of timeless elegance that did not date itself as quickly as more fussy, more modish styles.

"Thank you," she said.

"I fancy," he said, "that some artist must once have mixed his paints with care and used a fine brush in order to produce the particular color of your eyes. It is unusual, if not unique."

She smiled into the dancing flames. Men were always lavish in their compliments on her eyes, though no one had ever said it quite like this before.

"I have some Irish blood in me, my lord," she said.

"Ah. The Emerald Isle," he said softly. "Land of red-haired, fiery-tempered beauties. Do you have a fiery temper, Miss Heyward?"

"I also have a great deal of English blood," she told him.

"Ah, we mundane and phlegmatic English." He sighed. "You disappoint me. Come to the table."

"You like hot-tempered women, then, my lord?" she asked him as he seated her and took his place opposite.

"That depends entirely on the woman," he said. "If I believe there is pleasure to be derived from the taming of her, yes, indeed." He picked up the bottle of wine that stood on the table, uncorked it and proceeded to fill her glass and then his own.

While he was so occupied, Verity looked fully at him for the first time since they had left the theater. He was almost frighteningly handsome, though why there should be anything fearsome about good looks she would have found difficult to explain. Perhaps it was his confidence, his arrogance more than his looks that had her wishing she could go back to the greenroom and change her answer. They seemed very much alone together, though two waiters were bringing food and setting it silently on the table. Or perhaps it was his sensual appeal and the certain knowledge that he wanted her.

He held his glass aloft and extended his hand half-way across the table. "To new acquaintances," he said, looking very directly into her eyes in the flickering light of the candles. "May they prosper."

She smiled, touched the rim of her glass to his and drank. Her hand was steady, she was relieved to find, but she felt almost as if a decision had been made, a pact sealed.

"Shall we eat?" he suggested after the waiters had withdrawn and closed the door behind them. He indicated the plates of cold meats and steaming vegetables, the basket of fresh breads, the bowl of fruit.

She was hungry, she realized suddenly, but she was not at all sure she would be able to eat. She helped herself to a modest portion.

"Tell me, Miss Heyward," the viscount said, watching her butter a bread roll, "are you always this talkative?"

She paused and looked unwillingly up at him again. She was adept at making social conversation, as were most ladies of her class. But she had no idea what topics were suited to an occasion of this nature. She had never before dined tête-à-tête with a man, or been alone with one under any circumstances for longer than half an hour at a time or beyond a place where she could be easily observed by a chaperone.

"What do you wish me to talk about, my lord?" she asked him.

He regarded her for a few moments, a look of amusement on his face. "Bonnets?" he said. "Jewels? The latest shopping expedition?"

He did not, then, have a high regard for women's intelligence. Or perhaps it was just her type of woman. *Her type.*

"But what do *you* wish to talk about, my lord?" she asked him, taking a bite out of her roll.

He looked even more amused. "You," he said without hesitation. "Tell me about yourself, Miss Heyward. Begin with your accent. I cannot quite place its origin. Where are you from?"

She had not done at all well with the accent she had assumed during her working hours, except perhaps to disguise the fact that she had been gently born and raised.

"I pick up accents very easily," she lied. "And I have lived in many different places. I suppose there is a trace of all those places in my speech."

"And someone," he said, "to complicate the issue, has given you elocution lessons."

"Of course." She smiled. "Even as a dancer one must learn not to murder the English language with every word one speaks, my lord. If one expects to advance in one's career, that is."

He gazed silently at her for a few moments, his fork suspended halfway to his mouth. Verity felt herself flushing. What career was he imagining she wished to advance?

"Quite so," he said softly, his voice like velvet. He carried his fork the rest of the way to his mouth. "But what are some of these places? Tell me where you have lived. Tell me about your family. Come, we cannot munch on our food in silence, you know. There is nothing better designed to shake a person's composure."

Her life seemed to have become nothing but lies. In each of her worlds she had to withhold the truth about the other. And withholding the truth sometimes became more than a passive thing. It involved the invention of lie upon lie. She had some knowledge of two places—the village in Somersetshire where she had lived for two-and-twenty years, and London, where she had lived for two months. But she spoke of Ireland, drawing on the stories she could remember her maternal grandmother telling her when she was a child, and more riskily, of the city of York, where a neighborhood friend had lived with his uncle for a while, and about a few other places of which she had read.

She hoped fervently that the viscount had no intimate knowledge of any of the places she chose to describe. She invented a mythical family—a father who was a blacksmith, a warmhearted mother who had died five years before, three brothers and three sisters, all considerably younger than herself.

"You came to London to seek your fortune?" he asked. "You have not danced anywhere else?"

She hesitated. But she did not want him to think her inexperienced, easy to manipulate. "Oh, of course," she said. "For several years, my lord." She smiled into his eyes as she reached for a pear from the dish of fruit. "But all roads lead eventually to London, you know."

She was startled by the look of naked desire that flared in his eyes for a moment as he followed the movement of her hand. But it was soon veiled behind his lazy eyelids and slightly mocking smile.

"Of course," he said softly. "And those of us who spend most of our time here are only too delighted to benefit from the experience in the various arts such persons as yourself have acquired elsewhere."

Verity kept her eyes on the pear she was peeling. It was unusually juicy, she was dismayed to find. Her hands were soon wet with juice. And her heart was thumping. Suddenly, and quite inexplicably, she felt as if she had waded into deep waters indeed. The air fairly bristled between them. She licked her lips and could think of no reply to make.

His voice sounded amused when he spoke again. "Having peeled it, Miss Heyward," he said, "you are now obliged to eat it, you know. It would be a crime to waste good food."

She lifted one half of the pear to her mouth and bit into it. Juice cascaded to her plate below, and some of it trickled down her chin. She reached for her napkin in some embarrassment, knowing that he was watching her. But before she could pick it up, he had reached across the table and one long finger had scooped up the droplet of juice that was about to drip onto her gown. She raised her eyes, startled, to watch him carry the finger to his mouth and touch it to his tongue. His eyes remained on her all the while.

Verity felt a sharp stabbing of sensation down through her abdomen and between her thighs. She felt a rush of color to her cheeks. She felt as if she had been running for a mile uphill.

"Sweet," he murmured.

She jumped to her feet, pushing at her chair with the backs of her knees. Then she wished she had not done so. Her legs felt decidedly unsteady. She crossed to the fireplace again and reached out her hands as if to warm them, though she felt as if the fire might better be able to take warmth from her.

She drew a few steadying breaths in the silence that followed. And then she could see from the corner of one eye that he had come to stand at the other side of the hearth. He rested one arm along the high mantel. He was watching her. The time had come, she thought. She had precipitated it herself. Within moments the question would be asked and must be answered. She still did not know what that answer would be, or perhaps she did. Perhaps she was just fooling herself to believe that there was still a choice. She had made her decision back in the greenroom—no, even before that. This was a tavern, part of an inn. No doubt he had bespoken a bedchamber here, as well as a private dining room. Within minutes, then…

How would it feel? She did not even know exactly what she was to expect. The basic facts, of course…

"Miss Heyward," he asked her, making her jump again, "what are your plans for Christmas?"

She turned her head to look at him. Christmas? It was a week and a half away. She would spend it with her family, of course. It would be their first Christmas away from home, their first without the friends and neighbors

they had known all their lives. But at least they still had
one another and were still together. They had decided
that they would indulge in the extravagance of a goose
and make something special of the day with inexpensive
gifts that they would make for one another. Christmas
had always been Verity's favorite time of the year.
Somehow it restored hope and reminded her of the truly
important things in life—family and love and selfless
giving.

Selfless giving.

"Do you have any plans?" he asked.

She could hardly claim to be going home to that large
family at the smithy in Somersetshire. She shook her
head.

"I will be spending a quiet week in Norfolkshire
with a friend and his, ah, lady," he said. "Will you
come with me?"

A quiet week. A friend and his lady. She understood,
of course, exactly what he meant, exactly to what she
was being invited. If she agreed now, Verity thought, the
die would be cast. She would have stepped irrevocably
into that world from which it would be impossible to
return. Once a fallen woman, she would never be able
to retrieve either her virtue or her honor.

If she agreed?

She would be away from home at Christmas of all
times. Away from Mama and Chastity. For a whole
week. Could anything be worth such a sacrifice, not to
mention the sacrifice of her very self?

It was as if he read her mind. "Five hundred pounds, Miss Heyward," he said softly. "For one week."

Five hundred pounds? Her mouth went dry. It was a colossal sum. Did he know what five hundred pounds meant to someone like her? But of course he knew. It meant irresistible temptation.

In exchange for one week of service. Seven nights. Seven, when even the thought of one was insupportable. But once the first had been endured, the other six would hardly matter.

Chastity needed to see the physician again. She needed more medicine. If she were to die merely because they could not afford the proper treatment for her illness, how would she feel, Verity asked herself, when it had been within her power to see to it that they *could* afford the treatment? What had she just been telling herself about Christmas?

Selfless giving.

She smiled into the fire. "That would be very pleasant, my lord," she said, and then listened in some astonishment to the other words that came unplanned from her mouth, "provided you pay me in advance."

She turned her head to look at him when he did not immediately reply. His elbow was still on the mantel, his closed fist resting against his mouth. Above it his eyes showed amusement.

"We will, of course, agree to a compromise," he told her. "Half before we leave and half after we return?"

She nodded. Two hundred and fifty pounds before

she even left London. Once she had accepted the
payment, she would have backed herself into a corner.
She could not then refuse to carry out her part of the
agreement. She tried to swallow, but the dryness of her
mouth made it well nigh impossible to do.

"Splendid," he said briskly. "Come, it is late. I will
escort you home."

She was to escape for tonight, then? Part of her felt
a knee-weakening relief. Part of her was strangely disappointed. The worst of it might have been over within
the hour if, as she had expected, he had reserved a room
and had invited her there. She felt a deep dread of the
first time. She imagined, perhaps naively, that after that,
once it was an accomplished fact, once she was a fallen
woman, once she knew how it felt, it would be easier
to repeat. But now it seemed that she would have to wait
until they left for Norfolkshire before the deed was
done.

He had fetched her cloak and was setting it about her
shoulders. She came to attention suddenly, realizing
what he had just said.

"Thank you, no, my lord," she said. "I shall see
myself home. Perhaps you would be so kind as to call
a hackney cab?"

He turned her and his hands brushed her own aside
and did up her cloak buttons for her. He looked up into
her eyes, the task completed. "Playing the elusive game
until the end, Miss Heyward?" he asked. "Or is there
someone at home you would rather did not see me?"

His implication was obvious. But he was, of course, right though not in quite the way he meant. She smiled back at him.

"I have promised you a week, my lord," she said. "That week does not begin with tonight, as I understand it?"

"Quite right," he said. "You shall have your hackney, then, and keep your secrets. I do believe Christmas is going to be more…interesting than usual."

"I trust you may be right, my lord," she said with all the coolness she could muster, preceding him to the door.

CHAPTER THREE

JULIAN WAS FEELING weary, cold and irritable by the time Bertrand Hollander's hunting box hove into view at dusk on a particularly gray and cheerless afternoon, two days before Christmas. He would feel far more cheerful, he told himself, once he was indoors, basking before a blazing fire, imbibing some of Bertie's brandy and contemplating the delights of the night ahead. But at the moment he could not quite convince himself that this Christmas was going to be one of unalloyed pleasure.

He had ridden all the way from London despite the fact that his comfortable, well-sprung traveling carriage held only one passenger. During the morning, he had thought it a clever idea—she would be intrigued to watch him ride just within sight beyond the carriage windows; he would comfort himself with the anticipation of joining her within during the afternoon. But during the noon stop for dinner and a change of horses, Miss Blanche Heyward had upset him quite considerably. No, that was refining too much on a trifle. She had *annoyed* him quite considerably.

And all over a mere bauble, a paltry handful of gold.

He had been planning to give it to her for Christmas. A gift was perhaps unnecessary since she was being paid handsomely enough for her services. But Christmas had always been a time of gift giving with him, and he knew he was going to miss Conway and all its usual warm celebrations. And so he had bought her a gift, spending far more time in the choosing of it than he usually did for his mistresses and instinctively avoiding the gaudy flash of precious stones.

On impulse he had decided to give it to her in the rather charming setting of the inn parlor in which they dined on their journey, rather than wait for Christmas Day. But she had merely looked at the box in his out-stretched hand and had made no move to grab it.

"What is it?" she had asked with the quiet dignity he was beginning to recognize as characteristic of her.

"Why do you not look and see?" he had suggested. "It is an early Christmas gift."

"There is no need of it." She had looked into his eyes. "You are paying me well, my lord, for what I will give in return."

Her words had sent an uncomfortable rush of tightness to his groin, though he was not at all sure she had intended them so. He had also felt the first stirring of annoyance. Was she going to keep him with his hand outstretched, feeling foolish, until his dinner grew cold? But she had reached out a hand slowly, taken the box and opened it. He had watched her almost anxiously.

Had he made a mistake in not choosing diamonds or rubies, or emeralds, perhaps?

She had looked down for a long time, saying nothing, making no move to touch the contents of the box.

"It is the Star of Bethlehem," she had said finally.

It was a star, yes, a gold star on a gold chain. He had not thought of it as the Christmas star. But the description seemed apt enough.

"Yes," he had agreed. He had despised himself for his next words, but they had been out before he could stop them. "Do you like it?"

"It belongs in the heavens," she had said after a lengthy pause during which she had gazed at the pendant and appeared as if she had forgotten about both him and her surroundings. "As a symbol of hope. As a sign to all who are in search of the meaning of their lives. As a goal in the pursuit of wisdom."

Good Lord! He had been rendered speechless.

She had looked up then and regarded him very directly with those magnificent emerald eyes. "Money ought not to be able to buy it, my lord," she had said. "It is not appropriate as a gift from such as you to such as I."

He had gazed back, one eyebrow raised, containing his fury. *Such as he?* What the devil was she implying?

"Do I understand, Miss Heyward," he had asked, injecting as much boredom into his voice as he could summon, "that you do not like the gift? Dear me, I ought to have had my man pick up a diamond bracelet instead. I shall inform him that you agree with my opinion that he has execrable taste."

She had looked into his eyes for several moments longer, no discernible anger there at his insult.

"I am sorry," she had surprised him by saying then. "I have hurt you. It is very beautiful, my lord, and shows that you have impeccable taste. Thank you." She had closed the box and placed it in her reticule.

They had continued with their meal in silence, and suddenly, he had discovered, he was eating straw, not food.

He had mounted his horse when they resumed their journey and left her to her righteous solitude in his carriage. And for the rest of the journey he had nursed his irritation with her. What the devil did she mean *it is not appropriate as a gift from such as you?* How dared she! And why was it inappropriate, even assuming that the gold star was intended to be the Star of Bethlehem? The star was a symbol of hope, she had said, a sign to those who pursued wisdom and the meaning of their own lives.

What utter balderdash!

Those three wise men of the Christmas story—*if* they had existed, and *if* they had been wise, and *if* there had really been three of them—had they gone lurching off across the desert on their camels, clutching their offerings, in hopeful pursuit of wisdom and meaning? More likely they had been escaping overly affectionate relatives who were attempting to marry them off to the biblical-era equivalent of the Plunkett chit. Or hoping to find something that would gratify their jaded senses.

They must all have been despicably rich, after all, to be able to head off on a mad journey without fear of running out of money. It was purely by chance that they had discovered something worth more than gold, or those other two commodities they had had with them. What the deuce were frankincense and myrrh anyway?

Well, he was no wise man even though he had set out on his journey with his pathetic handful of gold. And even though he was hoping to find gratification of his senses at the end of the journey. That was all he *did* want—a few congenial days with Bertie, and a few energetic nights in bed with Blanche. To hell with hope and wisdom and meaning. He knew where his life was headed after this week. He was going to marry Lady Sarah Plunkett and have babies with her until his nursery was furnished with an heir and a spare, to use the old cliché. And he was going to live respectably ever after.

It was going to snow, he thought, glancing up at the heavy clouds. They were going to have a white Christmas. The prospect brought with it none of the elation he would normally feel. At Conway there would be children of all ages from two to eighty gazing at the sky and making their plans for toboggan rides and snowball fights and snowman-building contests and skating parties. He felt an unwelcome wave of nostalgia.

But they had arrived at Bertie's hunting box, which

looked more like a small manor than the modest lodge Julian had been expecting. There were the welcome signs of candlelight from within and of smoke curling up from the chimneys. He swung down from his horse, wincing at the stiffness in his limbs, and waved aside the footman who would have opened the carriage door and set down the steps. His lordship did it himself and reached up a hand to help down his mistress.

And that was another thing, he thought as she placed a gloved hand in his and stepped out of the carriage. She was not looking at all like the bird of paradise he had pictured himself bringing into the country. She was dressed demurely in a gray wool dress with a long gray cloak, black gloves and black half boots. Her hair—all those glorious titian tresses—had been swept back ruthlessly from her face and was almost invisible beneath a plain and serviceable bonnet. There was not a trace of cosmetics on her face, which admittedly was quite lovely enough without. But she looked more like a lady than a whore.

"Thank you, my lord," she said, glancing up at the house.

"I trust," he said, "you were warm enough under the lap robes?"

"Indeed." She smiled at him.

One thing at least was clear to him as he turned with her toward Bertie, who was standing in the open doorway, rubbing his hands together, a welcoming grin on his face. He was still anticipating the night ahead with a great deal of pleasure, perhaps more so than ever. There was something unusually intriguing about Miss Blanche Heyward, opera dancer and authority on the Star of Bethlehem.

VERITY FELT embarrassment more than any other emotion for the first hour or so of her stay at Bertrand Hollander's hunting box, and what a misnomer *that* was, she thought, looking about at the well-sized, cozy, expensively furnished house that a gentleman used only during the shooting season. And, of course, for clandestine holidays with his mistress.

It was that idea that caused the embarrassment. Mr. Hollander appeared to be a pleasant gentleman. He had a good-looking, amiable face and was dressed with neat elegance. He greeted them with a hearty welcome and assured them that they must make themselves at home for the coming week and not even think of standing on ceremony.

He greeted her, Verity, with gallantry, taking her hand and raising it to his lips before tucking it beneath his arm and leading her into the house while begging her to call upon him at any time if he might be of service in increasing her comfort.

And yet there was something in his manner—a certain familiarity—that showed he was a gentleman talking, not with a lady, but with a woman of another class entirely. There was the frank way, for example, that he looked her over from head to toe before grinning at Viscount Folingsby. It was not quite an insolent look. Indeed, there was a good deal of appreciation in it. But he would not have looked at a lady so, not at least while she was observing him doing it. Nor would he have called a lady by her first name. But Mr. Hollander used hers.

"Come into the parlor where there is a fire, Blanche," he said. "We will soon have you warmed up. Come and meet Debbie."

Debbie was the other woman, Mr. Hollander's mistress. She was blond and pretty and plump and placid. She spoke with a decided Yorkshire accent. She did not rise from the chair in which she lounged beside the fire, but smiled genially and lazily at the new arrivals.

"Sit down there, Blanche," she said, pointing to the chair at the other side of the fire. "Bertie will send for tea, won't you, love? Ee, you look frozen, Jule. You'd better pull a chair closer to the fire unless you want to sit with Blanche on your lap."

She was addressing Viscount Folingsby, Verity realized in some shock as she took the offered chair and removed her gloves and bonnet, since no servant had offered to take them in the hall. She directed a very straight look at her new protector, but he was bowing over Debbie's outstretched hand and taking it to his lips.

"Charmed," he said. "I do hope you are not planning to order tea for me, too, Bertie?"

His friend barked with laughter and crossed the room to a sideboard on which there was an array of decanters and glasses. The viscount pulled up a chair for himself, Verity was relieved to find, but Mr. Hollander, when he returned with glasses of liquor for his friend and himself, raised his eyebrows at Debbie. She sighed, hoisted herself out of the chair, and then settled herself on his lap after he had sat down.

Verity refused to feel outrage. She refused to show disapproval by even the smallest gesture. These were two gentlemen with their mistresses. She was one of the latter, by her own choice. There was already more than two hundred pounds safely stowed away in a drawer at home. The rest of the advance payment had been spent on another visit to the physician for Chastity and more medicine. A small sum was in her purse inside her reticule. It was too late to go back even if she wanted to. The money was not intact to be returned.

And so she resigned herself to what must be. But she had made one decision during the days since she had accepted Viscount Folingsby's proposition. She was not going to act a part besides what she had already committed herself to. She spoke with some sort of accent to disguise the refinement of her lady's voice. She had invented a family at a smithy in Somersetshire. But beyond those things she was not going to go. She was not going to try to be deliberately vulgar or stupid or anything else she imagined a mistress would be.

She had brought with her the clothes she usually wore at home. She had dressed her hair as she usually wore it there. She had kept her end of the bargain by coming here. She would keep it by staying over Christmas and allowing Viscount Folingsby to do *that* to her. Her mind still shied away from the details and from the alarming fact that she was ignorant of many of them. She had hardly been in a position to ask her mother, as she would have done had she been getting married and facing a wedding night.

She had told Mama and Chastity that Lady Coleman was going into the country for Christmas and required her presence. She had told them that she was being paid a very generous bonus for going, though she had not mentioned the incredible sum of five hundred pounds. They had both been upset at the prospect of her absence over Christmas, and she had shed a few tears with them, but they had consoled themselves with the belief that as a member of a house party she would have a wonderful time.

"Are you warmer now?" Viscount Folingsby asked suddenly, bringing Verity's mind back to Mr. Hollander's sitting room, into which a servant was just carrying a tea tray. He leaned forward and took one of her hands in both of his. His were warm; hers was not. "Perhaps I should have cuddled you on my lap after all."

"I believe the fire and the tea between them will do the trick nicely for now, my lord," she said before turning her attention to Mr. Hollander, who was smiling genially at them. "I have never before been into this part of the world, sir. Do tell me about it. What beauties of nature characterize it? And what history and buildings of note are there here?"

She would no longer be mute, wondering what topics of conversation were appropriate for an opera dancer and a gentleman's mistress.

"Ee, Bertie, love," Debbie said, "there is a right pretty garden out back. Tell Blanche about it. Tell her about the tree swing."

It was not tree swings exactly that Verity had had in mind, but she settled back in her chair with a smile as the servant handed her her tea. Viscount Folingsby relinquished her hand.

"For now," he murmured. "But later, Blanche, I beg leave to do service in place of the fire and the tea."

It took her a moment to realize he was referring to her earlier words. When she did so, she wished she were sitting a little farther back from the fire. Her face felt as if it were being scorched.

It did not seem, she thought suddenly, as if Christmas was close. Tomorrow would be Christmas Eve. For a few moments there was the ache of tears in her throat.

THERE MUST have been a goodly number of bedchambers in the house, Julian guessed later that night as he ascended the staircase with Blanche on his arm. But Bertie, of course, had assigned them only one. It was a large room overlooking the small wooded park at the back of the house. It was warmed by a log fire in a large hearth and lit by a single branch of candles. Heavy velvet curtains had been drawn back from the large canopied bed and the covers had been turned down.

He was glad he had not had her before, he decided as he closed the door behind them and extinguished the single candle that had lit their way upstairs. Pleasurable anticipation had been building in him for over a week. It had reached a crescendo of desire this evening. She had been looking almost demure in the green silk dress she had worn the evening they first supped together, her hair dressed severely but not unattractively.

And she had been acting the part of a lady, keeping the conversation going during dinner and in the sitting room afterward with observations about their journey, about the Christmas decorations and carol singers in London, and about—of all things—the peace talks that were proceeding in Vienna now that Napoleon Bona-parte had been defeated and was imprisoned on the island of Elba. She had asked Bertie what plans had been made for their own celebration of Christmas. Bertie had looked surprised and then blank. He obvi-ously had no plans at all beyond enjoying himself with his pretty, buxom Debbie.

Paradoxically Julian had found Blanche's demure appearance and ladylike behavior arousing. He consid-ered both erotic. She had too many charms to hide ef-fectively.

"Come here," he said now.

She had gone to stand in front of the fire. She was holding out her hands to the blaze. But she turned her head, smiled at him and came to stand in front of him. She was clever, he thought. She must know that an over-eagerness on her part would somehow dampen his own. Though there was just a chance she was not quite as eager as he. This was a job to her, after all. He would soon change that. He set his hands on either side of her waist and drew her against him, fitting her body against his own from the waist down. He could feel the slimness of her long legs, the flatness of her abdomen. His breath quickened. She looked back into his eyes, a half smile on her lips.

"At last," he said.

"Yes." Her smile did not waver. Neither did her eyes.

He bent his head and kissed her. She kept her lips closed. He teased them with his own and touched his tongue lightly to the seam, moving it slowly across in order to part her lips and gain entrance. Her head jerked back.

"What are you doing?" She sounded breathless.

He stared blankly at her. But before he could frame an answer to such a nonsensical question, her look of shock disappeared, she smiled again and her hands came up to rest on his shoulders.

"Pardon me," she said. "You moved just a little too fast for me. I am ready now." She brought her mouth back to his, her lips softly parted this time, and trembling against his own.

What the devil?

His mind turned cold with suspicion. He closed his arms about her and thrust his tongue deep into her mouth without any attempt at subtlety. She made no move to pull away, but she went rigid in every limb for a few moments before relaxing almost to limpness. He moved his hands forward quite deliberately and cupped her breasts with them, his thumbs seeking and pressing against her nipples. Again there was the momentary tensing followed by relaxation.

He was looking down at her a moment later, his eyes half-closed, his hands again on either side of her waist.

"Well, Miss Heyward," he asked softly, "how have you enjoyed your first kiss?"

"My first…" She gazed blankly at him.

"I suppose it would be strange indeed," he said, "if I were to discover in a few minutes' time on that bed that you are not also a virgin?"

She had nothing to say this time.

"Well?" he asked her. "Shall I put the matter to the test?" He watched her swallow.

"Even the most hardened of whores," she said at last, "was a virgin once, my lord. For each there is a first time. I will not flinch or weep or deny you your will, if that is what you fear. You are paying me well. I will do all that is required of me."

"Will you indeed?" he said, releasing her and crossing the room to the hearth to push a log farther into the blaze with his foot. He watched the resulting shower of sparks. "I am not paying for the pleasure of observing martyrdom."

"I was not acting the martyr," she protested. "You

took me by surprise. I did not know… I am perfectly willing to do whatever you wish me to do. I am sorry that I will be awkward at first. But I will learn tonight, and tomorrow night I will know better what it is you expect of me. I hope I… Perhaps under the circumstances you will decide that you have already paid me handsomely enough. I believe you have. I will try to earn it."

Did she realize, he wondered in some amazement, that she was throwing a pail of cold water over his desire with every sentence she uttered? Anger was replacing it—no, fury. Not so much against her. She had told him no lies about her experience, had she? His fury was all against himself and his own cleverness. He would keep her for Bertie's, would he? He would savor his anticipation, would he, until it was too late to change his mind, to go to Conway as he ought to have done? He would have one last fling, would he, before he did his duty by his family and name? Well, he had been justly served.

In the middle of the desert, far from home, had the wise men ever called themselves all kinds of fool?

"I do not deal in virgins, Miss Heyward," he said curtly.

"Ah," she said, "you do not like to face what it is you are purchasing, then, my lord?"

He raised his eyebrows in surprise and regarded her over his shoulder in silence for a few moments. This woman had sharp weapons and did not scruple to wield them. "Is your need for the money a personal one?" he asked her, turning from the fire. "Or is it your family that is in need?" He did not want to know, he realized after the questions were out. He had no wish to know Blanche Heyward as a person. All he had wanted was one last sensual fling with a beautiful and experienced and willing partner.

"I do not have to answer that," she said. "I will pay back all I can when we have returned to London. But I am still willing to earn my salary."

"As I remember," he said, "our agreement was for a week of your company in exchange for a certain sum, Blanche. There was no mention of your warming my bed during that week, was there? We will spend the week here. It is too late now for either of us to make other arrangements for Christmas. Besides, those were snow clouds this afternoon if ever I have seen any. We will salvage what we can of the holiday, then. It might be the dreariest Christmas either of us has ever spent, but who knows? Maybe not. Maybe I will decide to give you lessons in kissing so that your next, ah, employer will make his discovery rather later in the process than I did. Undress and go to bed. There is a dressing room for your modesty."

"Where will you sleep?" she asked him.

He looked down at the floor, which was fortunately carpeted. "Here," he said. "Perhaps you will understand that I have no wish for Bertie to know that we are not spending the night in sensual bliss together."

"You have the bed," she said. "I will sleep on the floor."

He felt an unexpected stirring of amusement. "But I have already told you, Blanche," he said, "that I have no wish to gaze on martyrdom. Go to bed before I change my mind."

By the time she came back from the dressing room a few minutes later, dressed in a virginal white flannel nightgown, her head held high, her cheeks flushed and her titian hair all down her back, he had made up some sort of bed for himself on the floor close to the fire with blankets he had found in a drawer and a pillow he had taken from the bed. He did not look at her beyond one cursory glance. He waited for her to climb into the bed and pull the covers up over her ears, and then extinguished the candles.

"Good night," he said, finding his way back to his bed by the light of the fire.

"Good night," she said.

What a marvelously just punishment for his sins, he thought as he lay down and his body registered the hardness of the floor. But why the devil was he doing this? She had been willing and he was paying her handsomely. Heaven knows, he had wanted her badly enough, and still did.

It was not any real reluctance to violate innocence, he decided, or any unwillingness to deal with awkwardness or the inevitable blood. It was exactly what he had said it was. He had no desire to watch martyrdom or to inflict it.

I will not flinch or weep or deny you your will.

If there were less erotic words in the English language, he could not imagine what they might be. Sheer martyrdom! If only she had wanted it, wanted *him* just a little bit, even if she had been nervous…

Miss Blanche Heyward, he was discovering to his cost, was not the average, typical opera dancer. In fact she was turning out to be a royal pain.

A fine Christmas this was going to be. He thought glumly of Conway and of what he would be missing there tomorrow and the day after. Even the Plunkett chit was looking mildly appealing at this particular moment.

"What would you have done for Christmas," a soft voice asked him as if she had read his thoughts, "if you had not come here with me?"

He breathed deeply and evenly and audibly.

Perhaps tomorrow he would teach her to see a night spent in bed with him as fitting a different category of experience from Christians being prodded into the arena with slavering lions. But unlike his usual confident self, he did not hold out a great deal of hope of succeeding.

Surprisingly he slept.

CHAPTER FOUR

VERITY DID NOT sleep well during the night. But as she lay staring at the window and the suggestion of daylight beyond the curtains, she was surprised that she had slept at all.

There were sounds of deep, even breathing coming from the direction of the fireplace. She listened carefully. There were no sounds from beyond the door. Did that mean no one was up yet? Of course, Mr. Hollander and Debbie had probably been busy all night and perhaps intended to be busy for part of the morning, too.

It should have been all over by this morning, she thought. She should be a fallen woman beyond all dispute by now. And he had been wrong. It would not have felt like martyrdom. Even in the privacy of her own mind she was a little embarrassed to remember how exciting his hard man's body had felt against her own and how shockingly pleasurable his open mouth had felt against her lips. All her insides had performed some sort of vigorous dance when he had put his tongue into her mouth. What an alarmingly intimate thing to do. It should have been disgusting but had not been.

Well, she thought with determined honesty, she had actually wanted to experience the whole of it. And deny it as she would, she had to confess to herself that there had been some disappointment in his refusal to continue once he had realized the truth about her.

And so here they were in this ridiculous predicament with all of Christmas ahead of them. How could she possibly earn five hundred pounds when one night was already past and he had slept on the floor?

All of Christmas was ahead of them. What a depressing thought!

And then something in the quality of the light beyond the window drew her attention. She threw back the bedcovers, ignored her shivering reaction to the frigid air beyond their shelter and padded across the room on bare feet. She drew aside the curtain.

Oh!

"Oh!" she exclaimed aloud. She turned her head and looked eagerly at the sleeping man. "Oh, do come and look."

His head reared up from his pillow. He looked deliciously tousled and unshaven. He was also scowling.

"What?" he barked. "What the devil *time* is it?"

"Look," she said, turning back to the window. "Oh, look."

He was beside her then, clad only in his shirt and last night's knee breeches and stockings. "For this you have dragged me from my bed?" he asked her. "I told you last night that it would snow today."

"But look!" she begged him. "It is sheer magic."

When she turned her head, she found him looking at her instead of at the snow beyond the window, blanketing the ground and decking out the bare branches of the trees.

"Do you always glow like this in the morning?" he asked her. "How disgusting!"

She laughed. "Only when Christmas is coming and there is a fresh fall of snow," she said. "Can you imagine two more wonderful events happening simultaneously?"

"Finding a soft warm bed when I am more than half-asleep and stiff in every limb," he said.

"Then have my bed," she said, laughing again. "I am getting up."

"A fine impression Bertie is going to have of my power to keep you amused and confined to your room," he said.

"Mr. Hollander," she told him, "will doubtless keep to his room until noon and will be none the wiser. Go to bed and go to sleep."

He did both. By the time she emerged from the dressing room, clad in the warmest of her wool dresses, her hair brushed and decently confined, he was lying in the place on the bed where she had lain all night, fast asleep. She stood gazing down at him for a few moments, imagining that if she had not been so gauche last night…

She shook her head and straightened her shoulders. Mr. Hollander had made no preparations for Christmas.

Doubtless he thought that spending a few days in bed
with the placid Debbie would constitute enough merry-
making. Well, they would see about that. She was not
being allowed to earn her salary in the expected way.
The least she could do, then, was make herself useful
in other ways.

TWO COACHMEN, one footman, one groom, a cook, Mr.
Hollander's valet and four others who might in a more
orderly establishment have been dubbed a butler, a
housekeeper and two maids were in the middle of their
breakfast belowstairs. A few of them scrambled awkwardly to their feet when Verity appeared in their midst.
A few did not. Clearly it was not established in any of
their minds whether they should treat her as a lady or
not. The cook looked as if she might be the leader of
the latter faction.

Verity smiled. "Please do not get up," she said. "Do
carry on with your breakfast. Doubtless you all have a
busy day ahead."

If they did, their expressions told Verity, this was the
first they had heard of it.

"Preparing for Christmas," she added.

They might have been devout Hindus for all the
interest they showed in preparing for Christmas.

"Mr. Hollander don't want no fuss," the woman who
might have been the housekeeper said.

"He said we might do as we please provided he has
his victuals when he is ready for them and provided the

fires are kept burning." The possible-butler was the speaker this time.

"Oh, splendid," Verity said cheerfully. "May I have some breakfast with you, by the way? No, please do not get up." No one had made any particular move to do so. "I shall just help myself, shall I?" She did so. "If you have been given permission to please yourselves, then, you may be pleased to celebrate Christmas. In the traditional way, with Christmas foods and wassail, with carol singing and gift giving and decorating the house with holly and pine boughs and whatever else we can devise with only a day's warning. Everyone can have a wonderful time."

"When I cook a goose," the cook announced, "nobody needs a knife to cut it. Even the edge of a fork is too sharp. It melts apart."

"Ooh, I do love a goose," one of the maids said wistfully. "My ma used to cook one as a treat for Christmas whenever we could catch one. But it weren't never cooked tender enough to cut with a fork, Mrs. Lyons," she added hastily.

"And when I make mince pies," the cook continued as if she had not been interrupted, "no one can stop eating after just one of them. *No one.*"

"Mmm." Verity sighed. "You make my mouth water, Mrs. Lyons. How I would love to taste just one of those pies."

"Well, I can't make them," Mrs. Lyons said, a note of finality in her voice. "Because I don't have the stuff."

"Could the supplies be bought in the village?" Verity suggested. "I noticed a village as I passed through it yesterday. There appeared to be a few shops there."

"There is nobody to go for them," Mrs. Lyons said. "Not in all this snow."

Verity smiled at the groom and the two coachmen, all of whom were trying unsuccessfully to blend into the furniture. "Nobody?" she said. "Not for the sake of goose tomorrow and mince pies and probably a dozen other Christmas specialties, too? Not for Mrs. Lyons's sake when it sounds to me as if she is the most skilled cook in all of Norfolkshire?"

"Well, I am quite skilled," the cook said modestly.

"There are pine trees and holly bushes in the park, are there not?" Verity asked of no one in particular. "Is there mistletoe anywhere?" She turned her eyes on the younger of the two maids. "What is Christmas without a few sprigs of mistletoe appearing in the most unlikely places and just over the heads of the most elusive people?"

The maid turned pink and the valet looked interested.

"There used to be some on the old oaks," the butler said. "But I don't know about this year, mind."

"The archway leading from the kitchen to the back stairs looks a likely place to me for one sprig," Verity said, looking critically at the spot as she bit into a piece of toast.

Both maids giggled and the valet cleared his throat.

After that the hard work seemed to be behind her, Verity found. The idea had caught hold. Mr. Hollander had given his staff carte blanche even if he had not done so consciously. And the staff had awakened to the realization that it was Christmas and that they might celebrate it in as grand a manner as they chose. All lethargy magically disappeared, and Verity was able to eat her eggs and toast and drink down two cups of coffee while warming herself at the kitchen fire and listening to the servants make their animated plans. There were even two volunteers to go into the village.

"You cannot all be everywhere at once, though," Verity said, speaking up again at last, "much as I can see you would like to be. You may leave the gathering of the greenery and just come to help drag it all indoors. Mr. Hollander, Lord Folingsby, Miss, er, Debbie and I will do the gathering."

Silence and blank stares met this announcement until someone sniggered—the groom.

"I don't think so, miss," he said. "You won't drag them gents out of doors to spoil the shine on their boots nor 'er to spoil 'er complexion. You can forget that one right enough."

The valet cleared his throat again, with considerably more dignity than before. "You will speak with greater respect of Mr. Hollander, Bloggs," he told the groom, who looked quite uncowed by the reprimand.

Verity smiled. "You may safely leave Mr. Hollander and the others to me," she said. "We are *all* going to enjoy Christmas. It would be unfair to exclude them, would it not?"

Her words caused a burst of merriment about the table, and Verity tried to imagine Julian pricking his aristocratic fingers in the cause of gathering holly. He would probably sleep until noon. But she had done him an injustice. He appeared in the archway that was not yet adorned with mistletoe only a moment later, as if her thoughts had summoned him. He was dressed immaculately despite the fact that he had not brought his valet with him.

"Ah," Julian said languidly, fingering the handle of his quizzing glass, "here you are, Blanche. I began to think you had sprouted wings and flown since there are no footprints in the snow leading from the door."

"We have been planning the Christmas festivities," she told him with a bright smile. "Everything is organized. Later you and I will be going out into the park with Mr. Hollander and Debbie to gather greenery with which to decorate the house."

Suddenly that part of the plan seemed quite preposterous. His lordship raised his quizzing glass all the way to his eye and moved it about the table, the better to observe all the conspirators seated there. It came to rest finally on her.

"Indeed?" he said faintly. "What a delightful treat for us."

JULIAN WAS SITTING awkwardly on the branch of an ancient oak tree, not quite sure how he had got up there and even less sure how he was to get down again without breaking a leg or two or even his neck. Blanche was standing below, her face upturned, her arms spread as if to catch him should he fall. Just a short distance beyond his grasp was a promising clump of mistletoe. Several yards away from the oak, Bertie was standing almost knee-deep in snow, one glove on, the other discarded on the ground beside him, complaining about a holly prick on one finger with all the loud woe of a man who had just been run through with a sword. Debbie was kissing it better.

A little closer to the house, in a spot sheltered by trees and therefore not as deeply covered with snow, lay a pathetically small pile of pine boughs and holly branches. Pathetic, at least, considering the fact that they had been outdoors and hard at work for longer than an hour, subjected to frigid temperatures, buffeting winds and swirling flakes of thick snow. The heavy clouds had still not finished emptying their load.

"Oh, do be careful," Blanche implored as Julian leaned out gingerly to reach the mistletoe. "Don't fall."

He paused and looked down at her. Her cheeks were charmingly rosy. So was her nose. "Did I imagine it, Blanche," he asked, using his best bored voice, "or did the drill sergeant who marched us out here and ordered me up here really wear your face?"

She laughed. No, she did not—she giggled. "If you kill yourself," she said, "I shall have them write on your epitaph—He Died In The Execution Of A Noble Deed."

By dint of shifting his position on the branch until he hung even more precariously over space and scraping his boot beyond redemption to get something of a toehold against the gnarled trunk, he finally succeeded in his mission. He had dislodged a handful of mistletoe. There was no easy way down to the ground. Indeed, there was no possible way down. He did what he had always done as a boy in a similar situation. He jumped.

He landed on all fours and got a faceful of soft snow for his pains.

"Oh, dear," Blanche said. "Did you hurt yourself?" He looked up at her and she giggled again. "You look like a snowman, a snowman whose dignity has been bruised. Do you have the mistletoe?"

He got to his feet and brushed himself off with one hand as best he could. His valet, when he got back to London, was going to take one look at his boots and resign.

"Voilà!" He held up his snow-bedraggled prize. "Oh, no, you don't," he said when she reached for it. He swept it up out of her reach. "Certain acts have certain consequences, you know. I risked my life for this at your instigation. I deserve my reward, you deserve your punishment."

She grinned at him as he backed her against the tree and held her there with the weight of his body. He was still holding the mistletoe aloft.

"Yes, my lord," she said meekly.

His mind was not really on the night before, but if it had been, he might have reflected with some satisfaction that she had learned well her first lesson in kissing. Her lips were softly parted when he touched them with his own, and when he teased them wider and licked them and the soft flesh behind them with his tongue, she made quiet sounds of enjoyment. The contrast between chilled flesh and hot mouths was heady stuff, he decided as he slid his tongue deep. She sucked gently on it. Through all the layers of their clothing he could feel the tautly muscled slenderness of her dancer's body. Total femininity.

Someone was whistling. Bertie. And someone was telling him to be quiet and not be silly, love, and come away to look at *this* holly.

"Well," Julian said, lifting his head and feeling a little dazed and more than a little aroused. He had not anticipated just such a kiss. "The mistletoe *was* your idea, Blanche."

"Yes." Her nose was shining like a beacon. She looked healthy and girlish and slightly disheveled and utterly beautiful. "And so it was."

He was cold and wet, from the snow that had slipped down inside his collar and was melting in trickles down his back, and utterly happy. Or for the moment anyway, he thought more cautiously when he remembered the situation.

Someone was clearing his throat from behind Julian's back—Bertie's groom, Julian saw when he looked. The man was looking for Bertie, who stuck his head out from behind the holly bushes at the mention of his name.

"What is it, Bloggs?" he asked.

Bloggs told his tale of a carriage half turned over into the ditch just beyond the front gates with no hope of its being hauled out again until the snow stopped falling and the air warmed up enough to melt some of it. And the snow was so deep everywhere, he added gloomily, that there was no going anywhere on foot, either, any longer, even as far as the village. He should know. He and Harkiss had had the devil's own time of it wading home from there all of two hours since, and the snowfall had not abated for a single second since that time.

"A carriage?" Bertie frowned. "Any occupants, Bloggs?" A foolish question if ever Julian had heard one.

"A gentleman and his wife, sir," Bloggs reported. "And two nippers. Inside the house now, sir."

"Oh, good Lord," Bertie said, grimacing in Julian's direction. "It looks as if we have unexpected guests for Christmas."

"The devil!" Julian muttered.

"Oh, the poor things!" Blanche exclaimed, pushing away from the tree and striding houseward through the snow. "What has been done for their comfort, Mr. Bloggs? Two children, did you say? Are they very young? Was anyone hurt? Have you…"

Her voice faded into the distance. Strange, Julian

thought before following her with Bertie and Debbie. Most women who had had elocution lessons spoke well except when they were not concentrating. Then they tended to lapse into regionalism and worse. Why did the opposite seem to happen with Blanche? Bloggs was trotting after her like a well-trained henchman, just as if she were some grand duchess ruling over her undisputed domain.

Funnily enough, she had just *sounded* rather like a duchess.

CHAPTER FIVE

THE REVEREND HENRY MOFFATT had been given unexpected leave from the parish at which he was a curate in order to spend Christmas at the home of his wife's family thirty miles distant. Rashly—by his own admission—he had made the decision to begin the journey that morning despite the fact that the snow had already begun to fall and he had the safety of two young children to concern himself with, not to mention that of his wife, who was in imminent expectation of another interesting event.

He was contrite over his own foolishness. He was distressed over the near disaster to which he had brought his family when his carriage had almost overturned into the ditch. He was apologetic about foisting himself and his family upon strangers on Christmas Eve of all days. Perhaps there was an inn close by?

"In the village three miles away," Verity told him. "But you would not get there in this weather, sir. You must, of course, stay here. Mr. Hollander will insist upon it, you may be sure."

"Mr. Hollander is your husband, ma'am?" the Reverend Moffatt asked.

"No." She smiled. "I am a guest here, too, sir. Mrs. Moffatt, do come into the sitting room so that you may warm yourself by the fire and take the weight off your feet. Mr. Bloggs, would you be so kind as to go down to the kitchen and request that a tea tray be sent up? Oh, and something for the children, as well. And something to eat." She smiled at the two little boys, who were gazing about with open curiosity. The younger one, a mere infant of three or four years, was unwinding a long scarf from his neck. She reached out a hand to each of them. "Are you hungry? But that is a foolish question, I know. In my experience little boys are always hungry. Come into the sitting room with your mama and we will see what Cook sends up."

It was at that moment that Mr. Hollander came inside the house with Debbie and Viscount Folingsby close behind him. The Reverend Moffatt introduced himself again and made his explanations and his apologies once more.

"Bertrand Hollander," that young gentleman said, extending his right hand to his unexpected guest. "And, er, my wife, Mrs. Hollander. And Viscount Folingsby."

Verity was leading Mrs. Moffatt and the children in the direction of the sitting room, but she stopped so that the curate could introduce them to his host.

"You have met my wife, the viscountess?" Julian asked, his eyes locking with Verity's.

"Yes, indeed." The Reverend Moffatt made her a bow. "Her ladyship has been most kind."

One more lie to add to all the others, Verity thought. Her new husband, having divested himself of his outdoor garments, followed her into the sitting room, where she directed the very pregnant Mrs. Moffatt and the little boys to chairs close to the fire. The viscount stood beside Verity, one hand against the back of her waist. But during the bustle of the next few minutes, she felt her left hand being taken in a firm grasp and bent up behind her back. While Julian smiled genially about him as the tea tray arrived and cups and plates were passed around and everyone made small talk, he slid something onto Verity's ring finger.

It was the signet ring he normally wore on the little finger of his right hand, she saw when she withdrew the hand from her back and looked down at it. The ring was a little loose on her, but with some care she would be able to see that it did not fall off. It was a very tolerable substitute for a wedding ring. A glance across the room at Debbie assured her that that young woman's left hand was similarly adorned.

One could only conclude that Viscount Folingsby and Mr. Hollander were born conspirators and had had a great deal of practice at being devious.

"I will hear no more protests, sir, if you please," Mr. Hollander was saying with all his customary good humor and one raised hand. "Mrs. Hollander and I will be delighted to have your company over Christmas. Much as we have been enjoying that of our two friends, we have been regretting, have we not, my love, that we did not invite more guests for the holiday. Especially those with children. Christmas does not seem quite Christmas without them."

"How kind of you to say so, sir," Mrs. Moffatt said, one hand resting over the mound of her pregnancy.

"Ee," Debbie said, "it is going to be right good fun to hear the patter of little feet about the house and the chatter of little voices. You sit down, too, Rev, and make yourself at home. Set your cup and saucer down on that table there. It must have been a right nasty fright to land in the ditch like that."

"We tipped up like *this*," the older of the little boys said, listing over sharply to one side, his arms outspread. "I thought we were going to turn over and over in a tumble-toss. It was ever so exciting."

"I was not scared," the younger boy said, gazing up at Verity before depositing his thumb in his mouth and then snatching it determinedly out again. "I am not scared of anything."

"That will do, Rupert," their father said. "And, David. You will speak when spoken to, if you please."

But Rupert was pulling at his father's sleeve. "May we go out to play?" he whispered.

"Children!" Mrs. Moffatt laughed. "One would think they would be glad enough to be safe indoors after that narrow escape, would you not? And on such a cold, stormy day. But they love the outdoors."

"Then I have just the answer for them," Julian said, raising his eyebrows and fingering the handle of his quizzing glass. "There is a pile of Christmas greenery out behind the house in dire need of hands and arms to carry it inside. We will never be able to celebrate Christmas with it if it remains out there, will we?" He leveled his glass at each of the boys in turn, a frown on his face. "I wonder if those hands and arms are strong enough, though. What do you think, Bertie?"

Two pairs of eyes turned anxiously Mr. Hollander's way. *Please yes, please yes,* those eyes begged while both children sat with buttoned lips in obedience to their father's command.

"What do I think, Jule?" Mr. Hollander pursed his lips. "I think— But wait a minute. Is that a muscle I spy bulging out your coat sleeve, lad?"

The elder boy looked down with desperate hope at his arm.

"It is a muscle," Mr. Hollander decided.

"And have you ever seen more capable fingers than this other lad's, Bertie?" Julian asked, magnifying them with the aid of his glass. "I believe these brothers have been sent us for a purpose. You will need to put your scarves and hats and gloves back on, of course, and secure your mama's permission. But once that has been accomplished, you may follow me."

Verity watched in wonder as two rather bored and jaded rakes were transformed into kindly, indulgent uncles before her eyes. The two boys were jumping up and down before their mother's chair in an agony of suspense lest she withhold her permission.

"You are too kind, my lord," she said with a weary smile. "They will wear you out."

"Not at all, ma'am," he assured her. "It is a sizable pile."

"Oh," Verity said, beaming down at the children, "and after you have it all inside and dried off, you may help decorate the house with it. There are mistletoe and holly and pine boughs. And Mrs. Simpkins has found ribbons and bows and bells in the attic. Deb—Mrs. Hollander and I will sort through them and decide what can be used. Before Christmas comes tomorrow, this house is going to be bursting at the seams with good cheer. I daresay we will have one of the best Christmases anyone ever had."

Her eyes met Viscount Folingsby's as she spoke. He regarded her with one raised eyebrow and a slightly mocking smile. But she was no longer fooled by such an expression. She had seen him without his mask of bored cynicism. Not just here with the two little boys. She had seen him climb a tree like a schoolboy, not just because she had asked him to do so, but because the tree was there and therefore to be climbed. She had seen him with a twinkle in his eye and a laugh on his lips.

And she had—oh, dear, yes—she had felt his kiss. It was not one she could censure even if it had occurred to her to do so. He had earned it, not with five hundred pounds, but with the acquisition of mistletoe. The mistletoe had sanctified the kiss, deep and carnal as it had been.

"It seems," the Reverend Moffatt said as the other two gentlemen left the room with the exuberant children, "that we are to be guests here at least until tomorrow. It warms my heart to have been stranded at a place where we have already been made to feel welcome. Sometimes it seems almost as if a divine hand is at play in guiding our movements, taking us where we had no intention of going to meet people we had no thought of meeting. How wonderful that you are all preparing with such enthusiasm to celebrate the birth of our Lord."

"I am going to make a kissing bough," Debbie announced, looking almost animated. "We had kissing boughs to half fill the kitchen ceiling when I was a girl. Nobody escaped a few good bussings in our house. I had almost forgotten. Christmas was always a right grand time."

"Yes, Mrs. Hollander," Mrs. Moffatt said with a smile. "It is always a grand time, even when we are forced to spend it away from part of our families as I assume we are all doing this year. Your husband is being very kind to our boys. And yours, too, my lady." She turned her smile on Verity. "They have been in the carriage all day and have a great deal of excess energy."

"There will be no going into the village tonight or tomorrow morning if what you said is true, Lady Folingsby," the Reverend Moffatt said. "You will be unable to attend church as I daresay you intended to do. I shall repay a small part of my debt to you, then. I shall conduct the Christmas service here. We will all take communion here together. With Mr. Hollander's permission, of course."

"What a splendid idea, Henry," his wife said.

"Ee," Debbie said, awed into near-silence.

Verity clasped her hands to her bosom and closed her eyes. She had a sudden image of the church at home on the evening before Christmas, the bells pealing out the news of the Christ child's birth, the candles all ablaze, the carved Nativity scene carefully arranged before the altar, her father in his best vestments smiling down at the congregation. Christmas had always been his favorite time of the liturgical year.

"Oh, sir," she said, opening her eyes again, "it is we who will be in your debt. Deeply in your debt." She blinked away tears. "I would like it of all things. I am sure Mr. Hollander and Vi—and my husband will agree."

"It is going to be a grand Christmas, Blanche," Debbie said. "I did not expect it, lass. Not in this way, any road."

"Sometimes we come to grace by unexpected paths," the Reverend Moffatt commented.

"DO YOU EVER have the impression that events have galloped along somewhat out of your control, Jule?" Bertie asked his friend just before dinner was served and they stood together in the sitting room waiting for everyone else to join them. They were surrounded by the sights and smells of Christmas. There was greenery everywhere, artfully draped and colorfully decorated with red bows and streamers and silver bells. There was a huge and elaborate kissing bough suspended over the alcove to one side of the fireplace. There was a strong smell of pine, more powerful for the moment than the tantalizing aromas wafting up from the kitchen.

"And do you ever have the impression," Julian asked without answering the question, which was doubtless rhetorical anyway, "that you ought not to simply label a woman as a certain type and expect her to behave accordingly?" Blanche, changing for dinner a few minutes before in the dressing room while he made do with the bedchamber, had informed him with bright enthusiasm that the Reverend Moffatt was planning to conduct a Christmas service in this very room sometime after dinner. And that the servants had asked to attend. And that they were going to have to see to it on the morrow that the little boys had a wonderful Christmas. If there was still plenty of snow, they could...

He had not listened to all the details. But Miss Blanche Heyward, opera dancer, would have made a superlative drill sergeant if she had just been a man, he had thought. Consider as a point in fact the way she had organized them all—*all* of them—over the decorations. They had rushed about and climbed and teetered and adjusted angles at her every bidding. She had been flushed and bright-eyed and beautiful.

On the whole, he concluded as an afterthought, he was glad she was not a man.

"And have you ever had a cook for all of three or four years, Jule," Bertie continued, "and suddenly discovered that she could *cook?* Not that I have tasted any of the things that go with those smells yet, but if smell is anything to judge by…well, I *ask* you."

The staff, it seemed, had been as busy belowstairs as all of them had been above. But their busyness had had the same instigator—Miss Blanche Heyward. Julian even wondered if somehow she had conjured up the clergyman and his family out of the blizzard. What a ghastly turn of events that had been.

"Do you suppose," he asked, "anyone noticed the sudden appearance of rings on our women's fingers, Bertie?"

But the door opened at that moment to admit their mistresses, who had come down together. Debbie clucked her tongue.

"Now did I do all that work on the kissing bough just to see it hang over there and you men stand here?" she asked. "Go and get yourself under it, Bertie, love, and be bussed."

"Again?" he said, grinning and waggling his eyebrows and instantly obeying.

They had all sampled the pleasures of the kissing bough after it had been hung. Even the Reverend Moffatt had kissed his wife with hearty good humor and had pecked Debbie and Blanche respectfully on the cheek.

"Well, Blanche." Julian looked her up and down.

She was dressed in the dark green silk again. Her hair was neatly confined at the back of her head. She should have looked drably dreary but did not. "Are you enjoying yourself?"

Some of the sparkle that had been in her eyes faded as she looked back at him. "Only when I forget my purpose in being here," she said. "I have already taken a great deal of money from you and have done nothing yet to earn it."

"Perhaps I should be the judge of that," he said.

"Perhaps tonight I can make some amends," she said. "I have had a day in which to grow more accustomed to you. I may still be awkward—I daresay I will be because I am very ignorant of what happens, you know—but I will not be afraid and I will not act the *martyr.* Indeed, I believe I might even enjoy it. And it will be a relief to know that at last I have done something to earn my salary."

If Bertie and Debbie, now laughing like a pair of children and making merry beneath the kissing bough, had been the only other occupants of the house apart from the servants, Julian thought he might have excused Blanche and himself from dinner and taken her up to bed without further ado. Despite the reference to earning salaries, he found her words arousing. He found *her* arousing. But there were other guests. Besides, he was not sure he would have done it anyway.

If this stay in Norfolkshire had proceeded according to plan, he would have enjoyed a largely sleepless night with Blanche last night. They would have stayed in bed until noon or later this morning. They would have returned to bed for much of the afternoon. By now he would have been wondering how long into the coming night his energies would sustain him. But there would have been all day tomorrow to look forward to—in bed.

The prospect had seemed appealing to him all last week and up until just last night. Longer than that. He had felt disgruntled and cheated all through the night and when he had woken this morning. Or when she had awoken him, rather, with her excited discovery that it had snowed during the night.

But surprisingly he had enjoyed the day just as it had turned out. And the kiss against the oak tree had seemed in some strange way as satisfying as a bedding might have been. There had been laughter as well as desire involved in that kiss. He had never before thought of laughter as a desirable component of a sexual experience.

"You are disappointed in me," Blanche said now. "I am so sorry."

"Not at all," he told her, clasping his hands at his back. "How could I possibly be disappointed? Let me see. A night spent on the floor, an early wake-up call in the frigid dawn to watch snow falling, an expedition out into the storm in order to climb trees, murder my boots and risk my neck. The arrival of a clergyman as a houseguest, an hour spent finding occupation for two energetic infants, another hour of climbing on furniture and pinning up boughs only to move them again when it was discovered that they were half an inch out of place, a church service in the sitting room to look forward to. My dear Miss Heyward, what more could I have asked of Christmas?"

She was laughing. "I have the strangest feeling," she said, "that you *have* enjoyed today."

He raised his quizzing glass to his eye and regarded her through it. "And you believe that you might enjoy tonight," he said. "We will see, Blanche, when tonight comes. But first of all, Bertie's guests. I believe I hear the patter of little feet and the chatter of little voices approaching, as Debbie so poetically phrased it. I suppose we are to be subjected to their company as well as that of their mama and papa since there is no nursery and no nurse."

"For all your expression and tone of voice," Blanche said, "I do believe, my lord, you have an affection for those little boys. You do not deceive me."

"Dear me," Julian said faintly as the sitting room door opened again.

THERE WAS a spinet in one corner of the sitting room. Verity had eyed it a few times during the day with some longing, but its lid was locked, she had discovered. While the Reverend Moffatt was setting up the room after dinner for the Christmas service, his wife asked about the instrument. Mr. Hollander looked at it in some surprise, as if he were noticing it for the first time. He had no idea where the key was. It hardly mattered anyway unless someone was able to play it.

There was a short silence.

"I can play," Verity said.

"Splendid!" The Reverend Moffatt beamed at her. "Then we may have music with the service, Lady Folingsby. I would lead the singing if I had to, but I have a lamentably poor ear for pitch, do I not, Edie? We would be likely to end a hymn several tones lower than we started it." He laughed heartily.

Mr. Hollander went in search of the key. Or rather, he went in search of a servant who might know where it was.

"Where did you learn to play, Blanche?" Debbie asked.

"At the rectory." Verity smiled and then wished she could bite out her tongue. "The rector's wife taught me," she added hastily. That was the truth, at least.

Mr. Hollander came back in triumph, a key held aloft. The spinet was sadly out of tune, Verity discovered, but not impossibly so. There was no music, but she did not need any. All her favorite hymns, as well as some other favorite pieces, had been committed to memory when she was still a girl.

A table had been converted into an altar with the aid of a crisp white cloth one of the maids had ironed carefully, candles in silver holders and a fancy cup and plate the housekeeper had found somewhere in the nether regions of the house and the other maid had polished to serve as a paten and chalice. The butler had dusted off a bottle of Mr. Hollander's best wine. The cook had found time and space in her oven to bake a round loaf of unleavened bread. The Reverend Moffatt had clad himself in vestments he had brought with him and suddenly looked very young and dignified and holy.

The sitting room, Verity thought, gazing about her, had become a holy place, a church. Everyone, even the children, sat hushed as they would in a church, waiting for the service to begin. Verity did not wait. She began to play quietly some of her favorite Christmas hymns.

It was Christmas, she thought, swallowing and blinking her eyes. She had not thought it would come for her this year except in the form of an ugly self-sacrifice. But for all the lies and deceptions—with every glance down at her hands she saw the false wedding ring—Christmas had come. Christmas, she reminded herself, and the reminder had never been more apt, was for sinners, and they were all sinners: Mr. Hollander, Debbie, Viscount Folingsby and her. But Christmas had found them out, despite themselves, in the form of the clergyman and his family, stranded by a snowstorm. And Christmas was offering all its bound-less love and forgiveness to them in the form of the bread and the wine, which were still at this moment just those two commodities.

A child had been born on this night more than

eighteen hundred years ago, and he was about to be born again as he had been each year since then and would be each year in the future. Constant birth. Constant hope. Constant love.

"My dear friends." The clergyman's voice was quiet, serene, imposing, unlike the voice of the Reverend Moffatt who had conversed with them over tea and dinner. He smiled about at each one of them in turn, bathing them—or so it seemed—in the warmth and peace and wonder of the season.

And so the service began.

It ended more than an hour later with the joyful singing of one last hymn. They all sang lustily, Verity noticed, herself included. Even one of the coachmen, who was noticeably tone-deaf, and the housekeeper, who sang with pronounced vibrato. Mr. Hollander had a strong tenor voice. Debbie sang with a Yorkshire accent. David Moffatt sang his heart out to a tune of his own devising. They would not have made a reputable choir. But it did not matter. They made a joyful noise. They were celebrating Christmas.

And then Mrs. Moffatt spoke up, a mere few seconds after her husband had said the final words of the service and wished them all the compliments of the season.

"I do apologize, Mr. and Mrs. Hollander," she said, "for all the inconvenience I am about to cause you. Henry, my dear, I do believe we are going to have a Christmas child."

CHAPTER SIX

HENRY MOFFATT was pacing as he had been doing almost constantly for the past several hours.

"One would expect to become accustomed to it," he said, pausing for only a moment to stare, pale faced and anxious eyed, at Julian and Bertie, who were sitting at either side of the hearth, hardly any less pale themselves, "after two previous confinements. But one does not. One thinks of a new child—one's own—making the perilous passage into this world. And one thinks of one's mate, flesh of one's own flesh, heart of one's heart, enduring the pain, facing all the danger alone. One feels helpless and humble and dreadfully responsible. And guilty that one does not have more trust in the plans of the Almighty. It seems trivial to recall that we have hoped for a daughter this time."

He resumed his journey to nowhere, back and forth from one corner of the room to the other. "Will it never end?"

Julian had never before shared a house with a woman in labor. When he thought about it, about what was going on abovestairs—and how could he *not* think about it?—he felt a buzzing in his ears and a coldness in his nostrils and imagined in some horror the ignominy of fainting when he was not even the prospective father. He remembered how glibly just a few days before he had planned to have a child of his own in the nursery by next Christmas or very soon after.

It must hurt like hell, he thought, and that was probably the understatement of the decade.

There was no doctor in the village. There was a midwife, but she lived, according to the housekeeper, a mile or so on the other side of the village. It would have been impossible to reach her, not to mention persuading her to make the return journey, in time to deliver the child who was definitely on its way.

Fortunately, Mrs. Moffatt had announced with a calm smile—surely it had been merely a brave facade—she had already given birth to two children, as well as attending the births of a few others. She could manage very well alone, provided the housekeeper would prepare a few items for her. It was getting late. She invited everyone else to retire to bed and promised not to disturb them with any loud noises.

Julian had immediately formed mental images of someone screaming in agony.

Debbie had looked at Bertie with eyes almost as big as her face.

"If you are quite sure, ma'am," Bertie had said, as white as his shirt points.

"Come, Henry," Mrs. Moffatt had said, "we will put

the children to bed first. Perhaps I can see you in here for a few minutes afterward, Mrs. Simpkins."

Mrs. Simpkins had been looking a delicate shade of green.

That was when Blanche had spoken up.

"You certainly will *not* manage alone," she had assured the guest. "It will be quite enough for you to endure the pain of labor. You will leave the rest to us, Mrs. Moffatt. Sir," she said, addressing the clergyman, "perhaps you can put the children to bed yourself tonight? Boys, give your mama a kiss. Doubtless there will be more than one wonderful surprise awaiting you in the morning. The sooner you fall asleep, the sooner you will find out what. Mrs. Lyons, will you see that a large pot of water is heated and kept ready? Mrs. Simpkins, will you gather together as many clean cloths as you can find? Debbie—"

"Ee, Blanche," Debbie had protested, "no, love."

"I am going to need you," Blanche had said with a smile. "Merely to wield a cool, damp cloth to wipe Mrs. Moffatt's face when she gets very hot, as she will. You can do that, can you not? I will be there to do everything else."

Everything else. Like delivering the baby. Julian had stared, fascinated, at his opera dancer.

"Have you done this before, Blanche?" he had asked.

"Of course," she had said briskly. "At the rectory— ah. I used to accompany the rector's wife on occasion. I know exactly what to do. No one need fear."

They had all been gazing at her, Julian remembered

now. They had all hung on her every word, her every command. They had leaned on her strength and her confidence in a collective body.

Who the hell *was* she? What had a blacksmith's daughter been doing hanging around a rectory so much? Apart from learning to play the spinet without music, that was. And apart from delivering babies.

Everyone had run to do her bidding. Soon only the three men—the three useless ones—had been left in the sitting room to fight terror and nausea and fits of the vapors.

The door opened. Three pale, terrified faces turned toward it.

Debbie was flushed and untidy and swathed in an apron made for a giant. One hank of blond hair hung to her shoulder and looked damp with perspiration. She was beaming and looking very pretty indeed.

"It is all over, sir," she announced, addressing herself to the Reverend Moffatt. "You have a new…baby. I am not to say what. Your wife is ready and waiting for you."

The new father stood very still for a few moments and then strode from the room without a word.

"Bertie." Debbie turned tear-filled eyes toward him. "You should have been there, love. It came out all of a rush into Blanche's hands, the dearest little slippery thing, all cross and crying and—and human. Ee, Bertie, love." She cast herself into his arms and bawled noisily.

Bertie made soothing noises and raised his eyebrows at Julian. "I was never more relieved in my life," he said.

"But I am quite thankful I was not there, Deb. We had better get you to bed. You are not needed any longer?"

"Blanche told me I could go to bed," Debbie said. "She will finish off all that needs doing. No midwife could have done better. She talked quietly the whole time to calm my jitters and Mrs. Simpkins's. Mrs. Moffatt didn't have the jitters. She just kept saying she was sorry to keep us up, the daft woman. I have never felt so—so honored, Bertie, love. Me, Debbie Markle, just a simple, honest whore to be allowed to see *that*."

"Come on, Deb." Bertie tucked her into the crook of his arm and bore her off to bed.

Julian followed them up a few minutes later. He had no idea what time it was. Some unholy hour of the morning, he supposed. He did not carry a candle up with him and no one had lit the branch in his room. Someone from belowstairs had been kept working late, though. There was a freshly made-up fire burning in the hearth. He went to stand at the window and looked out.

The snow had stopped falling, he saw, and the sky had cleared off. He looked upward and saw in that single glance that he had been wrong. It was not an *unholy* hour of the morning at all.

He was still standing there several minutes later when the door of the bedchamber opened. He turned his head to look over his shoulder.

She looked as Debbie had looked but worse. She was bedraggled, weary and beautiful.

"You should not have waited up," she said.

"Come." He beckoned to her.

She came and slumped tiredly against him when he wrapped an arm about her. She sighed deeply.

"Look." He pointed.

She did not say anything for a long while. Neither did he. Words were unnecessary. The Christmas star beamed down at them, symbol of hope, a sign for all who sought wisdom and the meaning of their lives. He was not sure what either of them had learned about Christmas this year, but there was something. It was beyond words at the moment and even beyond coherent thought. But something had been learned. Something had been gained.

"It is Christmas," she said softly at last. Her words held a wealth of meaning beyond themselves.

"Yes," he said, turning his face and kissing the untidy titian hair on top of her head. "Yes, it is Christmas. Did they have their daughter?"

"Oh yes," she said. "I have never seen two people so happy, my lord. On Christmas morning. Could there be a more precious gift?"

"I doubt it," he said, closing his eyes briefly.

"I held her," she said softly. "What a gift that was."

"Blanche," he asked after a short while, "where was this rectory you speak of? Close to the smithy?"

"Yes," she said.

"And you went to school there," he said, "and were given lessons in playing the spinet and delivering babies."

"Y-yes." She had the grace to sound hesitant.

"Blanche," he said, "I have the strange suspicion that you may be the biggest liar of my acquaintance."

She had nothing to say to that.

"Go and get ready for bed," he told her. "I am not sure whether it would be more accurate to say it is late or early."

She lifted her head then and looked at him. "Yes, my lord," she said—the martyr being brave.

He was in bed when she came from the dressing room, wearing the virginal nightgown again with her hair down her back. She was still looking brave, he saw in the dying light of the fire. She approached the bed without hesitation.

"Get in," he told her, holding back the bedcovers and stretching out his other arm beneath her pillow.

"Yes, my lord."

He turned her as she lay down, and drew her snugly against him in order to warm her. He tucked the bedcovers neatly behind her. He found her mouth with his own and kissed her with lingering thoroughness.

"Go to sleep now," he told her when he was done.

That brought her eyes snapping open. "But—" she began.

"But nothing," he said. "You are at the point of total exhaustion, Blanche, and would be quite unable either to enjoy or to be enjoyed. Go to sleep."

"But—" she began again, a protest he silenced with another kiss.

"I have no desire to hear about five hundred pounds and the necessity of earning it," he said. "You promised to be mine for a week, obedient to my will. This is my command for tonight, then. Go to sleep."

He waited for her protest. All he heard instead was a quiet, almost soundless sigh, deepened breathing and total relaxation. She was asleep.

And the funny thing was, he thought, feeling her slim, shapely woman's body pressed to his from toes to forehead, he did not feel either frustrated or deprived. Quite the contrary. He felt warm and relaxed and sleepy, more like a man who had just had good sex than one who had had none at all.

He followed her into sleep.

VERITY AWOKE a little later than usual in the morning. She snuggled sleepily into the warmth of the bed and then came fully awake when she realized that she was alone. She opened her eyes. He was gone. He was not in the room, either, she saw when she looked about.

It was Christmas morning.

He had slept with her last night. Just that. He had *slept* with her. He had had her in bed with him, he had held her close and he had told her to go to sleep. It had not taken her long to obey. But had there been tenderness in his arms and his kiss? Had she imagined it? Certainly there had been no anger.

He was a likable man, she thought suddenly, throwing back the covers and making for the dressing room.

It was a surprising realization. She had thought him impossibly attractive from the start, of course. But she had not expected to find him a pleasant person. Certainly not a *kind* one.

She washed in the tepid water that stood on the washstand and dressed in the white wool dress she had made herself back in the autumn to wear after she left off her mourning. It was very simply styled, with a high neckline, straight, long sleeves and an unadorned skirt flaring from beneath her bosom. She liked its simplicity. She brushed her hair and dressed it in its usual knot at the back of her head. She took one last look at herself in the looking glass and hesitated.

Should she? She looked at the plain neckline of her dress.

She opened the drawer in which she had placed most of her belongings and stared at the box before drawing it out and opening it. It really was beautiful. It must have cost a fortune. Not that its charm lay in its monetary value. It was well crafted, tasteful. The chain was fine and delicate. It was easily the most lovely possession she had ever owned. She touched a finger to the star, withdrew, and then, after hesitating a moment longer, lifted the chain from its silken nesting place. She undid the catch, lowered her head and lifted her arms.

"Allow me," a voice said from behind her, and hands covered her own and took the chain from her.

She kept her head bent until he had secured the chain.

"Thank you," she said, and looked up into the glass.

His hands were on her shoulders. He was dressed with his usual immaculate elegance, she could see.

"It is beautiful," she told him. It really was the perfect ornament for the dress.

"Yes." He turned her to face him. "Is that sadness I see in your eyes, Blanche? It is where it belongs, you know. You have earned the right to wear the Christmas star on your bosom."

She smiled and touched a hand to it. "It is a lovely gift," she said. "I have something for you, too."

She had spoken entirely on impulse. When she left London, she had given no thought to a Christmas gift. She had expected him to be merely an employer, who would pay her for the unlimited use of her body. She had not expected him to become…yes, in some strange way he had become her friend. Someone she cared about. Someone who had shown her care.

She turned to the drawer and reached to the back of it. She could not believe she was about to give away such a treasure and to *him* of all people. And yet she knew that she wanted to do it, that it was the right thing to do. Not that it was either an elaborate or a costly gift. But it had been Papa's.

"Here," she said, holding it out to him on her palm. It was not even wrapped. "It is precious to me. It was my father's. He gave it to me when I left home. I want you to have it." All it was was a handkerchief, folded into a square. It was of the finest linen, it was true. But still only a handkerchief.

He transferred it to his own palm and then looked into her eyes. "I believe," he said, "your gift might be more valuable than mine, Blanche. Mine only cost money. You have given away part of yourself. Thank you. I will treasure it."

"Happy Christmas, my lord," she said.

"And to you." He leaned toward her and set his lips against hers in what was a gentle and achingly sweet kiss. "Happy Christmas, Blanche."

And she felt happy, she thought, even though her thoughts had gone to her mother and Chastity, celebrating the day without her. But they had each other, and she had...

"I wonder how the baby is this morning," she said eagerly. "I can scarcely wait to see her again. Did she sleep? I wonder. Did Mrs. Moffatt sleep? And have the little boys met their new sister yet? I wonder if their papa will have time to spend with them today. It is Christmas Day, such an important day for children. Perhaps—"

"Perhaps, Blanche," Viscount Folingsby said, looking and sounding his bored, cynical self again suddenly, "you will conceive ideas again, as you did yesterday, for everyone's delectation. I do not doubt that the boys and the rest of us will be worn to a thread by the time you have finished with us."

"But did you not enjoy yesterday?" she asked him. Surely he had. "It is *Christmas,* my lord, and Mr. Hollander had made no plans to celebrate it. What choice did I have? Poor man, I daresay he has always had a mother or some other relatives to plan the holiday for him."

"Precisely." He sighed. "It was our idea to escape such plans this year, Blanche. To spend a quiet week instead with the women of our choice. Not gathering greenery in the teeth of a blizzard, but making love in a warm bed. Not loading down the house with Christmas cheer and making merry noise with Christmas carols and entertaining energetic little boys and delivering babies, but—well, making love in a warm bed."

"You did *not* enjoy yesterday," she said, dismayed. "And you *are* disappointed. I *have* failed you. And I have ruined the holiday for Mr. Hollander, too. And—" He had set two fingers firmly against her lips.

"The baby slept through the night," he said, "and has only just begun to fuss. Mrs. Moffatt had a few hours of sleep and declares herself to be refreshed and in the best of health this morning. The Reverend Moffatt is in transports of delight and proclaims himself to be the most fortunate man alive—as well as the cleverest, I do believe—to have begotten a daughter.

"The little boys have been given their gifts and have met their sister, with whom they seem far less impressed than their papa. They are roaring around the sitting room, obeying the paternal command to confine their energies to it until they hear otherwise. Cook is banging around the kitchen with great zeal and has every other servant moving at a brisk trot. Bertie and

Debbie have not yet put in an appearance. I daresay they are making love in a warm bed. And you are looking more beautiful than any woman has any right to look. Virginal white becomes you."

"I am sorry it is not the Christmas you intended," she said.

"Are you?" He smiled lazily. "I am not sure I am, Blanche. Sorry, I mean. It is an interesting Christmas, to say the very least. And it is not over yet. *Do* you have plans for us?"

She felt herself flush. "Well," she said, "I did think that since there are children here and their mother is indisposed and their father will wish to spend much of the day with her…and I thought that since there are still heaps of snow out there even though no more is falling…and I thought that since the rest of us have nothing particular to do all day except…" Her cheeks grew hotter.

"Make love in a warm bed?" he suggested.

"Yes," she said. "Except that. I thought that perhaps we could…that is, unless you wish to do the other. I am quite willing. It is what I came here to do, after all."

He was grinning at her. "Outdoor sports," he said. "I wonder how Bertie and Debbie will greet the happy prospect?"

"Well," she said, "they cannot spend *all* day in bed, can they? It would not be at all polite to the Reverend and Mrs. Moffatt."

He merely chuckled. "Let the day begin," he said,

offering her his arm. "I would not miss it for the world, you know, or even for all the warm beds in the world, for that matter."

CHAPTER SEVEN

JULIAN did not change his mind all through the day though he had hardly exaggerated when he had predicted that Blanche would have run them all ragged before they were done with Christmas.

As soon as breakfast was over, they took the children outside to play in the snow. *They* being he and Blanche until Bertie and Debbie came out to join them. They romped in the snow for what seemed only minutes but must have been hours until Bloggs appeared to inform them that their Christmas dinner was ready. His expression suggested also that Cook would have their heads if they did not come immediately to partake of it.

But long before that they had engaged in a vigorous snowball fight, which turned out to be grossly unfair in Julian's estimation—and he complained loudly about it—as he and Bertie were pitted against both boys as well as both the ladies, two against four. And if Debbie had ever been a member of a rifle regiment, there would surely not be a Frenchman left in France without a hole through his heart. She had a deadly accurate aim and was wildly cheered by her side, and herself, whenever she demonstrated it.

They built snowmen. Or at least Julian and Bertie did while the boys danced around "helping" and Debbie ran off to beg ashes and carrots and one ancient straw hat from the kitchen. Blanche, reclining on a snowbank, declared that as judge she had the hardest job of all. She awarded the prize of one leftover carrot to Bertie and David.

They made snow angels until Rupert declared with loud disgust that it was a girl's game. Blanche and Debbie continued with the sport notwithstanding while the men constructed a long slippery slide on a bit of a slope and risked their necks zooming along it. Somehow Julian ended up with David on his shoulders, clinging to his hair after his hat had proved to be an untrustworthy anchor. The child whooped with mingled fright and glee.

Debbie sought out the tree swing, brushed the snow off it and cleared a path beneath it before summoning everyone else. They all sampled its delights, singly and in pairs, all of them as noisy and exuberant as children. The adults continued even after the children had rushed away at the appearance of their father to bury him up to his neck in snow.

"The snow is starting to melt," Blanche said wistfully as they were going indoors for dinner. "How sad."

"It is in the nature of snow," Julian said, wrapping one arm about her waist. "Just as it is in the nature of time to pass. That is why we have memories."

"The children have had a marvelous morning, have they not?" she said, beaming happily at him.

"Now to which children are you referring?" he asked, kissing her cold red nose. "To the very little ones? Or to the rest of us? For myself I would as soon have been sitting with my feet up before a roaring fire."

She merely laughed.

Christmas dinner proved to be a culinary delight beyond compare. They all ate until they were close to bursting and then Bertie sent for the cook and made a rather pompous speech of congratulation.

But that was not enough for Blanche, of course. If Mr. Hollander would be so good, she suggested, perhaps all the staff could be invited to the sitting room for a drink of the excellent wassail. She for one would like to thank them all for the hard work they had put into giving everyone such a wonderful Christmas.

"I can only echo your sentiments, Lady Folingsby," the Reverend Moffatt remarked. "Though by my observations, the servants are not the only ones who have been hard at work. My wife and I will not soon forget the warm welcome we have received here and the efforts you have all put into entertaining our children. Not to mention last night, for which we will never be able to repay you, my lady, and you, Mrs. Hollander. We will not try, of course, as we know that you acted out of the goodness of your hearts. We humbly accept the gift from two true ladies."

Debbie sniffled and blew her nose in the handkerchief Bertie handed her. "That is one of the nicest things anyone ever said to me," she said. "But it was Blanche who did all the work."

The servants spent the best part of an hour in the sitting room, eating cakes and mince pies and drinking wassail and accepting Christmas bonuses from their employer, as well as from both Julian and the Reverend Moffatt. Julian was never afterward sure who suggested singing Christmas carols again, though he did not doubt it was Blanche. They did so anyway to her accompaniment on the spinet and sang themselves into a thoroughly genial and sentimental mood.

And then after the servants had gone back belowstairs, Mrs. Moffatt made a surprise appearance in the sitting room with the baby.

Julian had always been fond of children. He had had to be, for there had always been enough of them at family gatherings to make life miserable for anyone who was not. But he had never been much for infants or newborns. They were a woman's preserve, he had always thought, needing only to be fed and rocked and sung to and changed.

But he felt a certain proprietary interest in the little Moffatt girl, he discovered. Her birth had somehow brought Christmas alive for him more than ever before. And Blanche had delivered her. And now Blanche was holding her and gazing down at her with such a look of tenderness in her face that he felt dazzled. She looked so right thus, dressed with simple elegance, glowing with health and vitality and warmth, holding a newborn infant in her arms.

If it were her child, his…

He jerked his mind free of such an alarming daydream and found himself gazing deep into her eyes. She smiled at him.

Ah, Blanche. It was hard to believe that just a week ago he had looked on her only as a desirable candidate for his bed. He had seen her beauty—the long, shapely legs, the taut slender body, the glorious hair and lovely face—and not given even one moment's consideration to the fact that there must be a person behind the facade.

And what a person was there. Even more beautiful, perhaps, than the body in which she resided.

He was in love with her, he thought in some astonishment. He had never been in love before. He had been in lust more times than he could recall and had sometimes called it love, especially when he had been younger. But he had never before felt this ache of longing for a *person*. It was not just that he wished to bed her, though he did, of course. It was more than that. Much more. He wanted to be a part of her, a part of her life, not just a very temporary occupant of her body.

He smiled back at her a little uncertainly.

"I daresay," Mrs. Moffatt said, having noticed perhaps the exchange of smiles, "you and her ladyship have not been married long, my lord." Not long enough for the union to have been fruitful, her words implied.

"Not long, ma'am," he agreed.

He was glad, he thought some hours later, after tea, after the vigorous indoor games Blanche and the Reverend Moffatt had organized for the amusement of the children and everyone else, that he had not gone to Conway for Christmas. He had been thinking about it on and off all day and had been missing his family. Had his Christmas gone according to plan, he realized now, he would be regretting his decision. The sort of activity he had planned would not have been any way to celebrate such an occasion. But as events had turned out, he had discovered everything one was surely meant to discover at Christmas—love, hospitality, merriment, kindness, sharing, decency… The list could go on and on.

Sometimes it seemed almost as if one were led blind by some guiding hand toward something for which one had not known one searched. By a star perhaps. To the stable at Bethlehem perhaps. Perhaps he had more in common with the wise men than he had realized until this moment.

The children, yawning and protesting, were finally led away by their father to bed after hugging their adopted "uncles" and "aunts" as if they had known them all their lives.

"I do not believe we will be far behind them, Deb," Bertie said, yawning hugely after they had left. "Have you enjoyed Christmas?"

"Ee, love," Debbie said, "it has been the grandest Christmas since I left home. Maybe grander than then. The Rev is the kindest of gents and the boys are darlings. And the baby! I will never forget last night. I never will. It has been a Christmas to end Christmases."

"I believe," Bertie said, pulling her down onto his lap, perhaps feeling free to do so since the clergyman had expressed his intention of joining his wife and the baby after he had put the boys to bed, "we have you to thank for much of the joy of the past two days, Blanche."

"Oh," she said, "how foolish. It is Christmas. Christmas has a way of happening without any assistance from anyone."

"Nonsense," Julian said. "It needed a whole host of angels to get the shepherds moving off their hillside. It has taken one angel to set us off on a similar pilgrimage."

"Do you mean me?" she asked, blushing. "A strange angel indeed. One with very tarnished wings."

He got to his feet and held out a hand for hers. "It has been a long day," he said, "and you had only a few hours of sleep last night. It is bedtime."

Her eyes met his as she took his hand. There was not even a hint of martyrdom in their expression.

"Good night, Mr. Hollander," she said as the two couples took their leave of one another. "Good night, Debbie. Thank you for helping make Christmas such a joy."

HE WAS STANDING at the window when she came out of the dressing room. He was wearing a nightshirt. The room was warm from the fire that had been built high.

"Is the star still there?" she asked him, going to stand at his side and looking up.

"Gone," he said. "Or merely hidden by clouds. It is warming up out there. The snow will disappear rapidly tomorrow."

"Ah." She sighed. "Christmas is over."

"Not quite." He set an arm about her, and she rested her head on his shoulder. It felt perfectly right to do so. She felt strangely comfortable with him as if, perhaps, she had come to believe the myth that they belonged together. She had even found herself imagining downstairs during the afternoon that that newborn baby was hers, theirs.

"Blanche," he said softly.

And then they were in each other's arms, pressed together, kissing each other with such passion that it seemed indeed that they were one, that they were not meant to be two separate beings, that they would find wholeness and happiness and peace only together like this.

"Blanche." He was kissing her temples, her jaw, her throat, her mouth again. "Ah, my dear one."

It was not enough to touch him with her mouth, her tongue, her arms, her hands. She touched him with her breasts, her hips, her abdomen, her thighs. She wanted…ah, she wanted and wanted. He was warm and hard muscled. He smelled musky and male. And he felt safe, solid, dependable. He felt like a missing part of herself for which she craved. She wanted him. She wanted wholeness.

She did not know how her nightgown had become unbuttoned down the front. She did not care. She needed him closer. She needed his hands and then his mouth on her breasts. She needed…ah, yes.

"Ah, yes," she said from somewhere deep in her throat, and she twined her fingers in his hair and tipped her head back as he suckled first one nipple and then the other, sucking gently, laving the tips with his tongue, sending raw aches down between her thighs and up through her throat into her nostrils. "Ah, yes. Please." Her knees no longer quite belonged to her.

"Come, my love," he whispered against her mouth, lifting her into his arms. "Come to bed."

He slid her nightgown down over her feet after setting her down and pulled his nightshirt off over his head. She gazed at him in the flickering light of the fire, her eyes half-closed. He was beautiful, beautiful.

"Come." She lifted her arms to him. "Come."

His hands and his mouth moved over her, worshiping her, arousing her. She touched him, explored him, rejoiced in the feel of him, the heat of him. But she could not touch him *there,* though she became increasingly aware of that part of him, thick and long and hard. He touched her where she had never thought to be touched with a hand, with fingers. She felt an ache so intense it was pain and pleasure all strangely mixed together. And she heard wetness and was curiously unembarrassed.

She could not wait—for she knew not what.

"Please," she begged him, her voice sounding not quite her own. "Please."

"Yes," he said, coming to her open arms, coming down into them, coming down between her thighs, pressing them apart with his own, coming heavy and warm and eager to her nakedness. "Yes, my love. Yes."

She would not believe at first that it could be possible. He pressed against her and she was almost surprised, although she knew her own body, when he found an opening there and pushed into it, stretching her wide, not stopping, coming and coming.

"Don't tense," he murmured against her ear. "Just relax. Ah, my dear one, my love. I don't want to hurt you."

But it did not hurt. Not really. It only surprised her and filled her with wonder and gave her a moment's panic when she thought he could come no farther but he pressed on. There was what she expected to be pain, and then he pressed past it until he was deep, deep inside. She lifted her legs from the bed and twined them about his. He moaned.

And then, just when she thought ecstasy had been arrived at and finally relaxed, he moved. He moved to leave her.

"No," she murmured in protest.

He lifted his head, looked down into her face and kissed her. "Yes," he said. "Like this, you see." And from the brink of her he pressed deep again. And withdrew and pressed deep.

Final ecstasy came several minutes or hours later—

time no longer had any meaning—after they had loved together with sweet, strong rhythm, with a sharing of bodies and pleasure, with a mingling of selves. It came with a building of almost unbearable need, with an involuntary tightening of every inner muscle and with a final relinquishing of self, a final trust in the power of union. It came as shivering relaxation and quiet peace. It came with shared words.

"My sweet life," he whispered. "My dear angel."

"My love," she heard herself murmuring. "My love, my love."

She fell asleep moments later, after he had drawn out of her and rolled onto his side, taking her with him and keeping her against him. Just after he drew the bedcovers warmly about her.

JULIAN DID NOT fall asleep for a long while, even though he lay in a pleasant lethargy. He was sexually sated. He was also deeply happy.

He had never set much store by happiness. It was strange, perhaps, when for all his adult years he had directed almost all his energies into activities that would bring him pleasure or gratification in varying degrees. But he had never really believed in *happiness*. He had never either expected or craved it for himself.

Happiness, he thought, was a feeling of rightness, of having arrived at a place one had always sought, however halfheartedly, but never quite believed existed. With a person of whose existence one had always dreamed, even if not always consciously, but had never thought to find. Happiness was a moment in time when one was at peace with life and the universe, when one felt one had found the meaning of one's existence. And it was more than a moment. It was a direction for the rest of life, an assurance that the future, though not, of course, a happily ever after, would nevertheless be well worth living.

He had never really believed in romantic love.

But he was in love with Blanche Heyward.

There was more to it than that, though. He would perhaps, even now, have laughed at himself if that had been all. But it was not. He *loved* her. She had become in the course of a few days—though he felt he had known her from the eternity before birth—as essential to his life as the air he breathed.

Fanciful thoughts. He would be writing a poem to her left eyebrow if he did not watch himself. He mocked himself as he smoothed the hair back from her sleeping face and settled her head more comfortably in the hollow between his neck and shoulder. He had been teased by her for a few days, that was all, and had finally had very good sex indeed with her. In a few weeks' time, when they were back in London and he had set her up properly as his mistress, he would already be tiring of her. He had quickly tired of every mistress he had ever kept.

He kissed her brow and then her lips. She made little protesting sounds but did not wake.

No, it was not so. He wished it were. She was a blacksmith's daughter and an opera dancer. He was a viscount, heir to an earldom. No other relationship was possible between them but that of protector and mistress. He could not...

But as he stared into the darkness, lit only by the dying embers of the fire, he knew that there was one thing he would never be able to do. He could never marry anyone else. Ever. Even though he owed it to his father to secure the succession for the next generation. Even though he owed it to his mother and his sisters to secure their future. Even though he owed it to his birth, his upbringing, his position.

If he could not marry Blanche—and he did not see how he ever could—then he would not marry anyone.

Perhaps he would see things differently tomorrow, next week, next year. He did not know. All he did know now was that he loved, that he was happy, that—he had been led to one of those earth-shattering experiences one sometimes read about that changed the whole direction of his life.

He would wake her up later, he decided, and make slow, lazy love to her again. And if they stayed awake afterward, he would take the risk of telling her how he felt. It was no very great risk, he thought. She felt about him as he felt about her. That was a part of the miracle. Unworthy as he was of her, she felt as he did. *My love,* she had called him over and over again as he had spilled his seed into her. And her body had told him the same thing even if she had not spoken the words aloud, and their minds and their very souls had intertwined as their bodies had merged.

Later he would love her again. In the meantime he slept.

NOT FOR ONE moment did Verity feel disoriented when she awoke. Neither did she entertain any illusions.

She had given in to naiveté and passion and the sentimentality that had surrounded Christmas. She had given in to a practiced seducer. Not that she would have resisted even if she had realized the truth at the time. She would not have done so. She would have given her body just as unprotestingly. She would have done so as part of the bargain she had made with him in London. But she would have guarded her heart. She would not so foolishly have imagined that it was a love encounter.

He had been a man claiming his mistress.

She had been a woman at work, earning her pay.

And now, beyond all argument, she was a fallen woman. A whore. She had done it for Chastity. Strange irony, that. But that fact notwithstanding, she was and always would be a whore.

She could not bear to face him in the morning. She could not bear to see the knowing look in his eyes, the triumph. She could not bear to play a part. She could not bear to become his regular mistress, to be used at his convenience until he tired of her and discarded her. She could not even bear to finish out this week, after which she would be free to withdraw from any future commitment.

Perhaps at the end of the week she would not have the strength to do so.

She could not bear to face him in the morning and see from his whole attitude how little their encounter had meant to him.

She had no choice but to live out the week. Even if there were a way of leaving now, she still had two hundred and fifty pounds to earn. And he had already paid her that same amount. Had she earned that advance? With what had happened here a few hours ago? With her willingness to allow it to happen on the two previous nights? *Two hundred and fifty pounds?* If she were a governess, she would be fortunate to earn that amount in four years.

There *was* a way of leaving. There was a village three miles away. A stagecoach stopped there early each morning. She had heard the servants mention it. But there was snow on the ground. And would the stage run on the day after Christmas? The snow had been melting since yesterday afternoon. It had been a cloudy night, perhaps a mild night. Why would the stage *not* run?

She would surely wake him if she tried to get out of bed, if she tried to dress and creep away.

But now that the mad, impossible idea had entered her mind, she could not leave it alone. She *could* not face him in the morning. If she felt nothing for him, she would do so with all the cheerful good sense she could muster. She had taken this employment quite deliberately, after all, knowing what was involved. She had been prepared to do what she had done with him earlier as many times as he chose. It was not from that she shrank.

In her naiveté she had not realized that her feelings might become involved. It had not occurred to her that spending a few days in close proximity with a man would reveal him to her as a person, or that she would find this particular man likable, charming, lovable. She had never for one moment expected to fall in love. She had done even worse than that. She had *loved* and still did and always would.

After removing herself from his arms while he grumbled sleepily, she edged her way across and then out of the bed. The room was cold, she realized, shivering, and she was naked and stiff. She silently gathered up her nightgown from the floor and tiptoed to the dressing room, the door of which was fortunately ajar. She slipped inside and shut the door slowly. Fortunately the hinges were well oiled and made no sound.

She lit a single candle, washed quickly in the ice-cold water, dressed in her warmest clothes, packed her belongings and wondered if her luck would hold while she tried to leave the house undetected.

She had not packed everything. She had left his signet ring on the washstand. And one other thing. She wasted several precious moments gazing at it, spread across the top of the chest of drawers, where she had put it the night before. Should she take it? She wanted desperately to do so. It would be the one memento. But she would not need a memento. And it had been too extravagant a gift, especially under the circumstances.

She set one fingertip lightly to the gold star on its chain and then left it where it was. She did not go back into the bedchamber. There was a door leading directly from the dressing room to the corridor beyond.

It had always seemed rather silly, she thought as she made her way cautiously downstairs and let herself out of the front door, to talk about a heart aching. How could a heart *ache?* But this morning it no longer seemed silly. She hurried along the driveway to the road, past the still-stuck carriage, relieved to see that the snow had melted sufficiently that she should be able to walk to the village without any great difficulty.

Her heart ached for a little gold star and chain that would fit into the palm of her hand. And for the Christmas star that had brought such joy and such hope this year and had lured her into a great foolishness. And for the man whom she hoped was still asleep where she had slept with him a mere half hour ago.

She would never see him again, if only she was in time for the stage. *Never* could sometimes be a terrifying word.

She would love him forever.

CHAPTER EIGHT

IT TOOK Julian three months to find her. Though even then he had the merest glimpse of her only to lose her again without a trace, it seemed. Just as he had lost her on Christmas night.

He had woken up by daylight and been half amused, half exasperated to find her gone from bed and from their room. He had washed and shaved and dressed in leisurely fashion, hoping she would return before he was ready, and had then gone in search of her. Even when he had not found her in any of the day rooms or in the kitchen he had not been alarmed, or even when he had peered out of doors and not seen her walking there. He had assumed she must be in the only possible place left, Mrs. Moffatt's room, admiring the baby.

The morning had been well advanced before he had discovered the truth. She was gone and so were all her possessions except the star and chain. He had picked up the necklace, squeezed it tight in his palm and tipped back his head in silent agony.

She had left him.

Why?

He had returned to London the same day, having concocted a whole arsenal of new lies for the edification of Bertie, Debbie and the Moffatts. And so had begun his search for her. She had left her job at the opera without a word to anyone there. She had not gone to any other theater—he had checked them all. And none of her former coworkers knew of her whereabouts. They had not seen or heard of her since before Christmas.

Eventually he bribed the manager of the opera house to give him her address, but it was a false one. There was no one by the name of Blanche Heyward living there, the landlady informed him, and no one of her description, either, except that Miss Ewing, who used to live there, had been tall. But Miss Ewing had been no opera dancer and nor had any other lady who had ever rented her house. The very idea! She had glared at him with indignation. He became almost desperate enough to travel down to Somersetshire in search of the smithy that had been her home. But how many smithies must there be in Somersetshire?

Blanche clearly did not want to be found.

He tried to put her from his mind. Christmas had been an unusually pleasurable interlude, largely thanks to Blanche, and sleeping with her had been the icing on an already scrumptious cake. But really there was no more to it than that. One could not carry Christmas about all year long, after all. One had to get back to the mundane business of everyday life.

But he did at the end of January make a three-day visit to Conway, where he was greeted with such affection by his parents and such a scold from his youngest sister that he almost lost his courage. He found it again when sitting alone with his father in the library one afternoon. He would not marry Lady Sarah Plunkett, he had announced quite firmly. And before his father could draw breath to ask him—as he was obviously about to do—whom he *would* marry then, he had added that there was only one woman in the world he would consider marrying, but she would not marry him and anyway she was ineligible.

"Ineligible?" his father had asked, eyebrows raised.

"Daughter of a blacksmith," his son had told him.

"Of a *blacksmith*." His father had pursed his lips. "And *she* will not marry *you,* Julian? She has more sense than you."

"I love her," Julian had said.

"Hmm" was all the comment his father had made. Perhaps that was all the comment he had thought necessary since the marriage seemed in no danger of becoming a reality.

Back in London Julian had searched hopelessly, aimlessly, until the afternoon in March when he spotted her on a crowded Oxford Street. She was on the opposite side of the street, coming out of a milliner's shop. He came to an abrupt halt, unable to believe the evidence of his own eyes. But then her eyes locked on his and he knew he was not mistaken. He started forward as she turned abruptly and hurried away along the pavement.

At the same moment a gentleman's curricle and a tradesman's wagon decided to dispute the right-of-way along the street, whose width had been narrowed by the presence of a large carriage picking up two passengers loaded with parcels. They confronted each other head-on and refused to budge an inch for each other.

The tradesman swore foully and the gentleman only a little more elegantly; the horses protested in the way horses did best. A whole host of bystanders took sides or merely gathered to enjoy the spectacle, and Julian got caught up in the tangle for a few seconds too long. He was across the street in less than a minute, but during that minute Blanche Heyward had disappeared totally. He hurried along the street in the direction she had taken, peering into every shop and along every alley. But there was no sign of her. Or of the young girl who had been with her.

One thing was clear to him. If she had ever regretted running away from Bertie's hunting box, she regretted it no longer. She had no wish to be found. She had no wish even to claim the second half of her week's salary.

She had played the martyr after all, then, on that night and with such courage that he had not even known that she played a part. Fool that he was, he had thought her feelings matched his own. He had thought she enjoyed losing her virginity to a rake who had paid for her favors. What a fool!

He gave up looking for her. Let her live out her life in peace. He just hoped that the two hundred and fifty pounds had proved sufficient to cover whatever need at the smithy had impelled her to accept his proposition, and that there had been some left over for her.

But his resolve slipped when he attended a rout at his eldest sister's in April. Her drawing room and the two salons that had been opened up for the occasion were gratifyingly full, she told him, her arm drawn through his as she led him through. New families were arriving in town every day for the season. But he drew her to a sudden halt.

"Who is that?" he asked, indicating with a nod of the head a thin, pretty young girl who was standing with an older lady and with General Sir Hector Ewing and his wife.

"The general?" she asked. "You do not know him, Julian? He—"

"The young girl with him," he said.

She looked archly at him and smiled. "She *is* pretty, is she not?" she said. "She is the general's niece, Miss Chastity Ewing."

Ewing. *Ewing!* The name of the tall lady who had lived at the false address given to the opera house manager by Blanche Heyward. And Miss Chastity Ewing was the young lady who had been with Blanche on Oxford Street.

"I have an acquaintance with the general, Elinor," he said, "but not a close one. Present me to Miss Ewing, if you please."

"Smitten after one glance," his sister said with a laugh. "This is *very* interesting, Julian. Come along, then."

"WHO?" Verity asked faintly. She had waited up for Chastity even though it was late and even though they no longer shared a room. She was sitting on her sister's bed.

"Viscount Folingsby," Chastity said. "At least I think I have the name correct. He is Lady Blanchford's brother. He is *very* handsome and *very* charming, Verity."

There was a slight buzzing in her head. It had been almost inevitable, of course. She knew that he was in London—she had *seen* him—and that therefore, he would attend ton events, especially now that the season was beginning. Since her uncle had returned from Vienna the week after Christmas, brought them all to live with him and was now undertaking to introduce Chastity to society, then Chass would surely attend some of the same balls and parties as him. Verity had just hoped that pretty and healthy as Chastity was, she would be just too youthful to attract the notice of Viscount Folingsby.

"Is he?" she said in answer to her sister's words.

But Chastity was smiling at her with bright mischief and came to sit on the bed beside her, still clad in her evening gown. "Of course he is," she said. "You know him, Verity."

Her heart performed a somersault. "Oh?" she said. "Do I?"

Chastity laughed merrily and clapped her hands. "Of course you do," she said, "and I can tell from your guilty expression that you remember him very well. He *told* us. About Christmas."

Verity could feel the blood draining out of her head, leaving it cold and clammy and dizzy.

Chastity took one of her sister's cold, nerveless hands in her own. "Dear Verity," she said. "I daresay you have convinced yourself that he did not really notice you. But I knew it would happen sooner or later. I *told* you, did I not? How could any gentleman look at your beauty and not be struck by it and by *you*. No matter who you were."

"Does Mama know?" Verity was whispering.

"Of course," Chastity said, laughing gleefully. "She was there with me and our uncle."

"*Uncle* knows?" They would all be turned out on the street tomorrow, she thought. Was there any way of persuading him to dismiss her alone? She had already displeased him by refusing to participate in any of the social entertainments of the season. She had pleaded advanced age. Could Mama and Chastity be saved?

"The viscount knew that Lady Coleman went to Scotland the day after Christmas," Chastity said. "He assumed you had gone with her. Imagine his surprise and gratification to learn that you had not, that you were here in London."

"*What?*" There *was* no Lady Coleman, and he did not know her as Verity Ewing.

"Oh, Verity, you silly goose." Chastity raised her sister's hand to her cheek and held it there. "Did you think he would not notice you because you were merely a lady's companion? Did you think he would not wish to renew the acquaintance? He told Mama how you quietly set about making everyone's Christmas comfortable and joyful, not just Lady Coleman's. He told us about the clergyman's family being stranded and about you delivering the baby. Oh, Verity, why did you not tell us about that? And he confessed to Mama that he had kissed you beneath the kissing bough. He has the most roguish smile."

"Oh," Verity said.

"And you thought he would forget you?" Chastity said. "He has not forgotten. He asked Mama if he might call upon you. And he asked Uncle for a private word. They went walking off together. Verity, he is *wonderful*. Almost wonderful enough for you, I do believe. Viscountess Folingsby. Yes." She laughed again. "It will suit. I declare it will. And *now* I know why you have refused to go into society. You have been afraid of meeting him. You have been afraid he would not remember you. You goose!"

Verity could only cling to her sister's hand and stare wide-eyed. He knew who she was! Somehow Mama or Chastity must have mentioned Lady Coleman to him and he had played along with the game. And he wanted to see her. Why? To pay her the rest of her salary? But she had not earned it. To demand part of the other half back, then? The irony of that was that her sacrifice had been unnecessary. Her uncle had taken over their care and the payment of Chastity's medical bills within two days of her return to London.

Perhaps he wanted her to earn what he had already paid her. Perhaps he wanted her to be his mistress here, in town. But he knew she was General Sir Hector Ewing's niece.

She did not *want* to see him. The very thought of doing so was enough to throw her into a panic, as the reality had that afternoon on Oxford Street.

And yet in almost four months the pain had not diminished even one iota. It only seemed to grow worse. She had even found herself bitterly disappointed, as well as knee-weakeningly relieved, when she had discovered that their one encounter had not borne fruit.

"Verity." Her sister's eyes were softly glowing. "You *have* remembered him. You are in love with him. Do not think you can deceive me. How splendid this is. How very romantic. It is like a fairy tale."

Verity snatched her hand away and jumped to her feet. "Foolish girl," she said. "It is high time you were asleep. You have recovered your health even if you are still just a little too thin, but you must not tax your strength. Go to bed now. Turn around and let me undo your buttons."

But Chastity was not so easily distracted. She got to her feet, too, and flung her arms about her sister. Her eyes shone with tears. "I am healthy because of the sacrifice you made for me," she said. "I will never *ever* forget what I owe you, Verity. But you are going to be rewarded. You never would have met him if you had not taken employment with Lady Coleman and if you had not given up your Christmas with us to go away with her. So you see it is a just reward. And I am so happy I could *weep*."

"Go to bed and to sleep," Verity said firmly. "You are drawing far too many conclusions from Viscount Folingsby's courtesy this evening. Besides, I do not like him above half."

Chastity was laughing softly as she left the room.

Verity stood against the door of her own room after she had closed it behind her, her eyes tight shut.

He had found her. But did she want to be found? Perhaps, after all, she needed to be. There was a yawning emptiness in her life, a sense of something unresolved, unfinished. Perhaps it should be finished. She did not know quite why he wished to see her—certainly not for any of the reasons Chastity imagined—but perhaps she should find out. Perhaps if she saw him again, if she found out exactly what it was he wanted of her, she would finally be able to close the book on that episode from the past and move on into the future.

Perhaps she would be able to stop loving him.

HE HAD SPOKEN with her uncle the evening before. He had met him again during the morning in order to discuss and settle details. And now, this afternoon, he had spoken with her mother. Mrs. Ewing had gone to send her daughter down to the visitors' salon in which he waited, feeling more nervous than he had ever felt in his life before.

The door opened and closed quietly. She stood against it, her hands behind her, probably still gripping the knob. She was dressed in pale green muslin, a dress of simple design. Her hair was dressed plainly, too. She had lost some weight and some color. But even if she tried twice as hard she would never be able to disguise the fact that she was an extraordinarily beautiful woman. He made her his most elegant bow.

"Miss Ewing?" he said.

She stared at him for several moments before releasing her hold on the knob and curtsying. "My lord."

"Miss *Verity* Ewing," he said. "You were misnamed."

She had nothing to say to that.

"Verity," he said.

"I have two hundred pounds left," she told him then, her voice soft, her chin up, her shoulders back. "I have not needed it after all. I will return it to you. I hope you will agree to forget the fifty pounds. I did partly earn it, after all."

The younger girl had been ill. Verity Ewing had taken employment in order to pay the physician's bills and to buy medicines. She had worked as a companion to Lady Coleman. She had done it for her sister.

"I believe your virginity was worth fifty pounds," he said. "Where is the rest?"

"Here."

She carried a small reticule over her arm, he saw. She opened it and took a roll of banknotes from it. She held them out to him and then brought them to him when he did not move. He took the money with one hand and the reticule with the other and set them down on the chair beside him.

"You are satisfied now?" he asked her. "It is all finished now?"

She nodded, looking down at the money. "I should have returned it to you before," she said. "I did not know quite how. I am sorry."

"Verity," he said softly. "My love."

She closed her eyes and kept them closed. "No," she said. "It is finished. I will not be your mistress. I will always be a…a fallen woman, but I will not be your mistress. Please leave now. And thank you for not exposing me to my mother and sister. Or to my uncle."

"My love." He was not at all sure of himself. Verity Ewing, alias Blanche Heyward, was, as he knew from experience, a woman of strong will and firm character. "Must I go? Or may I stay—forever? Will you marry me?"

She opened her eyes then and raised them to his chin. She smiled. "Ah," she said, "of course. I am a gentleman's daughter and you are a gentleman. No, my lord, you do not have to do the decent thing. I will not expose you, either, you see."

"It was your first time," he told her. "I could not

expect you to understand. You had not the experience. Usually when sex is purchased, it is simply for pleasure, on the man's part at least. It was pleasing, was it not? For both of us? But it was more. In a sense it was my first time, too, you see. I had never made love before.

"What happened *was* love, Verity. I knew with my body while we loved, with my mind after it was over, that you had become the air I breathed, the life I lived, the soul I cherished. I thought you felt the same. It did not occur to me that perhaps you did not until I discovered that you had left me. Did you feel as much pain on that day, I wonder, as I did? I have never felt an agony more intense."

"I was a blacksmith's daughter," she said, "an opera dancer and a whore. What you would have offered then would have been far less than marriage. I have not changed, my lord. I am the daughter of a clergyman, but I am still a whore. I will not be your mistress or your wife."

He possessed himself of both her hands. They were like ice. "You will scrape together the money," he said fiercely. "The fifty pounds. Every penny of it. I want it returned. And then I will hear you take back that ugly name you call yourself. Tell me something. And tell me the truth, *Verity*. Why did you allow me to bed you that night? Were you a working girl earning her pay? Or were you a woman making love, giving and receiving love without a thought to money? Which was it? *Look* at me."

She raised her eyes to his.

"Tell me." He was whispering, he realized. The whole of his future, the whole of his happiness depended upon her reply. He was far from sure of what it would be.

"How could I not love you?" she said. "They were magical days. And I was taken off guard. I went there with a cynical, arrogant rake. And I discovered there a warm, gentle, fun-loving, caring man. I have no experience with such situations, my lord. How could I not love you with my body and my heart and everything that is me? It did not once occur to me as *that* was happening that I was becoming a whore."

"You were not," he told her. "You were becoming mine as I was becoming yours. What we did was wrong. It should not have been done outside wedlock. But worse sins than that can be forgiven, I believe. Let me say one more thing before I plead with you again. I visited my father at Conway Hall after Christmas. He is the Earl of Grantham. Did you know that? I am his heir.

"He has been very eager for some time for me to marry and produce an heir since I have no brothers. I love my father, Verity. And I know my duty to him and to my position. But I told him that I could never marry anyone but you. That was when I still thought you the daughter of a blacksmith and an opera dancer. I *never* thought of you as a whore. What we did in bed together was love, not business."

"And how did your father reply?" she asked.

He smiled at her. "My father loves me, Verity. My happiness is important to him. In our family love has always been of more importance than duty. He would have given his blessing—a little reluctantly, it is true—to my marriage even to a blacksmith's daughter."

She dropped her glance again to stare down at their joined hands. He squeezed hers tightly and his heart hammered painfully against his chest.

"My love," he said. "Verity. Miss Ewing. Will you do me the great honor of marrying me?"

She kept her head down. "It was Christmas," she said. "Everything looks different at Christmas. More rosy, more possible, more unreal. This is a mistake. You should not have come. I do not know how you discovered who I am."

"I believe," he said, "the mistake is ours, Verity. We act as if Christmas is for one day of the year only, as if peace and hope and happiness can exist only then. It was not meant to be that way. Was all that business at Bethlehem intended to bring joy to the world for just one day of the year? What little trust we have in our religion. How little we demand of it and give to it. Why can it not be Christmas now, today, for you and me?"

"Because it is not," she said.

He released her hands then and reached into an inner pocket of his coat. "Yes, it is," he said. "It will be. How about this?" He held in his palm the linen handkerchief she had given him as a gift. He unfolded it carefully until she could see the gold star on its chain nestled within.

"Oh," she said softly.

"Do you remember what you said about it when I gave it to you?" he asked her.

She shook her head. "I hurt you."

"Yes," he said. "You did. You told me the Star of Bethlehem belonged in the heavens to bring hope, to guide its followers to wisdom and the meaning of their lives. Perhaps some power did not quite agree with you. Here it is, lying here between us. I believe we did follow it at Christmas, Verity, perhaps with as little understanding as the wise men themselves of where exactly it was leading us and to what. It led us to each other. To hope. To love. To a future that could hold companionship and love and happiness if we are willing to follow it to the end. Come with me. All the way. That one more irrevocable step. Please?"

Her eyes, when they looked up into his, were swimming with tears. "It can be Christmas today?" she said. "And every day?"

"But not in any magical sense," he said. "We can *make* every day Christmas. But only if we work hard at it. Only if we remember the miracle every day of our lives."

"Oh, my lord," she said.

"Julian."

"Julian." She gazed at him and he could feel his anxiety ease as she slowly smiled.

"Marry me," he whispered.

She lifted her hands then and framed his face with them. "I should have trusted my heart more than my head," she said. "My heart told me it was a shared love. My head told me how foolish I was. Julian." Her arms twined about his neck. "Oh, Julian, my love. Oh yes, if you are quite sure. But I know you are. And I am, too. I have loved you with so much pain, so much longing, so little trust. I *love* you."

He stopped her babbling with his mouth. He wrapped his arms about her and held her tightly to him. He held everything that was most dear in his life and vowed that he would never ever let her go, that he would never even for a single moment forget the strange, undeserved chance that had led him out into the desert to follow a star along an unknown route to an unknown destination. He would never cease marveling that he had been led, bored and cynical and arrogant, to peace and redemption and love.

In one palm, clasped tightly at her back as they kissed eagerly, joyfully, passionately, he held the linen handkerchief, which had been a treasured memento of her father, and the gold star, which he would hang about her neck in a few minutes' time.

The gifts of Christmas.

The gifts of love.

THE SEASON
FOR SUITORS
Nicola Cornick

CHAPTER ONE

THE LETTER arrived with his breakfast.

It was written in an unmistakably feminine hand and it smelled faintly of jasmine perfume.

Sebastian, Duke of Fleet, was not pleased to see it. Letters from ladies, especially those that arrived early in the morning, usually presaged bad news. Either some misguided woman was threatening to sue him for breach of promise, or his great-aunt was coming to stay, and he welcomed neither.

"Perch, what is this?" the duke asked, tapping the parchment with his finger.

His butler continued to unload the breakfast from the silver tray, placing the coffeepot at an exact degree from the cup, and the milk jug at the perfect angle from both. Perch was a butler of precision.

"It is a letter from a lady, your grace."

The duke's brows drew together in an intimidating frown. He had spent much of the previous night at White's; both the drink and the play had been heavy, and this morning his mind was not very clear. At least he had had the sense to reject the amorous advances of one of

London's latest courtesans. He had had no wish to wake up with her painted face beside him.

He had an unwelcome suspicion that he was getting too old for drinking and debauchery, a superannuated rake. Once he started to wear a wig and use face paint to cover the ravages of age, he would have to ask Perch to shoot him.

He pushed aside the dispiriting thought. Without the wine and the gambling and the women there was little left for him, except a rambling old mausoleum of a house that, on this December day, was particularly difficult to heat. Indeed, his hot water bottle had burst in the night, adding another unpleasant dimension to his night's slumber.

"I *perceive* it is from a lady," he said coldly. "I simply wondered which lady was attempting to communicate with me?"

Perch's expression suggested that his master might consider breaking open the seal in order to find out, but after a moment he answered him.

"The letter was delivered by a man in the Davencourt livery, your grace."

The duke reached thoughtfully for the coffeepot and poured for himself, then he slid his knife under the seal, scattering little bits of wax across the table, where they mixed with the crumbs from the toast. Perch winced at the mess. Seb ignored him. What benefit was there in being a duke if one could not scatter crumbs as one pleased? After all, he attended to his ducal respon-

sibilities in exemplary fashion. He had improved the
family seat at Fleet Castle, he was generous to his
tenants, he had even been known to attend the House
of Lords if there was a particularly important debate
taking place. His days were perfectly ordered—and
damnably boring. Life was hard when one had done
everything there was to do.

He unfolded the letter and looked at the signature.

Yours sincerely, Miss Clara Davencourt.

He was aware of rather more pleasure than seemed
quite appropriate. He had not seen Clara Davencourt for
almost eighteen months and had not known she was
currently in London. He sipped his coffee, rested the
letter on the table and swiftly scanned the contents.

Your Grace…

That was rather more formal than some of the things
Miss Davencourt had called him during their last encounter. Arrogant, conceited and rude were the words
that sprang immediately to his memory.

I find myself in something of a dilemma…

Seb's blue eyes narrowed. The combination of Miss
Davencourt and a dilemma was sufficient to strike
dread into the strongest constitution.

I find that I need some paternal advice…

A smile curled the corner of Seb's firm mouth. Paternal advice indeed! If Miss Clara Davencourt had deliberately set out to depress his pretensions as the most notorious rake in town she could not have done a better job. He was only twelve years her senior and had not begun his life of dissipation at so young an age that he was qualified to be her father.

My brother is preoccupied with affairs of state and all the more suitable of his friends are un-available at present, which only leaves you…

Seb winced. The minx. She knew how to deliver a neat insult.

I therefore have no alternative than to beg your help. If you would call at Davencourt House at the earliest opportunity I should be most grateful.

Seb sat back in his chair. Calling on young ladies in order to play the role of paternal confidant was so foreign to him as to be ludicrous. He could not imagine what had possessed Clara even to ask. Of course, he would not comply. It was out of the question. If she needed advice she should be sending for a female friend, not the greatest rake in London.

He glanced out the window. The winter morning

looked crisp and bright. There was a dusting of frost on the rooftops. There were so many possibilities for a clear Yuletide morning. He could go riding. He could go to Tattersalls and spend more money on horses. He could go to White's and read the paper, chat with his cronies, drink some more fine brandy. He yawned.

He could go to Collett Square and call upon Miss Clara Davencourt.

It would be something to do. He could teach her that summoning rakes to one's drawing room was in every way a poor idea.

He folded the letter and slid it into his pocket. Draining his coffee cup, he stood up and stretched. He was aware of a most unfamiliar feeling, a lifting of the spirits, a sense of anticipation. He took the stairs two at a time, calling for his valet as he went.

MISS CLARA DAVENCOURT was sitting in the library of the house in Collett Square, listening with a quarter of an ear while her companion, Mrs. Boyce, read to her from the *Female Spectator*. She checked the little marble clock on the mantelpiece. The Duke of Fleet would surely have received her letter by now. She wondered when he might call. Then she was struck by the thought that perhaps he might not call at all. Given that they had parted on the worst possible terms eighteen months before, she supposed it was quite possible he would not wish to see her again. She fidgeted with the material of her skirt, smoothing away imaginary creases. Seb Fleet was a rogue, but on this occasion that was what she needed. A gentleman simply would not do.

Clara wrinkled her nose slightly as she recalled their last meeting. She had called Fleet a callous, coldhearted scoundrel when he had rejected her admittedly unconventional but honest offer of marriage. It had taken all her courage to propose in the first place, and to be turned down had been a dreadful blow. In her pride and unhappiness she had told him that she never wished to see him again so she could understand if he chose not to respond to her plea now.

"The Duke of Fleet, ma'am." Segsbury, the Davencourt butler, was bowing in the doorway. Clara jumped. Despite the fact that she had been half expecting him, she felt shock skitter along her nerves. Mrs. Boyce jumped, too. She dropped the newspaper and her hand fluttered to her throat. Clara noted the pink color that swept up her companion's neck to stain her cheeks, and the brightness that lit Mrs. Boyce's eyes. She bit her lip, hiding a smile. She had seen Sebastian Fleet have this effect on many ladies, no matter their age.

The duke was bowing to Mrs. Boyce and smiling at her in a way that made the woman's hands flutter like nervous moths. Clara watched with a certain cynicism. Charm was as effortless to Fleet as breathing.

Nevertheless, as he turned toward her she could not quite repress the flicker of awareness that he kindled inside her. She had assured herself that the previous eighteen months had taught her indifference where the Duke of Fleet was concerned. Now she knew that she lied.

It was impossible to be indifferent to Sebastian Fleet. He was a big man, both tall and broad, and his command of any room and any situation appeared natural. Despite his size he moved with a nonchalant grace that compelled the gaze. Clara reminded herself not to stare. She dropped her eyes to the embroidery that rested in her lap. She hated embroidering and would leave the material sitting around for months with absolutely no work done on it at all, but at a time like this it was a useful subterfuge.

Fleet was standing before her now. She could see the high polish of his boots. She resisted the urge to look up sharply. Instead she raised her chin slowly, composedly, every inch a lady of quality.

His eyes were very blue and lit with a devilry that told her more clearly than words that he was remembering their last meeting. Her heart thumped once with a mixture of nostalgia and relief. Now, she was sure, they could behave as mere acquaintances.

She saw the look in his eyes and amended the thought. She was far too aware of his physical presence to be comfortable with him. She felt her color rise and silently cursed him. He had taken her hand although she had not offered it. Neither of them were wearing gloves, and his fingers were warm and strong against hers, sending a shiver along her nerves.

"It is a great pleasure to see you again, Miss Davencourt." He held her hand for a moment longer than was quite respectable. A rakish smile curved his firm mouth. "I was afraid we might never meet again."

Clara cast her gaze down. "I regret there was no other course open to me, your grace."

The Duke's smile grew. He turned to Mrs. Boyce. "I wondered whether I might have a little time alone with Miss Davencourt, ma'am? We are old friends."

For a moment Clara thought her companion was so swept away by Fleet's charm that she was actually going to agree. Then the happy light died from Mrs. Boyce's eyes. Clara had impressed upon her many times that she was not to leave her alone with any gentleman, least of all a certified scoundrel. This, the one time Clara *did* wish to be left alone, was the first occasion on which Mrs. Bryce had remembered what her duty entailed.

"I am sorry, your grace, but that would not be in the least proper of me."

Mrs. Boyce sat up straighter, looking fully prepared to take up residence on the gold sofa until the duke had departed.

It took more than a mere refusal to stop Seb Fleet. "I had actually intended to take Miss Davencourt driving, ma'am," he said. "It is such a beautiful day."

Mrs. Boyce's face cleared. "Driving! Oh, I see. Well, in that case there can be no objection. Nothing untoward could possibly take place in a curricle."

Fleet smiled broadly. Clara knew with an instant's insight that he was thinking of all the disreputable things that *could* happen in a curricle. No doubt he had indulged in them all at one time or another. But he spoke quite gravely.

"I assure you that Miss Davencourt will be completely safe with me, ma'am. I view her in a strictly paternal fashion."

Clara cast him a demure, sideways glance, which he met with his bland blue gaze. She had hoped that her reference to his paternal advice in the letter would vex him, since he had spent so much time at their last meeting telling her that he was too old for her.

"Then I shall fetch my cloak," she said, dropping a slight curtsy. "Thank you, your grace."

The flash of amusement in Fleet's eyes told her that he was not fooled by this show of meekness. She felt his gaze follow her out and almost shivered under the cool blue intensity of it.

She kept him waiting only a few minutes and he was openly appreciative when she rejoined him in the hall.

"It is a rare woman who does not take an hour over her preparations, Miss Davencourt."

"I was concerned not to keep your horses waiting in the cold, your grace," Clara said, with an expressive lift of the brows.

"Rather than not wishing to inconvenience me? I take the snub, but your concern for my team is still admirable."

Clara gave him a little smile and accepted the arm that he offered. He handed her up into the curricle, tucked a thick rug about her and offered her a hot brick for her feet. Despite the chill of the day she felt snug. Fleet leaped up beside her and took up the reins. Clara noticed immediately that they did not travel with a groom and prayed that Mrs. Boyce had not observed the fact from her vantage point behind the drawing room curtains. It certainly made matters easier for her, for she wished to have no eavesdropper on their conversation; on the other hand it also made her a little nervous. She could not expect standard decorum from Fleet. In fact, she never knew what to expect from him. That was half the trouble.

"I confess I was a little surprised to hear from you, Miss Davencourt," Fleet said with a quizzical smile, as he moved the horses off at a brisk trot. "The terms of our parting left me in no doubt that you wished never to see me again."

Clara smiled back with dazzling sweetness. "You are quite correct, your grace. As I intimated in my letter, only the direst need led me to contact you. I hoped that out of the friendship you have for my brother, you would agree."

Fleet sketched an ironic bow. "And here I am, Miss Davencourt, at your service. How comforting it must be to know that you may appeal to my sense of honor and know that I will respond immediately."

Clara's lips twitched. "You are all generosity, your

grace." She looked up and met the intense blue of his eyes. "I hope," she added politely, determined to get the awkward part out of the way as soon as possible, "that we may put the past behind us. I am older and wiser now, and you—"

"Yes?"

"You, I suspect, are exactly as you were two years ago."

Fleet inclined his head. "I suspect that I am."

"So we may understand each other and be friends?" Clara finished.

There was a pause before Fleet spoke, as though he were weighing her words and found them lacking in some way she could not quite understand. "If you say so, Miss Davencourt," he said slowly.

He shot her another look. Clara felt her nerves tingle. She had always known Sebastian Fleet to be shrewd; those members of the ton who declared the duke to be nothing more than an easygoing rake did not understand him at all. The sharpness of mind behind those cool blue eyes had been one of the things that had attracted Clara to him in the first place. But she should not be thinking on that now. Dwelling on his attractions was foolish. She was no longer a green girl of one and twenty to fall in love with the most unobtainable duke in society.

The breeze ruffled Seb Fleet's dark golden hair, and he raised a hand absentmindedly from the reins to smooth back the lock that fell across his forehead. Contrary to both fashion and common sense, he wore no hat. The very familiarity of his gesture jolted Clara with a strange pang of memory. They had been in company a great deal together at one time but it was illusory to imagine that they had ever been close. Fleet had squashed that aspiration very firmly when he had rejected her proposal of marriage. No one ever got close to Sebastian Fleet. He did not permit it.

She knew she should not raise old memories but Clara had never done as she should. "When I proposed to you…" she began.

Fleet's brows snapped down in a thoroughly intimidating way. "I thought we were not speaking of the past, Miss Davencourt."

Clara frowned. "I would like to say my piece first."

Fleet sighed with resigned amusement. "I was under the impression you said your piece when we parted. *Arrogant, proud, rude, vain* and *self-satisfied* were all epithets I took to heart at the time and have not forgotten since."

"And," Clara said, "I imagine you have not altered your behavior one whit as a result."

"Of course not." Fleet flashed her a glance. "Naturally I was flattered by your proposal but I made it clear I am not the marrying kind."

"Being too much of a rake."

"Precisely."

"I thought it was worth asking you anyway," Clara said, with a small sigh.

Seb smiled at her, a dangerously attractive smile. "I

know," he said. "It is one of the reasons I like you so much, Miss Davencourt."

Clara glared at him. "You like me—but not enough to marry me."

"You are mistaken. I like you far too much to marry you. I would be the devil of a husband."

They looked at each other for a moment. Clara sighed. She knew he liked her, which was half the trouble. They liked each other very much and it was a perilous form of friendship, forever in danger of toppling over into forbidden attraction.

Fleet turned the conversation decisively. "Tell me what I may do to help you, Miss Davencourt."

Clara hesitated. "I suppose it was unorthodox of me to write to you."

Fleet glanced at her. There was a smile in his eyes. "In so many ways. Most young ladies, particularly with the history that is between us, would think twice before pursuing so rash a course."

They had turned into the park. It was too cold a morning for there to be many people about, but Clara found it pleasantly fresh, if chilly. Autumn leaves and twigs, turned white with frost, crunched beneath the horses' hooves. The sky was a pale, cloudy blue with faint sunshine trying to break through. Clara's cheeks stung with the cold and she burrowed her gloved hands deeper under the fur-lined rug.

Fleet slowed the curricle to a pace that required little concentration and turned his head to look at her directly.

"Perhaps," he added dryly, "you will satisfy my curiosity when the time is right?"

Clara's throat was suddenly dry. Feeling nervous was an unusual experience for her.

"I have a proposition for you." Clara looked at him out of the corner of her eye. He was starting to look a little exasperated.

"You are dissembling, Miss Davencourt," he said. "Could you be more specific?"

Clara swallowed hard.

"I need a rake," she said bluntly, "so I sent for you."

It was impossible to shock the Duke of Fleet. He was far too experienced to show any reaction to such a statement. After a pause, he said, equally bluntly, "Why do you need a rake?"

Clara drew a deep breath. "I need a rake to teach me how to outwit all the other rakes and scoundrels," she said. "I used to think I was up to all the tricks that a rogue might play, but I am sadly outwitted. I was almost abducted in broad daylight by Lord Walton the other day, and at the theater Sir Peter Petrie tried to back me into a dark corner and kiss me. If I am not careful I shall find myself compromised and married off to save the scandal before I have even realized it. It is intolerable to be so beset!"

Fleet gave a crack of laughter. "You are a sensible girl, Miss Davencourt. I cannot believe you unable to depress the pretensions of the worst scoundrels in town! Surely you exaggerate?"

"Sir, I do not," Clara said crossly. "Do you think I should be asking you for help were it not absolutely necessary? Now that I am an heiress, matters are threatening to get out of hand."

"How thoughtless of your godmother to die and leave you so much money," Fleet said sardonically. He dropped his hand lightly over her gloved ones. "If only you were not so pretty and so rich, Miss Davencourt. You have become irresistible!"

Clara turned her shoulder to him. "Oh, I should have known better than to ask you for help! You always laugh at me. But you know it is true that one is seldom the toast of society if one's parents are poor."

Fleet's grip tightened for a moment and she looked up to meet his eyes. "I do understand," he said. "Your situation is not so different from being a duke subject to the wiles of matchmaking mamas and their daughters. You would be astounded at the number of young ladies who have twisted their ankles outside the portals of Fleet House," he added ruefully. "The pavement must be unconscionably uneven."

Clara stifled a giggle. "I do recall that you are unsympathetically inclined toward twisted ankles. When I sprained mine that day we had the picnic at Strawberry Hill you refused to believe me, and I was left to hop back to the carriage!"

She thought Fleet looked suitably contrite. "I apologize. That was very uncivil of me."

Clara sensed a moment of weakness. "So you see the

difficulty I face," she said, spreading her hands in a gesture of pleading. "Will you help me?"

The weakness had evidently been an illusion. Fleet gave a decisive shake of the head. "Certainly not. This is nothing more than a blatant attempt to trap me into marriage."

Clara was outraged. Her lavender-blue eyes flashed. "I might have known you could not disabuse yourself of the idea that I might *still* wish to marry you, your grace! Despite everything I have said you cannot believe yourself resistible! Of all the arrogant, conceited, vain and self-satisfied *old* roués!"

There was a look in his eyes that suggested he admired the spirited nature of her outburst—but it was clear that the word *old* had stung him.

"That is most unfair of you," he said. "I am only three and thirty. Hardly in my dotage!"

Clara gave an exaggerated sigh. "Let us ignore your tragic obsession with age for a moment, your grace. The whole point of what I am asking is for you to teach me how to outwit a rake, not fall into his arms. You need have no concerns that I intend to importune you. I have no romantic feelings for you whatsoever!"

There was a heavy silence between them. The horses had slowed to a standstill beneath the bare branches of an oak tree as Seb Fleet turned his full attention toward her. Despite the cold air, Clara felt a fizzing warmth inside her that was not merely irritation. Under his slow and thorough scrutiny the color rushed to her face in an even hotter tide. Breathing seemed unconscionably difficult.

"No feelings for me," he drawled. "Can that be true?"

"No," Clara said, gulping down a breath. "I lied. I feel exasperated and infuriated and downright annoyed and you are the cause of all of those feelings."

"Strong emotions indeed."

"But not of the warmer sort." Clara evaded his gaze and picked at the threads of the tartan rug. "I have everything I desire in life at the moment. Why should I wish to marry anyone, least of all you?"

She saw the flash of something hot and disturbing in his eyes and added hastily, "Do not answer that! It was a rhetorical question!"

"Of course." Fleet's smile was wicked. "I doubt that you would appreciate my answer anyway."

"Very likely not. It is bound to be improper."

"What do you expect when you are talking to a rake? You cannot have it both ways, Miss Davencourt."

Clara sighed sharply. "Which is exactly why you would be the perfect person to help me," she said. "You are an out-and-out rogue. When we met, you took my hand before I was even aware of what you were doing. You charmed my companion into giving you time alone in my company. Those are precisely the things I wish to learn to avoid."

Fleet shook his head. "The answer is still no, I am afraid."

"Why?" Clara felt indignant.

"Because, my very dear Miss Davencourt, it would not serve," Fleet said. "You may not have realized it—" he turned toward her and his knee brushed against hers "—but I am behaving very much against type in refusing your request. Your average rake would accept, with no intention of keeping matters theoretical and every intention of seducing you."

Clara looked at him skeptically. "You actually claim to be acting from honorable motives?"

"The very purest, I assure you. But then, I am no average rake."

Clara did not need to be told. Sebastian Fleet was not average in any way. The languid arrogance, the dangerous edge, the sheer masculine power of him—all of these things made him exceptional. She shivered deep within her cloak.

To ask him to help her had been a reckless idea from the first; she recognized that. But her need had been genuine. She had been under siege and she was tired of it. She was also very stubborn.

"Can I not persuade you otherwise?" she begged. "I am not asking you to escort me about town, merely to tell me those dangerous behaviors to guard against."

She saw him shake his head decisively.

"To do so would be extremely perilous, Miss Davencourt. I might forget I was a gentleman and a friend of your brother and act on instinct. And I do not mean a paternal instinct."

Clara looked into his eyes. The instinct was there,

masculine, primitive, wholly dangerous. She felt her senses spin under the impact of his gaze. She knew that he wanted to kiss her. Right here. Right now. He had never pretended he did not find her attractive. She knew that had their circumstances been different he would have tried to seduce her without a qualm.

He had been ruthlessly open with her in the past, telling her he intended never to marry, did not wish for the responsibility, and that he was incapable of being faithful. It had been her disillusion and disappointment that had led her to rail at him for not being the man she had wanted him to be. And now he was rejecting her again, albeit for a very different proposal, and once again she could recognize his reasons and even appreciate them, in a way.

She cleared her throat and made a little gesture of acceptance. "Very well. I understand what you are saying and…I admire your honesty."

His eyes opened wider with surprise and then, echoing her thoughts, he said, "It is no difficulty to admit I find you very attractive, Miss Davencourt. I would have the most dishonorable intentions toward you if matters had fallen out differently."

He sighed, picked up the reins and gave the horses a curt word of encouragement. The curricle picked up speed.

It was a moment or two before Fleet broke the slightly uncomfortable silence between them. "Do you truly intend never to marry?"

Clara raised her brows. "I cannot say never, but for now I am very happy as I am."

"It would be a tragic waste for you to remain single."

Clara felt a sharp stab of anger then that he could appreciate the qualities that might make her a good wife—for someone else.

"I doubt you are a good judge of that," she said. The words came out more sharply than she had intended and, although his face did not register any emotion, she sensed he was hurt. He did not pursue the point, however, and once again a silence fell.

She was on the point of apologizing when he said abruptly, "You are genuinely happy as you are?" There was an odd note in his voice. "By which I mean to ask if you truly have everything you wish for?"

Clara ignored the small voice that told her she had everything she wished for *except him.*

"Of course," she said firmly. "I have my family and my friends and plenty to occupy myself. I am very happy." She fixed him with a direct look. "Aren't you?"

She saw him hesitate. "Not precisely. Happiness is a very acute sensation. I suppose you could say I am content."

"Content." Clara thought about it. There was a comfortable feeling to the word but no high excitement about it. "That is good."

"It is good enough, certainly." Fleet had turned his face away from hers and as a result she could not read his expression. He was difficult to read at the best of times, with that bland blue gaze and those open features. He appeared to be straightforward when in fact the reverse was true. Frustration stirred in her at how opaque he was, how difficult to reach. But then she had no reason to try to reach him. She had tried before and been rebuffed. She reminded herself that no one ever got close to the Duke of Fleet. This difficult friendship was as good as she would get. She had to decide whether it was worth it or not.

"If your rakes and fortune hunters are causing such a problem, I would suggest that you appeal to your sister-in-law, Lady Juliana, for help," Fleet said, breaking into her thoughts. "I doubt there is a rake in town who can out-maneuver her."

Clara shook her head sadly. "That would be the ideal solution but Juliana is entirely engrossed with the babies at present. That was really why I contacted you. We are to go to Davencourt for Christmas in a couple of weeks, but until then I imagine I am very much left to fend for myself."

"With the help of the redoubtable Mrs. Boyce, of course."

"Yes, and you have seen how much use she is!" Clara laughed. "I love her dearly but she conceives that she will have failed in her duty if she does not marry me off, and so makes a present of me to every passing rake and fortune hunter. I believe they view me as the ideal Christmas gift."

Fleet looked at her. His blue gaze was warm enough to curl her toes.

"I can imagine why, and it is nothing to do with your money."

Clara raised her chin.

"Since you are not to give me the benefit of your theoretical experience, your grace, I refuse to permit you to flirt with me. Rather I suggest you take me home." She looked around. "Indeed, I have no notion where we are!"

The path was narrow here and wended its way through thick shrubbery. Even in winter the trees and bushes grew dark and close overhead, enclosing them in a private world. It was a little disconcerting to discover just how alone they were in this frosty, frozen wilderness.

Fleet was smiling gently. "Take this as a free piece of advice, Miss Davencourt," he said. "Always pay attention to your surroundings. The aim of the rake will always be to separate you from company so that he may compromise you."

He put up a hand and touched one gloved finger lightly to her cheek. Her gaze flew to his as the feather-light touch burned like a brand.

"And once he has you to himself," the duke continued softly, "a rake will waste no time in kissing you, Miss Davencourt."

For what seemed like an age they stared into each other's eyes. Clara's heart twisted with longing and regret. Could he look at her like that if he did not care for her? He would deny it of course. Lust was easy for him to admit, love impossible.

Her body ached for him with a sudden, fierce fire. His presence engulfed her. She felt shaky, hot with longing. She raised her hand and brushed his away. Her fingers were not quite steady.

"Your point is well made, your grace." Her voice was husky and she cleared her throat. "I shall guard against that possibility."

Fleet's hand fell and he straightened up in his seat. Clara breathed again, a little unevenly.

"Take me home," she said again, and there was more than a little entreaty in her voice.

They came out from under the trees and joined the main path. A gentleman on a very frisky bay rode past, touched his hat to Clara and bowed slightly to Fleet, then pirouetted away with a fine display of horsemanship.

"Coxcomb," Fleet said.

His face was set in grim planes, the line of his mouth hard. Clara's sore heart shrank to see it.

The next barouche to pass them contained a gentleman and two painted ladies, who smiled and ogled in their direction, the gentleman in particular giving Clara a thorough scrutiny through his quizzing glass. Fleet cut them dead.

"Friends of yours?" Clara enquired politely.

"Not of the type that I would acknowledge when I am escorting you." Fleet paused perforce to avoid several young blades who had deliberately blocked their path in order to pay their respects to Clara.

"Walton, Jeffers, Ancrum and Tarver," Fleet said, when they had moved on. "I begin to see your difficulty, Miss Davencourt." He paused. "Perhaps if people see me squiring you about, that may dissuade the gazetted fortune hunters from pursuing you."

"I doubt that will dissuade anyone," Clara said. "It is well known that you have no intention of marrying, your grace, so it is more likely to encourage them if they think that I am prepared to spend time with a notorious rake."

Fleet cast her a look. "Nevertheless, Miss Davencourt," he said slowly, "perhaps I could help you."

Clara looked hopeful. "You have reconsidered?"

Fleet shook his head. "Not at all. I will not teach you about rakes. That would be foolhardy. But as it is only for a few weeks I *will* act as your escort while you remain in town and keep the gentlemen from troubling you." He smiled. "All in the most perfect and irreproachably paternal fashion, of course."

There was a thread of steel beneath his courteous tone, as though he would brook no refusal, and it brought Clara's chin up in defiance.

"Pray, do not conceive it to be your duty to help me, your grace," she said sharply. "I would detest the thought that I was a burden to you."

Fleet smiled a challenge. "If I cannot help you in one way, why not accept my assistance in another, Miss Davencourt?" he said persuasively. "I will protect you from unwanted attention and, since you have no wish to marry, I shall not be getting in the way of any gentleman you would consider a genuine suitor."

Clara bit her lip. In some ways it was a tempting proposition since it would free her from the odious attentions of insincere suitors. In other ways, though, his suggestion was sheer madness. To spend time in Fleet's company would only remind her of all the things she had loved about him, all the things she could not have. The cure had been hard enough last time. To invite trouble again now was plain foolish.

"No," she said, unequivocally.

Fleet shrugged and her heart shriveled that she meant so little to him one way or another.

"Very well, then." His tone was careless. "I shall take you home."

CHAPTER TWO

FLEET REFUSED to leave Clara at the door as she would have wished, but escorted her into the hall. There was high color in her face, both from the cold air and from their quarrel, and she refused to meet his eye. Her chin was raised and her whole body was stiff with haughtiness. Fleet found it amusing, provocative and downright seductive. He wanted to kiss the hauteur from her lips until her face was flushed with passion, rather than pride. He wanted to feel that voluptuous body softening, responding, under his hands. He shifted uncomfortably. He had always wanted Clara Davencourt in the most simple and fundamental way. It was unfortunate he simply could not have her and he had to learn to live with that. Under the circumstances it was probably the most foolish idea to offer her his escort and he should be grateful she had turned him down. He was uncomfortably aware that it had been the interest of Tarver and Walton and half a score others that had made him wish to keep her close. Allowing Miss Clara Davencourt to arouse his possessive instincts was a mistake. For that matter, allowing her to arouse any instincts at all was totally unsafe.

Lady Juliana Davencourt was in the hall, which broke the rather difficult silence between them. Juliana was dressed in an old striped gown and Fleet, remembering the wayward widow of the past, would never have believed she could have anything half so frumpish in her wardrobe. She was cradling a tiny baby in each arm and looked up with a smile as they came in at the door. Fleet thought she looked young and vibrant and alive with happiness. It was most odd. He had known Juliana Davencourt since she was a debutante, had once even thought that her particular brand of cynicism might be the perfect match for his, yet here she was transformed into someone he barely recognized. And why was she carrying the babies herself? Surely Davencourt was rich enough to employ a dozen nursemaids? This modern trend toward caring for one's children oneself made him shudder.

"Sebastian. How delightful to see you again!" Juliana did not offer him her hand, for which he could only be grateful since he was certain it was not clean. She turned to Clara, drawing them both with her into the warmth of the library, where a fire burned bright in the grate. Clara removed the enveloping cloak that she had been wearing, affording Fleet the opportunity to admire the luscious curves accentuated by her fashionable gown. It was all that he could do to keep his mind on the conversation.

"Did you enjoy your drive?" Juliana asked.

"Yes, thank you, Ju," Clara said. "I think it will snow

later, though. It is most unconscionably cold. How is little Rose's croup this morning?" She had taken one of the babies from her sister-in-law with a competence that both beguiled and appalled Fleet. He watched as the child opened its tiny pink mouth in an enormous yawn, then gave an equally enormous burp. Its eyes flew open in an expression of extreme surprise. Clara gave a delighted laugh.

"She is taking her food well enough, it seems!"

Fleet watched as Clara raised a gentle finger to trace the curve of the baby's cheek. She was smiling now, her face pink from the nip of the chill air outside, her hair mussed up by the hood of the cloak, escaping in soft curls about her face. Fleet stared, unable to look away. Something tightly wound within him seemed to give a little. He felt very odd, almost light-headed. It was as though he was seeing Clara in a different way and yet the revelation made her appear even more seductive. Clara with her own child in her arms...

Then he realized that Juliana was addressing him, and had been doing so for some time. He had no idea what she was talking about.

"We would be very pleased, Sebastian, although if you felt that you could not we would understand..."

"Of course," Fleet said automatically, forcing his gaze from Clara. "It will be my pleasure."

"You will?" Juliana sounded pleased, relieved and surprised at the same time. "But that is wonderful! Martin will be delighted!"

It was her tone that helped to focus his thoughts. What had he agreed to do? Juliana sounded far too excited for this to be a simple dinner invitation. He looked up to meet Clara's quizzical blue gaze. "You have surprised me," she said slowly, "but I, too, am delighted, your grace."

She gave him a smile so radiant that Fleet felt shaken and aroused. The fire seemed extremely hot and he was feeling very odd. He wondered if he had caught an ague.

Clara dropped a kiss on the baby's forehead.

"I think it is appropriate for your new godfather to hold you now," she murmured, moving toward him.

Understanding hit Fleet in a monstrous wave of feeling. He had just agreed to be the baby's *godfather!* He cast a terrified look at the little bundle Clara was holding out to him. Juliana was approaching in a flanking maneuver, murmuring something about him taking a seat so he could hold both babies at once. Both babies? Had he agreed to be godfather to the *pair* of them? He opened his mouth to protest, then closed it again, aware of the enormity of the situation in which he found himself. He could not in all conscience back out of the arrangement now. Juliana and Clara were both looking at him with shining eyes; it made him feel like a hero. He would have to wait until later—get Martin Davencourt alone over a glass of brandy, explain he had made a mistake, had thought he was being offered something much simpler, like a cup of tea or an invitation to a ball.

He was certain he could sort the matter out, but in the meantime he would have to play along.

He sank into the big armchair before the fire and sat as still as a statue while the infants were placed in his arms. If he moved he might drop them. Worse, they might vomit on his coat of blue superfine. He had heard babies were prone to do such things although he had never been near one in his life.

They smelled faintly of a milky sickness that turned his stomach, and yet at the same time they were the softest and sweetest things he had ever touched. He lowered his nose gently and sniffed the top of Rose's head. She moved a little and made a small mewing sound. The other baby opened his eyes suddenly and stared at him. He realized he did not even know the boy's name.

"What…" His voice had come out huskily. He cleared his throat. "What is his name?"

"Rory," Juliana said. She was smiling. "They are called Rory and Rose."

Fleet looked down on the tiny bodies nestling close. He felt as though they had fastened their little hands about his heart and were squeezing tightly. A whole wash of emotions threatened to drown him.

He had to escape, and quickly. He looked at Juliana, then Clara, in mute appeal.

"Well, I…"

"You have done very well for a first attempt," Clara

said, sounding like his childhood nanny, "although you do look utterly terrified."

To his inexpressible relief, she lifted Rory from his arms. Once Juliana had retrieved Rose he was free to stand, although his legs felt a little shaky. He made somewhat blindly for the door as though he could smell the fresh air and freedom.

"Thank you for the drive, your grace," Clara called after him. "Shall we see you tonight at Lady Cardace's Snow Ball?"

Fleet stared at her, trying to work out if he had heard the question correctly. He did not want to find himself accidentally agreeing to be godfather to yet more children or to something even more terrifying. He saw a tiny frown touch Clara's forehead at the length of time it was taking him to answer.

"Had you not been invited?" she inquired.

"Yes." Fleet took a grip on himself. "Yes, I shall be there."

Clara gave him another of her melting smiles. Much more of this and he would be quite undone. Clara and the twins between them had unmanned him.

"Good," she said. "I shall look forward to seeing you tonight."

FLEET TURNED the horses toward home. Some of the light seemed to have gone out of the day. Clara's vivid personality had set the air between them humming with life. Without her, everything seemed more dull and gray. He dismissed the thought as fanciful. It was simply that the weather had turned. Dark clouds were massing on the horizon, promising snow. The wind was sharper now, with a cutting edge. Despite the fact that he told himself it was just the effect of the weather, he found he missed Clara's warmth.

He remembered the twins with a shudder. He was not cut out to be anyone's godfather. He was scarcely an example for the younger generation. If it had simply been a matter of presenting suitably large gifts on birthdays and Christmases then he might have fulfilled the requirements, but he was depressingly aware that the role of godfather asked much more of him. It was a pity—Clara probably thought more highly of him now than she had ever done in their acquaintance. That should not be permitted to sway him, however. He did not seek her good opinion. Nevertheless, it would be a shame to lose it so swiftly.

The snow was starting to fall. In London it fell with sooty edges, to lie in a dirty slush on the streets. For a moment he recalled the pure brightness of Fleet in the snow, the way the icicles hung from the branches and the river froze over in intricate icy patterns and the snowdrifts lay ten feet deep in the lee of the hedges. He ached to be there.

The panic was rising in his throat, as it sometimes did when he thought of Fleet in the winter. He dashed the snowflakes from his eyes and tried to think of something else. The twins… No, that was a bad idea.

His panic heightened. Suppose something happened to Martin and Juliana? If he did not rescind his role as godfather he could conceivably end up with the care of two small children. The images crowded his mind. Babies crying, nursemaids fussing around… By the time he turned in to the stables at Fleet House he had got as far as redecorating one of the bedrooms as a nursery. He handed the curricle over to the grooms, hurrying inside, away from his fears.

The house was warm and quiet. The day's newspapers were waiting for him in the library. He sat down, but instead of picking up the *Morning Post* his hand strayed idly toward the bookcase. His eyes fell upon an ancient copy of Sterne's *Tristram Shandy* and he picked it up without thought. The book fell open at the title page, where there was an inscription in childish letters:

Oliver Fleet.

He shut the book with a sudden, violent snap that raised the dust from the pages. It had been about this time of year that his brother's accident occurred. He hated Christmas. He had never passed the holiday at Fleet since Oliver's death.

He settled back in his chair. The silence was almost oppressive. He could hear the brush of the snow against the windowpane. It was nine hours until Lady Cardace's rout. Then he would see Clara again. He tried not to feel too pleased and failed singularly. He liked Clara Davencourt immensely and that was his weakness; he found her hopelessly seductive and that was his danger.

With her corn-gold hair, huge blue eyes and voluptuous curves, Clara was ridiculously pretty and the embodiment of every masculine fantasy in which he had ever indulged. He suspected he was not the only gentleman to have had such musings, but he was fairly certain he was the only man who admired Clara for the shrewd intelligence that lurked beneath her charming exterior. She had a sharp mind, and most men would dislike that; Seb Fleet adored it. He loved their conversations. Such admiration had proved his downfall two years before when he had nearly fallen in love with her.

He must guard against falling in love with Clara Davencourt now. He had no desire to marry and he could not have her any other way. And yet the day did seem darker without her presence. He had an unnerving feeling that he was lost in some way and Clara was the only one who could save him. Total foolishness, of course. The business with the infant Davencourt twins had affected his judgment. He would regain his calm with strong coffee and the *Morning Post*. And when he saw Clara Davencourt that evening she would be just another debutante. A pretty debutante, a rich debutante, but like all the other pretty little rich girls. He rang for the coffee. He reached for the paper. But he could not banish Clara from his mind.

THE SNOW WAS ALREADY a foot deep by the time the Davencourt carriage turned onto the sweep in front of Cardace House that evening. The glare of the lanterns was muted by the swirling flakes and the guests were hurrying within to escape the bracing cold.

"Our slippers will be soaked," Juliana grumbled, gingerly accepting Martin's hand to help her down onto the damp red carpet that led up to the door. "If it were not that this is the most important ball of the season and I am on tenterhooks to see what Lady Cardace has in store for us, I would rather be curled up in the library at home with a cup of hot chocolate and a good book!"

Clara shivered as the icy wind found its way beneath her cloak and raised goose bumps on her arms. Her evening gown was so flimsy it felt as though the wind were cutting through it like a knife. She hoped Lady Cardace's arrangements for her guests included both a hot drink and a roaring fire. There was nothing worse than a cold ballroom in winter.

Lady Cardace was the leading hostess of the Little Season, and invitations to her Snow Ball were the most eagerly sought tickets of the year. Each winter she arranged something truly original and each year the lesser hostesses would copy her, driving Lady Cardace to ever more outrageous forms of entertainment the next time.

"Ah," Martin said, looking about them as they hastened into the house, "I think this year's theme is the traditional Christmas. How charming!"

They surrendered their coats to a footman and accepted the hot cup of negus proffered by another servant. Clara gratefully inhaled the richly alcoholic fumes and warmed her hands on the crystal glass. Lady

Cardace had exceeded herself this year. Sprays of holly and mistletoe adorned the ballroom walls, the deep green of the leaves contrasting richly with the red and white berries. The ceiling was hung with clouds of white gauze and sparkling snowflakes, a huge fire glowed behind the grates at each end of the hall and the orchestra was already striking up for the first dance of the night. From the refreshment room wafted the enticing scent of a richly warming beef soup. Martin immediately headed in that direction to fetch a bowl for each of them.

Despite the festive atmosphere, Clara felt blue-devilled. It was nearing midnight and a surreptitious first—and second—scan of the ballroom told her the Duke of Fleet was not in attendance.

She glanced about her a third time, taking pains to conceal the maneuver. It seemed that every other accredited member of the ton was pressed into Lady Cardace's mansion. The evening was a dreadful crush. But the only man Clara secretly wanted to be crushed against was absent.

She wished now that she had not written to Sebastian Fleet. She had managed perfectly well without seeing him for the past eighteen months. Now she had stirred up those old feelings once again and a part of her ached for his presence.

"You look as though you have chewed on a piece of lemon peel," Juliana said, slipping her arm through Clara's and guiding her toward the rout chairs at the end of the room. "It is Sebastian Fleet, I suppose. You never quite managed to cure yourself of that affliction, did you, Clara?"

Clara bit her lip. She had not realized her preference for Fleet's company was still so obvious after she had spent so much time and effort in trying to appear indifferent. But Juliana's eyes were kind so Clara shook her head ruefully and admitted the problem. "I fear not. I have tried, but I cannot help my feelings."

"Ah, feelings." Juliana's lips curved into a smile and Clara knew she was thinking of Martin. "What a blight they can be. No, there is absolutely no point in fighting how you feel."

"I thought," Clara said, "that you disapproved of my *tendre* for the Duke of Fleet?"

"I did," Juliana said cheerfully. "I do. One cannot approve of Fleet. He is too old for you, he is too experienced and he is too much of a rake."

Clara sighed. She knew Juliana was right, but in some deep and stubbornly instinctive way she believed that she was the right woman for Sebastian Fleet. She had always believed it, but his rejection of her had made her falter and question her conviction.

"I do not wish you to be hurt, Clara," Juliana said. "Fleet has had years of practice in keeping intimacy at bay. I understand because I did the same thing myself."

"And Martin helped you to see that it need not be so," Clara reasoned.

"That is true. But that does not mean the same thing

will happen for you." Juliana touched her hand briefly. "I am sorry, Clara. I want to help you—to save you the hurt." She shot a glance over Clara's shoulder. "Fleet is here now. Do you need a little time?"

Clara cast one swift glance toward the door then shook her head rapidly. "I am very well. I know you only mean to help me, Ju."

Juliana nodded and squeezed her arm, then they both turned to watch the Duke of Fleet approach. There was a prickle along Clara's skin, a mixture of fear and anticipation. He looked so autocratic, so easily in command.

Fleet had bumped into Martin in his journey across the room. Clara observed that Martin had managed to forget the refreshments. No doubt he had been distracted by some political discussion and had completely forgotten his original errand. She shook her head slightly.

The two men were coming toward them, deep in conversation. Juliana was beaming with a smile of warm pleasure as her husband approached her and Clara felt a pang of envy that she could not repress. She longed for such intimacy with Sebastian, but that was much more than he was prepared to give her.

Even so, she was scarcely indifferent to him. There was something about the way he moved that made the breath lock in her chest. She could swear her knees were trembling a little.

The duke had seen her now. He had also apparently noticed that a couple of gentlemen were hastening toward her, determined to get there before he did. A smile touched the corner of his mouth. The expression in his blue eyes made Clara feel ridiculously hot and bothered. She felt as though his gaze were stripping her naked. Damn the man. How could he work such mischief across a crowded ballroom?

Fleet had caught up to the two young men, Lords Elton and Tarver, and had diverted them from their original course toward Clara by grasping their arms, bending to have a word in their ears and then sending them packing in no uncertain terms. Clara's lips thinned. Though she had not particularly wished to be importuned by either Elton or Tarver, nor had she a need for Fleet to play the high-handed protector. Especially when she had earlier rejected his offer of help.

Fleet was upon them now. He bowed, first to Lady Juliana, then to Clara.

"How do you do, Lady Juliana, Miss Davencourt? It is a pleasure to see you this evening."

A faint smile curved Juliana's lips. "Thank you, Fleet. How pretty of you. Now, I sense you want something. How may we help you?"

Clara could sense Fleet watching her. She turned away and pretended a complete lack of interest. Surely there was some fascinating event occurring on the other side of the dance floor that she could focus upon…. Fleet took her hand. Her pulse jumped. He was smiling, very sure of himself.

"I was hoping you would grant me the pleasure of a dance, Miss Davencourt."

Lady Juliana was looking pointedly at their clasped hands. Fleet let go of Clara and she gave him a look of limpid innocence.

"I beg your pardon, your grace, but I do not dance this evening."

Both Fleet and Juliana looked startled.

"You do not dance tonight!" Fleet sounded thoughtful and not in the least put out. "How very dull for you to attend a ball and not indulge in the dancing."

Clara smiled. "I have no wish to indulge with you, your grace. You must forgive me. Pleasant as it is to see you, I told you earlier that I was not in need of your escort."

She sensed both Juliana's amusement and Fleet's chagrin, although he did not permit any expression to mar his features. Instead, he turned to Lady Juliana.

"If you were to recommend me as a suitable partner, ma'am, Miss Davencourt might be persuaded to relent."

Clara's lips twitched. She had to concede that it was clever of him to try an approach through Juliana but she was fairly certain her sister-in-law would not let her down.

Juliana laughed. "I cannot recommend you as suitable in any way, Fleet, at least not to a respectable young lady."

Fleet gave Clara a rueful smile that nevertheless held a hint of some other, more disturbing emotion in its depths. It promised retribution.

"Then if you will not consider me suitable, Lady Juliana," Fleet continued, "pray take pity on me."

Juliana flicked an imaginary speck from her skirts with disdainful fingers. "Pointless to appeal to my sense of pity, Fleet. You know I have none."

"I know your husband intends to dance with you, Lady Juliana," Fleet said, watching Martin finish his conversation with an acquaintance and make haste to join them. "A pity that Miss Davencourt denies herself—and me—a like privilege."

Juliana's whole face lit up at the sight of her husband. "When you are married, Fleet, then you may have the privilege of dancing with your wife. For now it is Miss Davencourt's right to deny a suitor if she chooses and she is weary of rakes. I suggest that you nurse your disappointment in the card room. Clara?"

Clara inclined her head. "Lady Juliana is in the right of it, your grace. I shall bid you good evening."

Fleet bowed gracefully. "Then I shall take you at your word. Good night, Lady Juliana, Miss Davencourt."

He went without a backward glance.

Clara watched him go. The lowering thing was that he radiated such indifference. She wished she had not given in to the childish impulse to thwart him. It was not that she wished to dance with either Lord Elton or Lord Tarver, but she had wanted to make that choice for herself. Once Fleet had dismissed them and presented himself as substitute she had vowed to reject him.

"A word of warning," Juliana said, turning back to Clara for a moment as Martin urged her toward the dancing. "Do not make a habit of playing these games with the Duke of Fleet. He *made* the game when you were still in the schoolroom."

"I think Clara was quite right to turn Fleet down," Martin said unexpectedly. "He can do nothing to enhance a lady's reputation."

"No, dear," Juliana said with an affectionate smile, "but as usual you have no notion of what is really going on." She led her spouse away to join the set that was forming for the quadrille.

He made the game…

Clara shivered a little. Fleet had told her that very morning he was no ordinary rake. She must be mad.

Everyone else was dancing and Clara realized she was the only girl left sitting out. It was not something that happened often, but whatever Fleet said to Elton and Tarver had evidently made the rounds, for although plenty of gentlemen were looking in her direction, none were making any move to engage her. How exceedingly annoying. Clara's exasperation with the Duke of Fleet grew stronger. Some of the debutantes were smiling behind their fans, clearly delighted the prettiest girl in the room was partnerless for once. Clara gritted her teeth. She would not stay to be laughed at. She would have to make a strategic retreat to the ladies' withdrawing room.

It felt like an unconscionably long time that she lurked in the shadows, pinning and repinning her silver brooch, tidying her already immaculate hair and smoothing her dress. Eventually she was so bored she could bear it no longer. She stalked out into the corridor wondering whether Juliana and Martin had concluded their dance and would provide her with some company.

The corridor was dark and quiet. Sprigs of holly and mistletoe adorned the walls here, as well, between the flaring lanterns. There was a scent of pine and citrus in the air, a smell so nostalgic of Christmases past that Clara paused for a moment and breathed in the heady scent, smiling. She was thinking of Christmas at Davencourt, when a door on her right opened abruptly and the Duke of Fleet stepped out directly in front of her.

"At last," he said. "I have been waiting for you."

SEB FLEET HAD BROKEN both his resolutions for the evening within two minutes of stepping inside Lady Cardace's ballroom. His plan to tell Martin he had changed his mind about being godfather to the twins fell at the first hurdle when his friend greeted him with such delight that Fleet found himself unable to disappoint him. He might have despised himself for such sentimental weakness—it was an affliction that he had not suffered previously—but then he caught sight of Clara and all other thoughts fled his mind.

Clara had long ago ceased to wear the white muslin of the very young debutante and tonight she was in a gown of delicate pale green. It swathed her soft curves with the sort of cunning elegance that accentuated rather than hid the body beneath. Her fine blond hair was swept up to reveal the tender line of her neck. She was smiling at something Juliana was saying. She looked radiant; Fleet felt it like a punch in the stomach. He vaguely remembered that he had resolved to avoid Clara that evening.

He had stopped, stared, and barely been able to conceal from Martin the fact that he was profoundly, outrageously, attracted to his sister. Then he had seen Elton and Tarver heading in the same direction with seemingly much the same thoughts as his own, and had ruthlessly stepped in to tell them that he was Miss Davencourt's escort that night unless they wished to challenge his right. Neither of them had done so.

He felt an almost uncontrollable compulsion to kiss her, to claim her, before the assembled company. The impulse appalled and excited him more than any other emotion he had ever experienced. Only the thinnest shred of self-control prevented him. Public response to such behavior would be to hound him into marriage or be cast out. So his desire for Miss Clara Davencourt would remain unslaked. Except…

Except that he could not resist. Part of a successful rake's strategy, of course, was cold calculation. He needed to be in control at all times. Seb Fleet had lost his control where Clara Davencourt was concerned. And now he had her where he wanted her.

Clara had stopped dead when she saw him. In the second it took for her to recover from her surprise,

Fleet leaned one hand against the wall, pinning her between his body and the door.

This was dangerous and foolhardy, but he felt an exhilaration that brooked no refusal. A strand of honey-colored hair had loosened from its clasp and lay against her cheek, heavy and smooth. He raised one hand to touch it and felt her jump. Her eyes were huge and dark in the shadows of the hall. When she spoke her voice was shaky and he felt a powerful rush of conquest.

"What do you mean when you say that you were waiting for me? You were playing cards."

Fleet shook his head. "I merely wanted you to think that."

There was silence between them. He kept her trapped between him and the door, so close he could feel the warmth of her body through the thin muslin of her gown. He leaned forward and brushed his lips against her ear. She jumped again and the response caused a jolt through his own body.

"Do not…" Her words were a whisper.

"I was intending to have you all to myself," Fleet said softly. "I knew you would not stay alone in the ballroom when you were devoid of admirers—what lady would expose herself to such humiliation? So I merely waited for you here."

He saw her expression change to anger.

"How conceited you are!" she exclaimed. "First you abandon me in the ballroom and then you presume you may pick up with me again whenever it suits you!"

Again she saw him smile. "I did not abandon you, Miss Davencourt. You rejected me."

She bit her lip. "Most gentlemen can comprehend a simple refusal, your grace."

"Alas, I have always been slower to understand than most." His breath stirred a tendril of her hair. The curve of her cheek was achingly sweet and the pure line of her jaw so tempting that he wanted to bury his face in its curve and breathe in the warm, feminine scent of her skin. His body tightened unbearably.

She turned her head slightly toward him. Their lips were no more than an inch apart now.

She whispered, "I have something to tell you, your grace."

Excitement kicked through his body. He could feel the caress of her breath against his cheek. She moistened her lips with the tip of her tongue and he almost groaned aloud to see it.

"You told me this morning that a lady should always be aware of her surroundings in order to thwart the evil plans of a rake." She raised her gaze to meet his. "I wanted to show you that I have taken you at your word. Good night."

He thought he had her trapped, but now he realized she had had one hand behind her back from the very beginning of their encounter. Indeed, he could read the triumph in her eyes. There was the softest of clicks as the doorknob turned in her palm. She gave him a smile that was pure provocation, stepped back into the ballroom and closed the door gently in his face.

CHAPTER THREE

SEB FLEET caught himself just before he slammed the palm of his hand against the panels of the closed door in sheer frustration. So, Clara Davencourt had out-played him for a second time that evening. He, on the other hand, had been taking his own game entirely too seriously. The constriction in his breeches told him just how desperately he wanted her. The physical ache was only matched by the aching disappointment of denial.

He shook his head slowly. He had been seduced by his own seduction. He had assumed he could outwit Clara and steal a kiss. But he wanted so much more from her; he could not pretend otherwise. He felt trapped between a rock and a very hard place.

"Are you all right, old fellow?"

Fleet straightened up. His host, Lord Cardace, had come out of the library farther down the passage and was looking at him with concern and no little curiosity. He realized he must have looked very odd, half-slumped against the wall.

"I am very well, thank you, Cardace," Fleet said.

"Just a trifle winded. The gout, you know. In my toes. Damnably painful when I try to dance."

Lord Cardace grimaced sympathetically. "The trials of age, eh, Fleet?"

"And of the bottle," Fleet agreed.

Cardace clapped him on the shoulder. "Then I'd find a seat if I were you. My wife has arranged for the mummers to entertain us. Can't abide all that old-fashioned singing and dancing myself and it's not for the old and infirm."

"Thank you for the advice," Fleet said with suitable gratitude.

He allowed Cardace to escort him with solicitude into the ballroom, then slipped away to the shelter of an alcove not, as his host assumed, to sit down and rest his aging bones, but to observe Clara without being observed. She was sitting between her brother and Lady Juliana in the demure pose of the perfect debutante. Fleet's lips twitched. She looked entirely composed. There was no hint that a few minutes before she had been within an ace of being ravished in a corridor by an out-and-out rake. The suitors were swarming around her again and Fleet felt the familiar wave of primitive possessiveness swamp him at the way the men were fawning, kissing her hand, whispering in her ear, smiling, toadying.

Until that moment, he had promised himself he would walk away. Clara Davencourt was not for him and well he knew it. He was full of good intentions. Then she gave her hand to Lord Elton to lead her into the dance, and a powerful wash of jealousy swept through Fleet. He started toward her.

One kiss. He would take one kiss and then he would leave her alone forever. He promised himself that.

He noted the precise moment she saw his approach. Her blue eyes narrowed with a disbelief she could not quite conceal. She caught her full lower lip between her teeth for a second before she turned aside to respond to something Elton was saying. The same honey-colored curl he had touched earlier in the darkness now curled in the hollow of her throat. She looked both fragile and determined. He could sense defiance.

Elton was no lady's champion. He saw Fleet approaching, turned pale, babbled something to Clara and shot away across the floor as though his coat were on fire. Clara turned on Fleet, ignoring the set that was forming around them, the curious ladies and gentlemen who had seen her abandoned before the dance even started.

"What on earth did you do to Lord Elton?" she whispered.

"I did nothing." Fleet was all innocence as he gained her side and took her arm.

"You know what I mean!" Clara's face was flushed with annoyance. "You spoke to him earlier! What did you say?"

"I warned him not to pester you with his false protestations of affection."

Clara snorted. "So that you could pester me instead?"

"You injure me."

"And you infuriate me!" Clara's blue eyes flashed. "Twice now I have bid you good-night."

"I am sorry. I never retire early from a ball."

"Oh!" Clara let go of her breath on an angry sigh. "Your high-handed interference first left me without partners and now has me standing alone in the middle of a set."

"I would offer to dance with you," Fleet said, "but you have already refused me and I do not wish to put my fate to the touch again."

Clara gave him a dark look and turned to stride off the floor. Her back was ramrod straight, her entire figure stiff with outrage. She ignored the raised brows and titters of amusement.

Fleet followed. Clara was standing with her back to him. He put a hand on her arm, leaned closer and spoke for her ears only.

"Do not be too complacent about escaping me earlier. I shall kiss you before the night is out. I swear it."

He felt her tremble. She spun around to face him. Her gaze was uncertain now, but behind her eyes he saw the flicker of something else: she was intrigued against her will, unwillingly fascinated, tempted… His blood fired at the thought.

"I do not believe you," she said, summoning all her will to steady herself.

"Believe me," Fleet said.

He had timed the matter to perfection. There was a shout that the mummers were coming and then a tide of people swept them to the edges of the ballroom as the dance broke up. The door was flung wide and the mummers marched in to the beat of the drum. The orchestra took up the tune with gusto and the crowd shifted and split as the dancing started again. Gone was the decorous elegance of the waltz. This music was fast and wild and, for a moment in the flickering fire and candlelight, amid the boughs of holly and mistletoe, it seemed as though they were in a medieval hall surrounded by all the pageantry and joy of Christmas.

Fleet grabbed Clara's wrist and drew her into his arms. Her body was soft against his and she came to him without demur. Perhaps she imagined they were to dance, for the strains of the music filled the air, mingled with laughter and voices.

Instead he drew her into the shadowed darkness of the window recess. It was colder here. Snow brushed the panes and the reflection of the candlelight shone in the glass. Without another moment's delay he bent his head and covered her mouth with his.

She stiffened with shock, but only for a moment. He felt her body soften against his, felt the instinctive response she could not hide. Her mouth opened beneath his and his mind spun even as a vise closed about his body, the desire he could barely control rampaging through him like wildfire.

He reined in his urgency and slid his tongue gently,

caressingly, along the inside of her lower lip, teasing a response from her. He must be gentle; this was not the time and the place for anything else. She made a small sound in her throat at the invasion of his tongue and he was shot through with lust so hot and primitive he was suddenly within an ace of tangling his hand in her hair, and slamming her back against the cold stone wall to kiss her within an inch of her life.

The beat of the music was in his blood now, primeval and intense. His mouth crushed hers again, his tongue sweeping deep. He wanted her naked in his bed. He wanted to strip away the layers of clothing between them and take her with an urgency and desire that made no concession to gentleness. He had wanted her for such a long time. He had denied that need and now he could deny it no longer. "Clara…"

He said her name on a ragged whisper as his lips met hers for a third time. Her eyes were closed, the lashes a dark sweep against her cheek. Her lips were swollen from the ruthless demands of his. She was trembling.

So was he. His emotions were frighteningly adrift. The way Clara was clutching at his jacket to pull him closer, the taste of her, the fusion of sweetness and desire, kindled in him sensations never previously experienced. She was his and his alone; he would never let her go.

He pressed her closer to him, one hand coming up very gently to caress her breast. He could feel the nipple harden through the muslin of her dress against the palm of his hand. The heat ripped through him.

Their lips parted slowly, reluctantly, one last time and he felt as though he were losing something. He felt cold.

She was looking at him with such dazed sensuality in her eyes that his heart turned over. He could not speak. A moment later she blinked and her expression warmed from bemusement into anger.

"When I asked for your help this morning," she said sharply, "I was *not* requesting lessons in kissing."

Sebastian, shaken by the unexpected intensity of the experience and by achieving the one thing he had dreamed of doing for the past two years, was rocked back.

"You scarcely need lessons, my dear," he said. Did she not understand her own power? If she could do that to him with one kiss he shuddered to think what would happen when he took her to bed. *When?* He forced his wild thoughts to slow down. He would *not* make love to Clara Davencourt.

He looked at her again as the heat drained from his body and a shred of sense took hold. He had not given much thought to her reactions, being so wrapped up in his own. Now, scanning her face, he made a stunning discovery that sent his thoughts into turmoil again.

"That was your first kiss," he said slowly. He felt a little regretful. While he had been swamped with lust and thoughts of ravishment, she was experiencing something quite different. Something new. Something shocking. He should have guessed. He should have realized how important the moment had been for her. He shut his mind to the thought of how important it had been to *him.*

"Yes, it was," she said.

Fleet was at a loss. He had taken greedily from her with no thought for her feelings. While he floundered, Clara had evidently regained full possession of her senses.

"Don't you dare say you are sorry," she said wrathfully.

Fleet smiled. "No. I'm not sorry." Her expression eased slightly. "It was nice," he added.

"Nice? *Nice!*" Clara took a deep breath.

He could see the hurt in her eyes. Nice was so bland a word for what had happened between them. Devil take it, how could he be making such a hash of this? He was supposed to be a man of the world. The trouble was that he was accustomed to dealing with women of the world, not inexperienced young ladies. He felt woefully out of his depth.

"Then I wish you a *nice* Christmas, your grace," she said, spun on her heel and walked briskly away.

SHE HAD BEEN KISSED for the first time. Thoroughly, expertly, ruthlessly kissed by a man who was a thorough, ruthless expert. She knew she should feel shocked or offended or both. The trouble was, it had been wonderful.

Clara curled up on her bedroom window seat and

watched the snow falling. The clouds were breaking now, shreds of moonlight showing in the blackness, glittering on the white branches of the trees as the tiny flakes fell softly then finally ceased. It was very late and the city was quiet. Clara leaned her head against the cold pane and thought of Sebastian Fleet.

She supposed she had been in love with him from the start. That realization did not excuse her behavior but it certainly explained it. She should have slapped his face. Instead she had pulled him closer with a hunger that had startled her as much as it had no doubt astounded him. The experience had been like feast after famine, joy after long nights of loneliness.

She sighed, wrapping her arms about her knees and curling up tighter still. When he let her go she had realized what had been an earth-shattering experience for her was for him no more than a pleasant encounter with a pretty girl. The vast gap between the two of them—the experienced rake and the never-been-kissed debutante—had never seemed starker.

Now was the moment to accept the truth and relinquish her fantasy.

Sebastian Fleet would never love her as she loved him.

As she wanted to be loved.

As she *deserved* to be loved.

She pressed her fingertips to the cold glass. Outside the night was beautiful but frozen. The trees were still as statues. Above the trees swung a little star, glittering in the deep dark of the night, sometimes obscured by the scurrying cloud, sometimes shining bright, growing in strength.

Have hope.

Have faith.

Clara shook her head slightly. She slid off the seat and let the curtain fall back into place. The room was warm and quiet. She felt lonely.

"Perch," the Duke of Fleet said, taking the pristine, pressed newspaper from the tray his butler offered, "would you be aware of those shops that sell Christmas gifts for infants?"

Perch's eyebrows shot up into his hair. "Gifts for infants, your grace?"

Fleet gave him a hard stare. "Nothing wrong with your hearing this morning is there, Perch?"

"No, your grace."

"Do you know the answer to the question?"

"No, your grace."

"But you could find out."

"Of course, your grace." Perch bowed. "Would you wish me to purchase something appropriate, your grace?"

"No," Fleet said absentmindedly, scanning the headlines, "I will do the purchasing myself. I merely need the direction."

"Of course, your grace," Perch said. "I shall see to it at once."

Fleet nodded, tucked the paper under his arm and

headed toward the library. He wondered what Miss Clara Davencourt was doing this morning. He would not call in Collett Square to find out. After the fiasco of the previous night it was best to leave matters to cool. Looking back, in the frozen light of day, he wondered what on earth had possessed him. Before he had gone to the ball he had made a perfectly reasonable resolution to avoid Clara's company, which he had broken as soon as he had seen her. It was incomprehensible. He must have been drunk. He must have been bewitched. He must have been both bewitched *and* drunk at the same time. It must not happen again.

Even so, he knew that his behavior had been shabby. He should send her some flowers to apologize. Except that she would probably cut off the tops and return the stems to him. He smiled a little at the thought.

Two portraits flanked the entrance to the library. They were of the previous Duke of Fleet and his Duchess. Sebastian rarely noticed them, for they were as much part of the fixtures and fittings of the house as a chair or a lamp. Now, however, he stopped and regarded the painted faces. His father looked noble, wrapped in scarlet and ermine and adorned with the ducal strawberry leaves. His mother had a gentler face beneath her coronet. Wise and kind, she had put the warmth into his childhood.

The huge ruby betrothal ring of the Fleets gleamed on her finger, alongside the simple wedding band. They were both in the vaults of his bank and there they would stay; it felt symbolic, somehow.

His mother had never really recovered from the loss of her youngest, Oliver. It was all wrong to bury one's child. Whenever he thought of the burden he had laid on his parents, he felt the same crushing cold. If he had saved Oliver it might all have been different, but he had failed.

He hurried into the library and sat down beside the fire. Perhaps it was time to rearrange the portraits in the house. A couple of landscapes might look attractive in the hall. At least there were no pictures of Oliver to haunt his waking nightmares.

There was a tap at the library door. Perch entered.

"Hamley's Emporium is the best shop to purchase children's gifts, your grace," he said.

"Hamley's," Fleet said. "Excellent. I shall go there at once."

He felt a profound relief to be occupied.

IT WAS LATE when the knock came at the door of the house in Collett Square. Clara had been reading alone in the library in the big armchair in front of the fire. Martin and Juliana were attending a dinner party and Mrs. Boyce had gone to bed. Clara had fully intended to follow, but had become caught up in Miss Austen's *Sense and Sensibility* and stayed before the dying fire as the clock ticked past midnight.

She heard the knock and looked up, surprised anyone would possibly be calling at this time of night. She heard Segsbury's footfall across the floor, followed by the creak of the hinges and a low-voiced exchange.

"I regret, your grace, that there must have been some mistake. Mr. Davencourt and Lady Juliana are not at home…."

Your grace?

Clara sat bolt upright, her book sliding off her lap with a thud. Could this be Sebastian Fleet come to call at this hour? Impossible, unless he had arranged to take a glass of brandy with Martin and discuss the latest legislation going through the Houses of Parliament….

"It is no matter, Segsbury. My mistake, I believe." Fleet sounded distinctly ill at ease now. "If you would be so good as to give this to Mr. Davencourt. It is a Christmas gift for the twins."

There was a rustling sound. Clara's curiosity gave her the excuse she needed. She opened the library door and went out into the hall.

"Miss…" Segsbury was as taken aback as a butler of his experience could be. "I apologize. I thought that you had retired."

"It is no matter, Segsbury," Clara said with a smile. "Good evening, your grace."

"Miss Davencourt." Fleet sketched a bow. He did not smile at her. In the barely lit hall Clara could not read his expression, although she fancied his mouth was set in grim lines.

Her heart was tripping with quick, light beats. She had wanted to see Fleet again despite everything. She had been compelled in some way to force this meeting when she could have stayed quietly in the library and allowed him to go on his way. Now she wished she had not given in to that impulse. This hard-faced stranger was not the man she had wanted to see. Already he had distanced himself from her. Already the events of the previous night seemed like a fevered dream.

"If you will excuse me," Fleet said, "I was merely delivering this parcel." He gestured to the package now in Segsbury's hand. "It is a Christmas gift for your young nephew and niece. I hope I have chosen appropriately. It is a little difficult when one is not accustomed to shopping for children."

Clara felt a jolt of surprise. "You chose it *yourself?*"

A rueful grin touched Fleet's mouth. "I did."

"And you delivered it yourself, too. How singular!"

She saw his smile deepen and felt a jolt of pleasure inside. "Perhaps you could put the parcel somewhere safe, Segsbury," she said, "while I show the Duke of Fleet out."

Segsbury gave her a hard stare. He had been butler to Lady Juliana before her marriage and so was no stranger to unconventionality, but he had a very definite way of showing his disapproval of such inappropriate behavior. He looked at Clara for a long moment and she looked back steadily, then he bowed slightly.

"Very well, miss."

Neither Clara nor Fleet moved as Segsbury walked away with stately displeasure. The hall was quiet as his footsteps died away.

"I wanted to see you," Clara said.

"So it seems. It was not, perhaps, your wisest decision." Fleet's entire body was taut with what Clara assumed was anger.

"Last night—"

"Miss Davencourt, we really must *not* discuss this."

"Not discuss it?" Clara felt something snap within her. "What do you want to do instead, your grace? Sweep it under the carpet because it is difficult for us to face up to so inconvenient an attraction?"

"No," Fleet ground out. "What I want is to have you."

Clara felt a sudden, treacherous excitement. It caught like a flare, blazing into shocking and sensual life. Fleet's eyes darkened with concentrated passion. He took one step forward, grabbed both her arms and his mouth captured hers, swift and sure.

Clara instinctively moved closer to him. All conscious thought fled her mind. Her arms went about him, fingers tangling in his hair. He tasted faintly of brandy and strongly of desire. The kiss grew frantic, then rough, almost brutal. The shock of it sent a blaze of feeling right to the center of Clara's body.

His impatient hands were already pushing aside silk and lace, and when he closed his hand over her breast, warm and hard against her bare skin, she gave a desperate moan as she felt her legs start to buckle. He half pulled, half carried her through the library door, slamming it shut behind them.

Then they were down on the rug before the fire and she was clutching at his shoulders. His tongue and teeth had replaced his fingers at her breast, and she squirmed and arched in quick delight to his touch.

She was shaking; so was he. Clara noticed it with astonishment, for surely this man was supposed to be an experienced rake. Yet he touched her with reverence as well as ferocious desire, as though he could not quite believe what was happening. The sense of power the thought gave her, the sheer unbelievable seduction of his hands on her body, roused a driving need.

His lips returned to hers with a passionate tenderness and urgency that inflamed her. He moved over her, throwing up her skirts, sliding a hand up her thigh, over the soft skin to find the hot, central core of her. Her body shivered like a plucked cord beneath his touch.

"Sebastian…"

She felt as though she were dissolving into some desperate pleasure, and when he moved down to meet her unspoken plea for release with the touch of his tongue against her most intimate place, the sensation was too hot and too sudden to resist. Her body was speared by so violent a delight that she rolled over, stifling a cry against his chest.

She could feel his arousal hard against her thigh but even as she reached blindly for him, intuitively knowing what was needed, he was withdrawing, wrapping his arms carefully about her. Although he held her close, she somehow knew he was putting distance between them. The pleasure and the astounding intimacy she felt turned cold and started to shrink.

"Clara… sweetheart…we must not…"

If Clara's thoughts had been clear, she would have noticed the harsh undertone in his voice, realized he was still trembling as much as she. Instead, she only knew that while her body still echoed with unfamiliar passion, Sebastian was trying to retreat, leaving her feelings too raw to bear.

"*We must not?* Sebastian, we already have!" Her voice cracked, and she felt him hesitate then draw her closer against him. The warmth of his arms should have been reassuring but it was not, for it already felt wrong. She had opened herself body and soul to this man, had allowed him the most shocking and unimaginable liberties. Now, in return, she had received nothing but humiliation.

She stifled a little sob and hid her face in her hands.

"Clara. Do not…"

Sebastian gently helped her to her feet as she pulled her disheveled dress tight around her. When he would have drawn her down to sit with him on the sofa she resisted, deliberately choosing a chair that set her apart from him.

"I am sorry." This time she realized that he sounded wretched. "I should not have done it."

"*You* should not have done it?" Clara's fingers scored the arms of the chair. "Do not take responsibility for something that I wanted as much as you! Indeed, if you had not stopped me…" Her voice trailed away as she realized she would have given herself to him totally, without reservation. But even then he had not been so emotionally engaged as she. He had known what he was doing. And he had stopped it. She bit her lip to stifle her anguish.

"I should never have sent for you yesterday," she said tonelessly.

"No." His word was uncompromising. "And I should never have come to you."

"It took me such a long time…" Clara gulped. "I thought I no longer had such strong feelings for you."

He was shaking his head but said nothing. She felt desolate.

"What are we to do?" she said. She looked at him properly for the first time and her heart turned over at the misery and self-loathing in his eyes. "I know that you cannot offer me what I want, Sebastian."

He closed his eyes for a moment. The pain was etched deep on his face. "Clara, to make you a promise and then break it would be intolerable."

She knew what he meant. He did not wish to have the responsibility of loving her. He could not swear to be faithful to her for the rest of his life. She remembered what she had thought the previous night: he could not love her as she wished to be loved, as she deserved to be loved.

"So what do we do?" she said again.

He did not pretend to misunderstand her.

"About this perilous attraction between us?" He smiled faintly and Clara's heart clenched with a combination of misery and longing. "There is nothing we can do. You are not a woman I can have by any means other than marriage. I accept that." His voice was calm but there was an undertone of emotion that seared Clara. She knew he wanted her and wanted her desperately.

The words fell into the silence. Despite the warmth of the room, Clara shivered. A little while ago, a mere half hour perhaps, she would have believed she was truly a woman bound by convention. Now she had tasted passion and her body ached for it. It would be fulfilling, overwhelming, to make love with Sebastian Fleet. She had sampled desire and it made her hungry.

"Sebastian."

He read her tone and she saw the leap of fire in his eyes. He came to his knees by her chair, taking her cold hands in his. "Clara…"

For a long moment they stared at each other, but then Clara shook her head. "I cannot do it, Sebastian. If it were only for myself I…" She broke off, unable even now, after all that had happened between them, to confess to what felt such an unmaidenly desire. She looked up again and met his eyes. "But you would lose my brother's friendship and gain nothing but the censure of those who had been your friends."

"It would be worth it for you." The sincerity in his tone was beyond question. His hands tightened on hers. "It would be worth it and more, a hundred times over, to have you even for a little while…."

For a moment, Clara's world spun on the edge of a different existence. She was a woman of independent means. There was no one else she would rather marry. She could not imagine there ever would be, for she loved Sebastian Fleet with all the stubbornness in her character. Yet upbringing and principle ran so deep. To lose her good reputation, to lose her family and friends, all the things she had once taken for granted, and to gain what? Not Sebastian's love, for he had sworn himself incapable of that. What was he really offering her? A few months of bliss perhaps, but with everlasting darkness at the end.

He released her suddenly and stood up, turning away. "No, I know it would not serve. I could not ask it of you, Clara, even if you were willing. You are not the kind of woman who could be happy with such an arrangement."

He was right. They both knew it. Clara felt her spirits sink like a stone. So this really was the end.

"So what do we do?" she asked hopelessly, a third time.

"We do not see each other again. It is the only way."

Clara shook her head. "That will not suffice. We are forever in the same company. We cannot avoid it. It will be unbearable."

The shadows made the planes of his face even more austere. "Then I will go away."

"No!" The cry was wrenched from Clara. That she could not bear. Not to see him again would be painful enough, but to think that he had exiled himself because of her…

"Perhaps," she said, after a moment, "it will become easier in time."

"I doubt it." There was a smile in Sebastian's voice now. "Not when I cannot even look at you without wishing to kiss you senseless and strip all your clothing from you and make love to you until you are exhausted in my arms."

Clara made a small sound of distress, squirming in her chair with a mixture of remembered desire and unfulfilled passion. "Do not!"

"I am sorry." She knew he was not only speaking of what had happened between them. He was speaking of his inability to give her what she desired.

The library door opened with shocking suddenness. Both Clara and Sebastian spun around like a couple of guilty schoolchildren. Engrossed in their own passions and anxieties, neither of them had heard the front door open or the sound of voices in the hall, or footsteps approaching.

Segsbury, Juliana and Martin were all poised in the doorway. Segsbury looked genuinely startled to see the Duke of Fleet in the house a full half hour after the man's supposed departure. Juliana looked shocked and Martin merely furious.

Clara felt a bubble of hysterical laughter rising inside her. She was seated; Sebastian was standing a good few feet away. There was nothing remotely compromising in their demeanor. And yet she wondered what on earth was showing on their faces.

"A curious time of the night to be making calls, Sebastian," Martin said, and although his voice was perfectly pleasant it held a distinct undertone of menace. "Segsbury implied that you had brought some gifts for the children."

"I did." Clara saw Sebastian pull himself together with an effort. "Excuse me. As you say, it is late. I should be leaving."

For a moment it looked to Clara, frozen in her seat, as though Martin were not inclined to let his friend go so easily. Then Juliana drifted forward. "Dear Sebastian," she said, putting one hand on Fleet's arm, "how thoughtful of you to bring presents." She steered him toward the door and after a moment, Martin stepped aside, though there was still an ugly look in his eyes. "Segsbury will show you out," Juliana continued, "and we shall see you soon, I am sure." She relinquished his arm and Segsbury stepped forward, perfectly on cue, just in case the duke had once again forgotten his way to the front door.

"This way, your grace."

Clara waited. Sebastian half turned toward her and Martin made an unmistakably threatening movement.

"Good night, Miss Davencourt," Sebastian said. There was nothing but darkness in his eyes. He inclined his head. "Davencourt, Lady Juliana…"

The library door shut with an ominous thud and

Martin took a purposeful step toward her. Clara shrank in her chair.

"Martin, darling," Juliana said clearly, "I wonder if you might check on the nursery? I would be relieved to know that all is well."

Clara saw the tiny shake of the head that Juliana gave her husband and, after a moment, to Clara's inexpressible relief, Martin went out. She was so thankful not to have to explain herself to her brother that she almost burst into tears.

"Oh, Ju!" She hurled herself into Juliana's arms and clung tight, careless of what her sister-in-law would think. And after a moment Juliana hugged her back fiercely, with no words until Clara had slackened her grip a little.

"I am sorry, Ju."

"Do not be." Juliana caught her hand and pulled her down to sit beside her on the sofa. "What happened, Clara?"

"He is to go away," Clara said, in a rush. "We think it is the only way."

"Yes," Juliana said quietly, "I think that may be true."

They sat for a moment in silence. "Perhaps you could go away for a little, too," Juliana said thoughtfully. "When your sister Kitty and Edward return to Yorkshire after Christmas."

"Yes," Clara said rapidly. "A change of scene. Perhaps that might serve."

"Clara—" There was anxiety in Juliana's voice now.

"Forgive me, but did you… I mean, surely you did not…"

At another time, Clara might have laughed at her notoriously outspoken sister-in-law being so timid at confronting her. She shook her head. "We did not." She knitted her fingers together. "I would have given myself gladly to Sebastian tonight," she said, "but he was not so careless as I."

"Thank God," Juliana said, and there was a wealth of relief in her voice.

"I suppose so." Clara stood up. Her heart felt as bleak as winter. "I must go to bed. I am so tired. Thank you, Juliana."

Juliana's expression was sad. "If you wish to talk to me tomorrow, Clara, you will, won't you?"

"Of course." Clara managed a smile. "I love having you for a big sister, Juliana."

Juliana's answering smile was vivid and bright. "Thank you, Clara. I will see you in the morning."

As she went slowly up the stairs, Clara worried she would not be able to sleep, but when she finally came to lie down she was so exhausted that she remembered nothing from the moment her head touched the pillow.

There were no stars that night.

CHAPTER FOUR

SEB FLEET RAN DOWN the steps leading from his lawyer's offices and out into the cold street, pulling on his gloves as he did so. Today was a perfect, clear, frosty winter's day with the air as sharp as a knife. It was the ideal day on which to leave London, the ideal way to remember the city, dressed in bridal white, its dirtiness hidden at least for a little beneath a blanket of snow.

It was two weeks since he had announced he was leaving England for an extended period of travel abroad. He had had no notion of the complexity of arrangements that would follow. Perch was attending to all the travel preparations, but Sebastian needed to settle his business affairs, from the authorizations needed to keep his estates running efficiently to a meeting with his anxious cousin and heir, who wished to know what would happen in the event of his untimely death abroad. It had reassured Seb to see Anthony, even if his cousin's thoughts were taking a morbid turn. It was good to know that with his passing, the Fleet succession would still be in safe hands. For half of Seb wished passionately for precisely that untimely death to which Anthony had alluded.

He felt trapped, and he hoped that different climes and fresh scenes might help him regain his perspective. All he had been able to think about in the fourteen days following his last meeting with Clara Davencourt was the sheer torment of wanting one thing and yet feeling incapable of gaining it. It was not so simple or so selfish as wanting Clara physically and being denied. He needed Clara in some deep sense that frightened him to analyze, and to tear himself away from her was to wrench out part of his soul. Yet to have her love and her trust felt such a huge burden and one of which he was not worthy. He would let her down; he would desert her. He could never meet her expectations or be what she deserved. The responsibility was too great and the image of Oliver was before him always. He had let Oliver die. He had let his parents down and caused them such a grief that could never be assuaged and he would never, ever, do that to another person again.

Sebastian had been walking with no fixed intention, so deep in thought was he. Now he found he had come out into the street by one of the pleasure gardens, the Peerless Pool. In summer it was the haunt of bathers who came to swim in the fresh spring waters. Now, the frozen lake was full of skaters. They circled beneath the high blue sky and their excited cries mingled with the cutting sound of skates on ice. The frozen branches of the lime and cherry trees seemed to catch the sound and send its echoes tinkling back.

Sebastian paused. It was a pretty scene and in the center of it skated a girl in crimson. He recognized Clara at once. She was surrounded by her family and friends. These were the very people with whom he would once have felt so comfortable. He found himself automatically moving to the marble steps that led down to the pool, then stopped. He had barely seen or spoken to Clara in the past fortnight, and to force himself on her party now felt awkward and wrong. Besides, now he looked more closely he saw that Lords Tarver and Elton were both in attendance, like twin ugly sisters waiting for Cinderella to choose between them. It made Sebastian feel ridiculously angry. Yet he knew that Clara might well be married by the time he returned from the continent and that he should feel relieved at the prospect. It was unfortunate that he was not even noble enough to want for her the thing that would achieve her greatest happiness. He did not want Clara enough to risk everything for her—the thought petrified him—and yet he did not wish her to find her happiness with anyone else. The tug of it was like an agonizing seesaw inside him. Risk all to gain all…he was so very close to it. And yet he turned aside to leave instead.

He almost missed it, had almost turned back through the gates where the doorman was still demanding his entry fee, when out of the corner of his eye he saw Clara fall. She had skated away from the others to the edge of the pool, where the ice ran beneath the branches of the bare trees. She was weaving her way under the trees, a snow queen all in red against the frosted white of the trunks. Then there was a harsh, horrible cracking sound and Sebastian saw the dark water run between the cracks in the ice, saw Clara clutch and miss the branch overhead, and did not wait to see more. He ran. The park keeper was still shouting for his money, unaware of the accident. The other skaters were still spinning and drifting on the other side of the pond. Sebastian scrambled down the bank, careless of the snow and the branches that tore at his coat and his face, and came down onto the ice near where Clara lay.

Someone else had seen now, and was shouting for help, but Sebastian reached her first. She was lying half on the ice and half in the icy water. She did not move. The ice cracked and shifted beneath his feet, but he ignored it. He caught a fold of her skirts and pulled fiercely.

"Clara!"

She moved then and tried to pull herself up out of the ice, but it broke beneath her hands. He grabbed one flailing wrist. There was a pain inside him so immense and a panic so smothering that he could not speak. Her wrist was wet and he could feel his grip slipping. She was sliding from his fingers and he was powerless to stop her. There was an immense crack as the ice gave beneath her and she tumbled from his grasp. Seb saw the water close over her head.

The dark images that he had thought buried forever

flashed across his mind with vividness. Oliver struggling against the ice, slipping away from him, disappearing from sight, his face white, his mouth open in a soundless scream... For a moment he was still with the horror of it and then he was lunging forward to seize hold of Clara before it was too late. His grasp met nothing but ice and air. He reached for her again and this time, to his inexpressible relief, he touched the material of her gown; he grabbed it and pulled. There was resistance, a ripping sound, and then her skirts were free of the clutching water and he was drawing her to him fiercely. They both tumbled backward onto the snowy bank, Clara held tight in his arms. He pressed his lips to her hair and tried to pull her closer still, until she made a muffled sound of protest.

The others were arriving now, full of questions and anxiety. Juliana and Kitty plucked Clara from his arms and fussed over her. Martin was shaking his hand and saying something, but Seb was not sure what it was. He felt sick and shaken and afraid. Martin carried Clara up the bank. Seb could hear her protesting that she was quite well and he felt breathless with relief. They were calling for a carriage to take her straight home. Clara turned to look at him and held out a hand in mute appeal, but he turned away. He was too dazed to speak to her, both by what had so nearly happened to Clara and by the tragic memories it had stirred for him. He did not want her thanks.

The fuss and bustle gave him the chance to escape.

He went to a nearby coffee house and, although he could see them looking for him out in the street, he stayed in his own dark corner until the last of their carriages had rolled away.

The coffee warmed him and gradually soothed his shaken emotions. He was able to force the fearsome images of the past back into the dark recesses of his mind where they belonged. Nevertheless, he knew that this was not the end. It could not be, now. For in those moments when he'd held her, he had confessed to Clara that he loved her. Not in words, perhaps, but in the expression in his eyes and the touch of his hands as he clutched her so fiercely to him; he had known it and so had she. And he knew she would seek a confrontation now, stubborn girl that she was. He would have to be ready.

CLARA CAME TO HIM that evening, as he had known she would. He could have gone to his club and avoided the confrontation, but he planned to leave first thing in the morning, as soon as it was light, and so he settled upon a final evening at home. Now he knew it would be a final reckoning, as well. When he left, it would be with the truth between them. He would tell Clara about Oliver and explain once and for all why he was not worthy of her. He sat in his study with a glass of brandy untouched on the table beside him and he stared into the fire and thought of Clara. Who had he been fooling when he pretended not to care for her? She had stripped away all but the last of his defenses now. He loved her. He loved her desperately and he had done so for a very long time.

"When Miss Davencourt arrives, please show her into the study," he told Perch, and he was on tenterhooks as the clock ticked on toward midnight. Perhaps she had been injured more than he had realized; perhaps she had taken a chill. It might be better if they did not meet. He could slip away in the morning and ask Perch to arrange for a message and a bouquet of flowers to be sent, wishing her a speedy recovery….

"Miss Davencourt, your grace."

Perch was ushering Clara into the room. She looked a little pale but he was glad to see that she appeared otherwise unharmed. He was quick to set a chair for her.

"You should not have come out tonight," he said. "You sustained a shock. Were you injured? You might have caught a chill…." He realized that he was rambling like a nervous youth. There was a spark of amusement in Clara's eyes.

"I am very well," she said. "I came to thank you, Sebastian. You disappeared so quickly this afternoon."

Sebastian shrugged awkwardly. He was feeling very ill at ease. Before she had arrived, he had been confident he would direct their conversation. Now he was not so sure. The balance of power between them seemed to have changed and he did not know how to change it back.

"Does Martin know that you are here?" he asked. "After last night…"

A shadow touched her face. "No one knows. I slipped out when they thought I was asleep."

He felt a rush of amusement followed by a jolt of despair. That was his Clara, so stubborn, so determined to do what she felt was right. Yet she was not really *his* Clara at all. He was about to tell her so.

She sat forward in the chair, looking directly at him. "Do you still intend to leave for the continent tomorrow, Sebastian?"

He looked away. "I do."

Her face fell. The bright light had gone. "I was hoping that you might have changed your mind," she said. "We all wished to thank you properly."

He looked up and met her eyes so sharply that she flinched a little. "Was that why you came here, Clara?" he said harshly. "To thank me?"

"No." She dropped her gaze. A shade of color stole into her cheeks. "I came here to tell you that I love you."

Sebastian looked at her. Her eyes were clear and steady. She was the most beautiful thing he thought he had ever seen. He felt an immense admiration for her courage, followed by a choking wave of love and an even sharper pang of despair. How many women would have had the honesty to behave as she had done?

She was regarding him directly but he knew she was nervous. She moistened her lips with her tongue. A tiny frown touched her forehead at his silence.

"My dear." He cleared his throat. He sounded

nervous. That was not good. He had to hide his feelings from her at all costs. "You know that I hold you in the greatest esteem."

She moved with a swift swirl of silk to kneel at his feet. She put one hand on his knee. "No, you do not, Sebastian. You do not hold me 'in esteem.'" Disdain colored her voice. "You *love* me."

He moved to raise her to her feet. He could not bear this closeness.

"You and I will never be equal, Clara," he said, trying to make her understand. "You are too open and truth-ful—damn it, you are too *good* for me. I am jaded. My soul is old."

Clara smiled. It devastated him. "You are making excuses, Sebastian. Do you think I do not know? You are afraid to let yourself love me."

He knew she was right. He had been building barriers against her from the moment they met, instinctively knowing that her love could be his undoing. And now the thing he feared most had happened. He was undone. He had to make her leave him before he disintegrated completely. He could not explain to her about Oliver. That would bring her too close and he would never recover.

"You are in love with love, Clara," he said, struggling to keep his voice neutral. "For me there is nothing between liking and lust. Do not try to dress up my desire for you as something it is not."

There was a stubborn spark of anger in Clara's eyes

now. "Why are you lying to me, Sebastian? What is it that you fear?"

He feared so much. He feared that he would offer her his love and she would then have the power to destroy him. But more than anything he feared taking responsibility for another life. He had failed once before when he had allowed Oliver to die. He could not risk that happening to Clara, his one and only love. He said nothing.

"I know you love me," Clara repeated. "I saw it in your face today at the pool. That is why I am here!" She spread her hands wide. "You have only to allow yourself to care for me and all will be well." Her tone was less forceful now, as his silence was starting to undermine her certainties.

"I do care for you," Sebastian said, "but I do not care for you enough." He hated himself for what he was doing. He could see the color draining from her face and the spirit leaching from her eyes, and knew how much he was hurting her. "I acknowledge that people can love each other with the sort of passion you describe," he said. He could barely hear his own false words over the desperate beating of his heart. "But I do not love you like that, Clara," he said starkly. "I do not love you nearly enough. It would not be fair to you to promise otherwise."

Clara scrambled to her feet. There was a blankness to her eyes. She stumbled a little, bumping clumsily into the small table on which stood his glass of brandy. He wanted to pull her into his arms then and never let her go, to comfort her and beg her forgiveness. He was too afraid to do it.

"Either you are lying or you do not know the truth," Clara said. She did not trouble to keep her voice from shaking and he loved her for it; he loved her for the strength of character that made artifice unimportant to her. "I was wrong when I called you coldhearted," she added. "Your heart is a desert, Sebastian, a dry, shriveled place where nothing can live, least of all love."

He could not look at her. He waited until he heard the soft patter of her footsteps receding and then he finally looked up. The face that looked back at him from the mirror was barely recognizable. He looked so haggard. He looked a broken man.

He had hurt Clara inexcusably. But he had succeeded in driving her away and protecting himself from the terrifying risk of loving and losing her. He knew that he should feel glad, but his heart felt like the desert that Clara had so accurately described.

"Miss Davencourt? Miss Davencourt!" Clara was heading for the front door, hampered by the fact that she was blinded by tears. She tripped over the edge of the Persian rug, grabbed a table for support and almost toppled the priceless vase that rested on it.

"Miss Davencourt!"

Her arm was caught in a reassuring grip and she found herself looking into the face of Perch, the butler.

She noticed, irrelevantly, what kind eyes he had. Then she also noticed that the door to the servants' stair was open and a row of anxious faces was peering at her from the gloom. Her curiosity was sufficient to overcome her misery for a moment.

"What on earth is going on?"

Perch steered her discreetly into the dining room, and the other servants trooped in silently. In the gothic shadowy darkness they lined up in front of her, candlesticks in hand, their expressions a mixture of hope and concern. Clara looked to the butler for enlightenment.

"Begging your pardon, Miss Davencourt," Perch said, "but we were thinking that you might have persuaded his grace…" He studied her face for a moment, shook his head and sighed. "No matter. Shall I procure you a cab to take you home, miss?"

The other servants gave a murmur of protest. It was clear they did not wish to let her go so easily without telling her their concerns.

"We thought you were to be the new Duchess of Fleet, ma'am," one of the housemaids, a girl with a round red face, said. "That's what Mr. Perch is trying to say. His grace has been sweet on you for as long as I've worked here."

Clara felt a rush of misery. She looked at their anxious faces and managed to raise a rueful smile. "Thank you, but I'm afraid I shall not be the next duchess."

"His grace must be mad," the hall boy whispered,

rolling his eyes expressively. Perch shot him a warning look.

"We are very sorry to hear that, ma'am," he said. "We should have liked it very much."

Clara's desolate heart thawed a little. She looked at them all properly for the first time, from the brawny under-gardener to the smallest scullery maid and realized how extraordinary it was that they had all pinned their hopes on her. "I had forgotten," she said. "The duke is to leave on the morrow, is he not? Are you—" she hesitated "—will he be closing the house?"

A row of doleful nods was her answer.

"We are looking for new positions, ma'am. All except Mr. Dawson, his grace's valet. He travels abroad with his grace."

So, most all of them would be out of work as soon as Fleet left for the continent, Clara thought. It was another consequence of his departure and one she had not even considered. She felt horribly guilty.

"I am sorry," she said.

"Not your fault, ma'am," one of the footmen said stalwartly. "His grace is a fine man but in this case his wits have gone a-begging, if you will excuse my saying so."

"His grace has a picture of you in his traveling case, ma'am," another of the maids put in, blushing. "I saw him pack it when he thought no one was watching."

There was a hopeful pause.

"I do not suppose, madam," Perch said weightily, "that you would be prepared to give his grace another chance?"

Clara looked at them all. "I have already given him several chances," she said.

Perch nodded. "We are aware, ma'am. What lady could be expected to do more?"

There was another rustle of disapproval from among the assembled ranks. Clearly they believed their esteemed employer had run mad.

"Unless you could think of a winning scheme," Clara said, "it is pointless. And even then I am not sure that his grace deserves it."

The housekeeper and several of the maids shook their heads. "Men!" one of the girls said. "Hopeless!"

"Get him at a moment of weakness," one of the footmen suggested. "He'll admit to his feelings when he's in his cups."

The valet nodded. "That's true, ma'am. If we could get him drunk."

Clara stifled a laugh. "I am not certain I would want a man who has to be drunk to admit his love for me."

The housekeeper shook her head. "Begging your pardon, ma'am, we're thinking it was the business with Master Oliver that made him this way. Those of us who have been with the family for years saw it happen. The master changed. Terrible shock, it was. After that he turned cold."

One of the older housemaids nodded sadly. "Aye, such an affectionate little boy he was, but he blamed himself from that day forward."

Clara raised her brows. "Who was Master Oliver?"

The servants shuffled uncomfortably. "Master Oliver was his grace's brother," Perch said. "There was an accident."

"Drowned," one of the footmen put in. "Terrible business."

Clara was so surprised that she was silent for a moment. She had never heard of Oliver Fleet, still less that the duke had ever had a brother. He had never, ever mentioned it to her and, she was sure, not to Martin, either. But then, he was good at keeping secrets.

"I had no notion," she said. "How dreadful. I am so sorry."

The servants nodded sadly.

"His grace blamed himself. He has been as cold as ice ever since," Perch explained. There was a long silence before he continued.

"We know that you are too good for his grace, ma'am, being a true lady and generous to a fault, but if you could see your way to giving his grace—and the rest of us—another chance…"

The eagerness of their expressions was heartbreaking. Clara thought of the stories behind the faces, the families that depended on their wages, the fear of being without a job or a roof over their heads, the uncertainty of a servant's life. And yet it was not only that that had prompted them to throw themselves on her mercy. They had seen her come and go through Sebastian Fleet's life for two years and the sincerity of their regard warmed her.

"If you have a plan," she said, "I am prepared to listen to it."

Perch checked the clock on the mantel. "In approximately two minutes his grace will decide to go out to drown his sorrows, ma'am. We shall give him a few hours to become cast adrift, and then we will escort you to fetch him home." He looked around at his fellow servants. "We believe he will admit his feelings for you very soon, ma'am. His grace has almost reached the point where they cannot be denied."

There was a crash out in the hall. Everyone jumped at the sound of the library door banging open and Seb Fleet's voice shouting irascibly for his butler. He sounded absolutely furious.

"Perch? Where the devil are you, man? I want to go out!"

"Perfectly on cue," one of the footmen said.

Perch smoothed his coat and trod slowly toward the door, opening it and closing it behind him with his usual grave deliberation.

"You called, your grace?" Clara heard him say.

"I am going out," Fleet repeated. She thought he sounded murderous.

"Might one inquire where, your grace?"

"No, one might not, damn you! Fetch my coat!"

"May I then remind your grace that you are to travel at first light?"

Fleet said something so rude that one of the housemaids gasped and clapped her hands over her ears.

"Sorry you had to hear that, ma'am," the housekeeper whispered. "His grace is in a proper mood and no mistake."

Clara bit her lip to stop a smile.

The front door slammed. There was a long pause while they all seemed to be holding their breath, then Perch appeared once more in the doorway of the dining room.

"I've sent Jackman to follow his grace," he said. "We shall soon know where he has gone. Miss Davencourt—" there was a smile in his eyes as he turned to Clara "—may we offer you some refreshment while we wait?"

CHAPTER FIVE

SEB FLEET did not choose to drown his sorrows at Whites, but instead went to the Moon and Goldfinch, a considerably less salubrious place on the Goldhawk Road where he could drink himself to hell and back without anyone caring. Indeed, once the landlord had seen that his money was good he kept him so well-supplied with alcohol that Sebastian found himself by turns maudlin, then merry, then maudlin again in the shortest possible time. By three in the morning he had made several dubious new friends, turned down eager kisses from the landlord's daughter and was comfortably asleep on the bar when he was shaken roughly awake. The door of the inn was open and a fresh burst of snow was swirling inside, pulling him from his welcome stupor.

"Sebastian! Wake up at once!" It was Clara's voice. Fleet groaned.

"This the missus, is it?" the landlord enquired affably.

"Not yet," Clara snapped.

Fleet shook the hair out of his eyes and tried to sit up. The room swam about him. His mouth felt like a cockpit. His eyes were gritty and his face was wet where he appeared to have fallen asleep in a pool of beer.

"You smell like a sewer," Clara grumbled. "Perch, Dawson, can you manage him?"

"Hello, my sweet love," Sebastian said with a slight slur, as his butler and valet struggled to lift him with all the finesse of a collier hefting a sack. He smiled at Clara as her cross-looking face swam before his eyes. He felt inordinately pleased to see her. He could not quite remember why, but he knew that earlier in the evening he thought he would never, ever see her again. Evidently he had been quite wrong. He struggled to remember the circumstances, failed completely and lurched heavily against Dawson's side.

"How splendid that you are here, my darling," he called as Perch and Dawson tried to maneuver him to the door. "I did not expect to see you." He staggered dangerously and almost knocked over the butler.

"Sorry, Perch. Don't know why you don't just leave me to sleep here."

"Yes, your grace." Perch sounded as though that was precisely what he would have done had he been permitted to have his way. "Miss Davencourt was concerned for you, your grace."

"Very wifely," Fleet observed. His head felt too heavy to think clearly. Here was Clara, turning his heart inside out again and making him feel as raw as an untried youth. He loved her so much that there was a lump in his throat at the thought of it. It was dreadful that she should see him this way. He must look terrible. He smelled. He was a disgrace. And yet she was still here, despite everything, and he really did not have the will to resist anymore.

"I am not certain it is the proper thing for you to be here, Miss Davencourt."

Clara smiled. "I am here to discover if you love me, Sebastian."

"Love you?" Fleet asked. The question seemed so absurd that he started to laugh. "Of course I love you! I love you so much it breaks my heart."

"Excellent," Clara said. "You are drunk, of course, so that may make a difference. Will you still love me when you are sober?"

"Of course I will." Fleet squinted, his head lolling against Dawson's shoulder. "'Course I will! I love you to perdition, you little fool! Why do you think I keep trying to make you go away?"

"Hmm. It lacks something for a declaration, I think," Clara said. "I shall not propose to you again, however. A lady has her pride."

"Marry me," Fleet said. He tried to get down on his knees but Perch and Dawson held him up. It was probably best they did; he had a feeling that once he was down there he would never stand again.

"We shall talk about it in the morning," Clara said.

"Now please be quiet, Sebastian, and get into the coach."

Fleet stumbled to the door, encouraged on his way by the profuse thanks of the landlord. The cold air sobered him somewhat and the falling snow on his face restored him to an unwelcome sense of reality. Clara was waiting patiently while Perch and Dawson hauled him into the carriage. She accepted Perch's hand up with perfect composure and settled herself opposite him, wrinkling her nose delicately at the combined scent of beer and tobacco.

"Clara," he said again, as the door shut on them. "This is no escapade for a lady. You really should not be here."

"If you were not here then neither should I be," Clara said calmly, wrapping the rug about them both. "I was worried about you, Sebastian."

Fleet pressed a hand to his aching brow. "I do not want you to worry about me!" The words came out almost as a shout and Clara put her gloved hands over her ears. "How many times do I have to explain this? This is exactly what I was trying to avoid!"

"It seems to me," Clara said, ignoring him, "that you have not permitted anyone to care for you in a very long time, Sebastian."

Fleet's head pounded. "Devil take it! Clara, have you not understood? I want you to leave me alone!"

His head was swimming, but in the dim light of the carriage lamps he saw that she was looking at him and there was a slight, satisfied smile on her lips. Fleet leaned his head against the seat cushions and closed his eyes in despair. He realized through the clearing fog of his inebriation that he'd declared his love to her. "Dash it, Clara, I am too befuddled to argue." He leant forward, suddenly urgent. "Yes, I love you to distraction, but I wish to the devil that I did not! I would go to the ends of the earth for you but I can hardly bear it! The responsibility of it terrifies me."

"It is perfectly simple," Clara said briskly. "I care for you and in return you care for me." She put one small hand against his chest and pushed gently. "Go to sleep, now."

He wanted to argue but he did not have the strength. To sleep seemed easier. So he did.

HE WAS AWOKEN by the white light of a snowy morning illuminating his bedroom. For a brief, blissful moment he could not remember anything, then he flung one arm across his eyes and let out a long groan.

"I have prepared a nice posset for you," Clara's voice said. "I thought perhaps you might need something restorative for your head."

Sebastian opened his eyes. He might have known Clara would still be here. No doubt she sat up all night at his bedside to make sure he was quite safe. He felt exasperated and deeply grateful at the same time. She looked as fresh as though she were stepping out to a ball. Her dress was uncreased and her eyes bright. He looked at her and felt a hopeless feeling swamp him.

"Your concern is most touching," he said, sitting up in bed to take the steaming cup of sweet liquid. "I have sunk more drink than last night, however. I shall survive."

"You told me that you loved me last night," Clara said. "Do you remember?"

He looked at her. It was too late now for denials and lies. Much too late.

"I remember," he said. "Oh, Clara, darling, of course I remember."

She took his hand. "There is no need to look so terrified, Sebastian. Love is not an illness. It will not kill you."

But to him it felt exactly as though he had contracted an unfamiliar and frightening disease. He had not tested love's boundaries yet. He did not know how far he could trust himself with it. Nevertheless, the need to tell Clara everything now was so acute he could not resist.

"When you fell through the ice yesterday I was so frightened," he said. His voice shook a little. "I thought that I was losing you, there in front of my eyes. It reminded me of when Oliver died." It had actually been worse than losing Oliver. Ten, twenty times more dreadful.

"Oliver was your brother," Clara said.

"Yes. He was four years younger than I was. I always protected him. Until the day I failed him."

The words came out in a torrent. He could not stop now if he tried.

"It was this time of year right before Christmas. We were supposed to be at our lessons but our tutor fell asleep and we crept out. It was too fine a day to stay indoors. We took our skates and went down to the old mill race." He swallowed painfully. "I can still see Oliver now. He skated out into the middle—the ice was hard, we did not realize the danger—and he was spinning around, his arms outstretched… And then he was simply not there." He stopped. Clara did not speak.

"I moved as fast as I could. The ice was cracking all around me. I shouted for help until I was hoarse but no one came. I could see him, under the ice, but I could not reach him. Every time I got close enough to grab him the ice would break beneath me and we would drift apart."

"What happened?" Clara whispered.

"Someone finally saw us. I do not know how long it took. The water was so cold. They brought ropes and ladders but I knew it was too late for Oliver. I was big and strong but he was only small. He was only eight years old! And I could not save him."

He half expected Clara to tell him that it had not been his fault. People had been saying that to him for years until they tired of reassuring him or thought that he was over the tragedy. But Clara did not say that. She held his hand and waited for him to continue.

"It was my fault," he said starkly. "I was the one who suggested we go skating that day. He always followed me. Then I could not help him when he needed me."

He gripped Clara's hand fast. "They rescued me first, you know. I was the heir." His mouth twisted bitterly. "The spare was sacrificed."

He was crying. He could not help it. He dashed the tears away with his hand and found they fell all the quicker for it. He spoke in gasps.

"I have never told anyone this before. I thought I could lock it away but you have unmanned me. You made me feel again. You made me love you. Oh, Clara—"

Clara moved from her chair to the edge of his bed. She caught him and pulled him to her, drawing him down so that his cheek rested against hers. Her arms were tight about him and it felt protected and safe. For a second he hesitated, but it was out of nothing more than habit. Then he let go and felt himself fall, mind and body, to a warm, safe place, where he was her strength and she was his.

He did not know how long they lay there, but when he opened his eyes, Clara's face was about an inch away from his, so he kissed her with love and gentleness. Her lashes lifted and she looked at him. He could see from her eyes that she was smiling.

"You need a shave," she said, running her fingers experimentally over the stubble that darkened his chin.

"And a wash. I fear I am most unwholesome."

"You are delightful." Clara rubbed her cheek against his rough one. "I love you, Sebastian."

He savored the words, tasted them. His entire body felt relaxed, released from a terrible torment. His eyes were heavy. He felt so tired. He did not want to resist and after a few moments, to his intense surprise, the sleep took him again.

CLARA DID NOT FALL ASLEEP. She lay looking at Sebastian with a small smile still on her lips. How ruffled and dishevelled he looked. If this was how he appeared when in a state of undress, how much more magnificent would he be when he was totally naked? And at least she might have a fighting chance of seeing that now. It had taken her a long time to realize that in permitting him to dictate her happiness she was helping neither of them.

She wriggled closer to the warmth of his body. He felt solid and strong. She ran a hand experimentally over his chest and he murmured something in his sleep and drew her deeper into the crook of his arm. He smelled faintly of leather and tobacco and lime cologne. Clara buried her nose in the curve of his neck and inhaled deeply. She felt almost light-headed with the warmth and the scent of him. It was a good job that he was asleep, for she felt exceedingly wide-awake. Her body tingled. She remembered the way Sebastian had kissed her, the way he had used his tongue and his teeth on her bare breast, and she was shot through with a pleasure that pooled deep within her and made her body tense and wanting.

Then he opened his eyes.

For a long moment she stared into that deep, slumberous blue and saw his gaze darken with desire as he rolled over to pin her beneath his weight.

There was a very sharp rap on the front door followed by the sound of raised voices in the hall.

For a moment Sebastian was still, his body poised above hers, then he sighed and eased himself off the bed.

"What sort of hour is this for visitors to call?"

Clara squinted at the clock on the mantelpiece. "It is past one, Sebastian. You have slept the clock around."

Sebastian stretched. Clara stared. She could not help it. He was still in his breeches and shirt and she was riveted by the deliciously tight fit of the buckskins over his thighs.

"You could avert your eyes," Sebastian said mildly.

"I could," Clara agreed, "but I am not going to."

He smiled. "Hussy."

"I know. But I have waited a long time—"

His eyes darkened again. "No more waiting, I promise you." He bent over and touched his lips to hers and Clara's senses leaped in response to the light caress. She grabbed his shirt and pulled him down to her, kissing him fervently.

The sound of voices was coming nearer. Through the pounding of the blood in her ears, Clara could hear Perch's tones, soothing and respectful, and in response a voice she recognized all too well—Martin, sounding dangerously angry, along with Lady Juliana, high and anxious.

"We know she is here, Perch. She left a note."

Sebastian eased his lips from Clara's. *"You left a note?"*

Clara hung her head, blushing a little. "I thought it was the right thing to do. I did not want anyone to worry about me."

"Whereas now that they know you have been all night at my bedside they will be delighted," Sebastian said dryly. "Your brother is about to call me to account for being a scoundrel and for the first time in my life I am entirely innocent of all wrongdoing."

The door flew open and Martin Davencourt erupted into the room, Juliana at his heels. Clara's heart sank as she saw in their wake her sister Kitty; Kitty's husband, Edward; Juliana's brother Joss; his wife, Amy; Edward's brother Adam; and Adam's wife, Annis, all jostling behind them on the landing.

"Why is everybody here?" she wailed.

A cacophony of noise broke over them and Clara put her hands over her ears.

"He is half-undressed!"

"She is fully dressed!"

"She is in his bed!"

"The place smells like a taproom!"

"Oh, Clara!" said Kitty, sounding both awed and disapproving.

"Scoundrel! Rogue!" Martin was not mincing his words. "To think I ever called you friend! To seduce my sister—" Before Clara could jump up, Martin had lunged at Sebastian and grabbed him by the remnants of his neck cloth, pulling tight. There was mindless fury in her brother's eyes. Clara heard Seb's breathing catch and saw his eyes start to bulge as, caught off balance, he tripped over backward onto the bed.

"I did no such thing, I swear!" he choked out, breaking off painfully as Martin pulled viciously on the cravat and brought tears to his eyes.

"Martin!" Clara leaped to her feet and hung on to Martin's arm. "Let him go! Nothing happened. I am the one to blame!"

Martin cast her one dark, angry look. "Oh, you need not think that I hold you blameless, Clara. I will settle with you when I have settled with him!"

Seb gave a despairing croak as the tourniquet tightened about his throat. Clara felt genuine alarm now. "Juliana!" She spun round to address her sister-in-law. "Do something! I promise nothing happened between us. Sebastian was too drunk—"

She realized this was not the most helpful defense, when Martin's breath hissed between his teeth with fury and he hauled Fleet to his feet, only to lay him flat out with one well-placed blow.

There was a silence.

"That was very unfair!" Clara said indignantly, scrambling to prop him up. "You have given Sebastian no opportunity to explain himself."

"It was the least I deserved," Sebastian said, fingering his jaw. "Would have done the same thing myself if I had a sister." He looked up at his angry friend and said, "Davencourt, my apologies. I have behaved abominably, even though it is true that your sister is quite unscathed."

"Because you were too drunk to seduce her," Martin said through shut teeth.

"Absolutely. And because I respect her and wish to make her my wife at the earliest possible opportunity."

There was a concerted gasp from the assembled company. Clara thought she saw a slight smile of satisfaction cross Perch's otherwise impassive expression.

"May I be the first to offer my congratulations, your grace," he said.

"Congratulations?" Martin's expression was like boiling milk. "Congratulations? I will *not* permit my sister to marry such a rogue."

"Martin, darling," Juliana said, putting a gentle hand on her husband's arm, "I completely understand your misgivings but I do think we should consider the matter calmly."

"Calmly!" Martin spun around. "I am not calm!"

"I think we all realize that, dearest," Juliana said. "Now, Clara, you will accompany us home. Sebastian, you will join us for dinner tonight, if you please. Great-Aunt Eleanor is staying and if you pass muster with her then I doubt anyone else will object to your suit."

She took Clara's arm and propelled her forcibly toward the door.

"Ladies and gentlemen," Sebastian said, raising his voice. "Might I beg one moment in private with my affianced wife?" He caught Clara's hand as Juliana escorted her past.

Martin, who had started to look vaguely placated, started frowning again. "Affianced? You try my patience too far, Fleet. You assume too much."

"One minute," Sebastian said. "Please." He kept tight hold of Clara's hand.

Everyone backed from the room with good-humored grumbling and Juliana dragged Martin out.

"One minute only," she warned.

As soon as the door closed behind them Sebastian pulled Clara into his arms.

"I asked you last night but you did not answer," he said. "Will you marry me?"

"Yes!" Clara said. "I am so glad that you asked. I had quite decided against putting my fate to the touch for a second time. A lady does not wish to appear too desperate."

Seb caressed her hair. "And the special license? Do you wish me to procure one?"

"Yes, please." Clara snuggled against his stroking hand. The latent sensuality of her behavior was doing terrible things to both his self-control and his clarity of thought.

"I am still a bit worried about your brother," he began, knowing there was another matter to be settled.

"We will persuade him," Clara said. She tilted her chin up. "Kiss me, please."

They were still engrossed when the door opened and Perch came back in.

"Mr. Davencourt requests his sister's presence at once," he said, straight-faced, "or he will go to fetch his duelling pistols."

SEB FLEET STOOD in the snow outside the house in Collett Square. It was late; the sky was black and cold, and the stars very bright. In all material terms the evening had been a vast success. Lady Eleanor Tallant, matriarch of the extended family, had given her seal of approval to the match between himself and Clara, and had dismissed Martin's objections in a few pungent words.

"Fleet is solvent, young enough to have his own hair and not require a corset, and influential enough to help your political career," she had said sharply. "You must have windmills in your head to object to such an offer." Then her face had softened. "He also dotes upon your sister, should that have more influence with you."

Martin had then reluctantly offered his hand, and Seb seized it gratefully.

"I do love her, you know, Davencourt," he said. "I would not wish to live without her."

He had seen the effort Martin had made to set aside the doubts and fears Seb knew were only for Clara's happiness. Things were *almost* back to normal.

Now he was supposed to go home and see his betrothed formally and respectably the next day, when arrangements would be made for him to join the family at Davencourt for Christmas, and for him and Clara to be married on Twelfth Night.

But there was one thing he had not done, one thing that required privacy rather than the benevolent observation of the family, one thing he wanted to give to Clara when they were alone.

He watched the lights go out in the house one by one and felt his feet freeze in the hard-packed snow.

Clara's room was at the back of the house and he let himself in through the small iron gate that led into the gardens. His footprints in the snow would give him away to anyone who spotted them, but this was too important not to take the risk. He suspected that for all their newfound harmony, Martin would allow him very little time alone with Clara until they were wed. Which was as it should be, of course. But he wanted her all to himself for a little.

He set his foot to the base of the ivy that climbed up the back of the house. It shivered under his weight but its branches were sturdy. At least the snow would break his fall if he misjudged the venture.

The ivy shook and trembled, sending showers of powdery snow to the ground, but he clung on as his fingers froze to the branches and he hauled himself up painfully to the first floor. The sharp twigs pricked at his hands and ankles.

He gained the ledge that ran around the first floor, then edged sideways past two windows until he came to Clara's chamber, at the end of the house. There was a faint light from behind the drapes. He hoped her maid was not still with her. He hoped she had not fallen asleep. He hoped he had not miscalculated and was outside Lady Eleanor Tallant's chamber instead.

He was wet and cold and scratched. The price of love. He smiled faintly and knocked at the windowpane.

Nothing happened. He knocked again, slightly more loudly. The vine creaked beneath his feet.

Clara's face appeared at the window, wide-eyed and astonished. In another moment she had thrown up the sash and was leaning out.

"Sebastian!" The whisper carried on the cold clear air. "What are you doing? You will fall!"

She grabbed his hand and pulled with all her might. Various parts of him caught on the latch or were squeezed in the aperture. Eventually he made a mammoth effort and half stumbled, half fell into the room and into Clara's arms.

"I came to tell you that I love you," he said, burying his face in her hair and holding her warm body against the coldness of his.

She eased back from him a little. The smile in her blue eyes was delicious. "You have told me that already today, Sebastian."

"I could not wait until tomorrow to tell you again. Besides," Sebastian said, gesturing toward the ivy, which would probably never recover from his onslaught, "I wanted to prove that I would do anything for you, even risk life and limb, flora and fauna, hauling my weight up to your balcony."

He released her and stood regarding her intently. In her flimsy peignoir and similarly transparent nightdress she looked luscious.

She gave a little giggle. "Dearest Sebastian, you have no need to prove anything to me. I know how much you love me."

He felt humbled by her generosity. "Clara, you do

not understand. I will always think of you as too good for me." He slid his hand into his pocket. "I brought you this. It is a betrothal gift. I wanted to give it to you in private. I hope that you understand."

Earlier that evening, in full, approving view of the family, he had given her the Fleet betrothal ruby ring, which he had retrieved from the bank that very day. Now she was looking puzzled.

"A gift? But I thought—"

He held the box out to her. "Take it. Please."

Clara took it slowly, ran her fingers over the smooth leather case, then opened the box.

"Oh!"

The huge ruby star pendant was nestling in the palm of Clara's hand now, its surface striking sparks from the candlelight. She looked up and her eyes were misty with tears.

"It is the most beautiful thing…"

She laid it reverentially in its box on the window seat, then came and took his hand and drew him down to sit on the bed beside her. She rested her head against his shoulder. "You know that there are things I need from you, Sebastian." She nestled closer. "You always claim that I am too good for you, but you are strong and courageous and loyal, and I admire those things."

Her nightgown slipped a little, the virginal white linen sliding from one rounded shoulder. Beneath it Sebastian knew that she would be soft and smooth, curved in all the most perfect places, warmly inviting.

He averted his eyes.

Her hair brushed his cheek—soft, confiding, innocent. She was tilting up her lips so that he could kiss her. His throat closed with nervousness. He gave her a tiny peck on the lips and withdrew hastily. Clara sat back, looking at him with a suddenly arrested expression.

"You do not intend to stay with me tonight?"

Sebastian stared at her in consternation. "Stay? Of course I will not stay." He knew that he sounded like a dowager. "That would be most inappropriate."

"So says the greatest scoundrel in London," Clara said.

"Clara, you are to be my *wife*. We must do these things properly." Seb wiped his brow. It was an excuse, of course. He wanted nothing more than to take her in the most improper ways imaginable, but he knew he could not do it.

Clara's lower lip quivered. "I am not certain I wish to marry you if you have become stuffy and proper all of a sudden. I do not want a reformed rake as a husband. I want a rake who will devote his attentions to me!"

Sebastian spread his hands helplessly. "You know I am yours, body and soul."

"And it is the physical side of you that intrigues me at present, I confess." She peeped at him. "No doubt I am shameless, but since you are to be my husband…"

She was tracing one finger down the line of his sleeve and when she touched the back of his hand, light as a breath of wind, he flinched as though scalded.

"No."

He could sense the uncertainty in her. She wanted him; she had courage, but in the face of his blank refusal she was too inexperienced to push for what she wanted. His heart twisted. He was hurting her again with a different sort of rejection now. He knew he had to explain to her. It was only fair. The difficulty was finding the words.

Clara covered her face with her hands. "Oh, dear! I was relying on you, Sebastian! I thought that one of us at least would know what to do."

"I do know the theory," Sebastian said. "Clara, I love you! I have never felt like this about anybody before—" He stopped.

Clara's eyes widened. She stared at him for a long moment. "Sebastian, you are afraid!"

He gave her a lopsided grin. "I confess it."

"When you said that I had unmanned you I did not think you meant…" Clara said, beginning to comprehend.

Sebastian looked down. He remained obstinately limp. He sighed.

"I am sorry."

"But what will happen on our wedding night?" Clara wailed.

Sebastian imagined that the longer their betrothal lasted, the more nervous he would become. Sebastian Fleet, the greatest rake in London, reduced to a quivering wreck by a slip of a girl.

Clara was looking at him, her blue eyes wide with apprehension. He felt a wave of hopelessness swamp him. Hell and damnation! The fact that he felt like ravishing her, the fact that he wanted to tear her clothes off and make mad, passionate love to her and yet he was somehow incapable of doing so was the last word in frustration. Theirs had been the most provocative courtship.

Then he saw a spark of amusement in Clara's eyes. The corner of her mouth lifted in a tiny smile. She traced a pattern on the edge of the sheet with her fingers and did not look at him as she spoke.

"Would you be prepared at least to try?" she asked demurely. "My governess always said that when one did not wish to do something it was better to grit one's teeth and take courage than to put off the moment."

Grit his teeth and summon all his courage. Seb drove his hands into his pockets in a gesture of contained fury. That was not how making love to Clara Davencourt should be.

"It is not that I do not *want* to, Clara," he said. "I want to kiss you and take you to bed and make love to you until dawn, but—" He broke off as he saw the rosy color suffuse her face.

"Do you really?" she said.

"Yes!" Seb almost shouted.

Clara looked around hastily. "Quiet! I do not wish Martin to find you here and have to explain that once again nothing has happened between us."

Seb gave an infuriated groan and sank down onto the bed. "This is humiliating."

He felt her wriggle across to sit beside him. Her breast pressed softly against his arm. She was warm and smelled faintly of jasmine and clean linen.

"Dear Sebastian." She was holding his hand in hers now and he let it rest there because it felt so comforting. "You must not worry about it. I shall not press you for my marital rights."

He looked up. She was so close that he could see the individual black eyelashes and the sweep of the shadow they cast on her cheek in the candlelight. Her cheek was round and smooth and he put up a hand to caress it. He smiled reluctantly.

"I suppose it is a little bit amusing…."

"Yes." She was nibbling at his fingers now, that full lower lip lush against the pad of his thumb. He felt a sudden fierce urge to kiss her that made him freeze on the spot. She withdrew slightly.

"I promise," she said solemnly, "to ask nothing of you that you are not prepared to give."

"Thank you." He started to relax. She gave him a little push and he lay back on the pillows, closing his eyes. When she lay down beside him he did not stir. Convention dictated that he should leave, but for once he was feeling completely at peace.

"Please hold me," Clara said, and he realized that in his selfish fears he had drawn so much on her strength and not given enough of himself back to her. He put his arms about her and drew her close so that her head rested beneath his chin and their hearts beat together.

After a moment he eased away a little and scattered little kisses across the soft skin of her face, paying special attention to those stubborn freckles that had always tempted him. He was trying not to think about what he was doing, trusting to instinct rather than past skill.

She turned her head slightly and her lips met his, then he felt the tip of her tongue touch the corner of his mouth. It set the blood hammering through his body and he opened his lips to hers, hesitantly at first, unprepared for the flash of desire that almost consumed him as their tongues touched, tangled.

Beneath the desire lay acute anxiety. He recognized it with incredulity. It almost paralyzed him. Clara was pressing closer, gently running her hands over his arms and shoulders, sliding the damp jacket from him so that he could feel the warmth of her touch through the linen of his shirt. She was resting her cheek against his chest now and he knew she would be able to hear the racing of his heart.

"I am sorry," he said, kissing her hair. "I do not wish to hurt you."

There was laughter in her voice. "I am no saint on a pedestal. You need not treat me like glass, Sebastian. I shall not break."

"No, but I am very afraid that I might."

She wriggled up until she was looking him in the eyes. "Then we shall break and mend together."

She saw the way his eyes darkened with sudden heat and felt a rush of the same excitement through her body with an undertow of fear. Now, at last, she sensed she was close to overcoming that last barrier that lay between them.

With one forceful movement he rolled her beneath him, his mouth crashing down on hers, scattering her own doubts and anxieties. Her senses reeled beneath the onslaught, her body arching, pleading for the fulfilment of pleasure. If he should hesitate now…

She felt his fingers rough on the fastenings of her chemise. He was trembling. She refused to give him time to think. She cast the chemise aside, caught his hand and placed it over her breast.

He groaned, but she knew with a flash of pure feminine triumph that she had won. His mouth was at her breast, hot and wet, and she ripped the shirt from his back so that she could touch his nakedness, skin to skin.

When he tore off his breeches and she felt the whole hard length of him against her for the first time, the shock splintered her. It was so strange but so exquisitely pleasurable. She arched again into his hands, and then his mouth was on hers as he came down over her, caressing her, parting her thighs to find that aching softness at the center of her.

He drew back a little.

"I will hurt you now…."

She sensed his reluctance and once again she was ruthless, straining for his touch.

"Then do so. Please…" Her voice broke on a ragged gasp. "Sebastian…"

The pause seemed agonizingly long, but then he was moving with one sure, hard thrust to claim her, and the pleasure and the pain raked her with fire and she gasped, but his mouth on hers silenced her cries. She clutched him to her, feeling her world shatter and reform as he took her with such thorough tenderness that her body melted into bliss. All she could be certain of was that she had his love and would never lose it.

"I LOVE YOU." Sebastian's face was turned into the damp curve of her shoulder. His breath tickled her skin. She could hear the profound relaxation and happiness in his voice and to her surprise it made the tears well up in her throat. Such a painful journey for a man who had rejected his feelings for so many years. She gave him a brief, fierce hug.

"I love you, too, Sebastian."

"I may not always be as good at showing my feelings as you are, my love. It was your sweetness and honesty that shamed me into such admiration for you. If I falter it will not be because I do not care for you."

She understood what he was trying to say. It would take time for him to unlock all the bitterness and unhappiness from the past. That did not matter for she would be there with him.

"As long as you can promise to love and be faithful to me alone," she said solemnly, "then there is nothing to fear."

She felt him smile against her skin. "I can promise that without a shadow of a doubt."

"Good." Clara turned to look at him. "This business between us, then—" she gave a little voluptuous wiggle "—this rather pleasant business of making love… Is it all settled now?"

His lips quirked into a smile. "I think it may well be."

She caressed his chest, feeling his muscles tense in sudden response to her touch. "Do you think that we should do it again, to make certain?" she whispered.

In reply he pulled her down on top of him, tangling a hand in her hair, bringing her mouth down to his.

"Yes," he whispered against her lips. "Yes, I do."

CLARA KNELT on the window seat, the ruby star in its box beside her. In the faint light before dawn it seemed to have a radiance of its own. She looked from her own particular star to the one she had seen that night a few weeks ago as it paled in the dawn sky over the roofs of London.

Have hope.

Have faith.

She smiled a little.

Sebastian stirred and she went across to the bed, slipping into the space beside him.

"How strange," she said, as she cuddled close to his warmth. "I never thought this would be the season in which I found a suitor."

He smiled, drawing her closer into his arms. "I never thought it would be the season in which I found a *wife*. Clara Davencourt, my love, my life."

THIS WICKED GIFT
Courtney Milan

*****

For Mass-yo (with a dash), the best little brother
that staged protests and hunger strikes can buy.
We wanted to do everything for you,
and you were too smart to let us.

P.S. You know that thing with the face, shoes,
Germany? Sorry about that. But can you stop
mentioning it every time we see each other?

CHAPTER ONE

London, 1822

IT WAS FOUR DAYS until Christmas and four minutes until the family lending library closed for the evening. Lavinia Spencer sat, the daily ledger opened on the desk in front of her, and waited for the moment when the day would end and she could officially remove her five pennies from the take. Every day since summer, she'd set aside a coin or five from her family's earnings. She'd saved the largesse in a cloth bag in the desk drawer, where nobody would find it and be tempted to spend it. Over the weeks, her bag had begun to burgeon. Now, she had almost two pounds.

Two pounds in small, cold coins to the rest of the world. For Lavinia, the money meant pies. Spices, sugar and wine to mull them with. And, once she scoured the markets, perhaps a goose—a small goose—roasted alongside their usual turnips. Her two pounds meant a Christmas celebration that would make Papa sit up and smile. Six months of planning—but the effort had been worth it, because Lavinia was going to deliver a holiday meal just like the ones her mother had prepared.

The business they'd conducted today had been frenetic. Lavinia finished adding columns in the day-book and nodded to herself. Today's take—according to her records—had been very fine indeed. If she hadn't miscalculated, today she'd let herself take *six* pennies from the till—half a shilling that made her that much more certain of goose, as opposed to mere stewing fowl. Lavinia took a deep breath. Layered atop the musk of leather-bound volumes and India ink, she could almost detect the scent of roast poultry. She imagined the red of mulled wine swirling in mugs. And in her mind's eye, she saw her father sitting taller in his chair, color finally touching his cheeks.

She reached for the cash box and started counting.

The bell above the door rang—at a minute to closing. A gust of winter wind poured in. Lavinia looked up, prepared to be annoyed. But when she saw who had entered, she caught her breath.

It was *him*. Mr. William Q. White—and what the *Q* stood for, she'd not had the foresight to demand on the day when he'd purchased his subscription. But the name rolled off the tongue. *William Q. White.* She could never think of him as simply a monosyllable last name. His name had rolled off her tongue, as it happened, far too many times in the last year for her own good.

He took off his hat and gloves at the threshold and shook droplets of water from the sodden gray of his coat. Mr. William Q. White was tall and his dark hair was cropped close to his skull. He did not dawdle in the doorway, letting the rain into the shop as so many other customers did. Instead, he moved quickly, purposefully, without ever appearing to rush. It was not even a second before he closed the door on the frigid winter and entered the room. Despite his alacrity, he did not track in mud.

His eyes, a rich mahogany, met hers. She bit her lip and twisted her feet around the legs of her stool. He spoke little, but what he said—

"Miss Spencer." He gestured with his hat in acknowledgment.

Unremarkable words, but her toes curled in their slippers nonetheless. He spoke in a deep baritone, his voice as rich as the finest drinking chocolate. But what really made her palms tingle was a wild, indefinable *something* about his accent. It wasn't the grating Cockney the delivery boys employed, nor the flat, pompous perfection of the London aristocracy. He had a pure, cultured voice—but one that was nonetheless from somewhere many miles distant. His *R*s had just a hint of a roll to them; his vowels stretched and elongated into elegant diphthongs. Every time he said "Miss Spencer," the exotic cadence of his speech seemed to whisper, "I have been places."

She imagined him adding, "Would you like to come with me?"

Yes. Yes, she would. Lavinia rather fancied a man with long…vowels.

And oh, she knew she was being foolish and giddy about Mr. William Q. White. But if a girl couldn't be foolish and giddy about a man when she was nineteen, when *could* she be foolish? It was hard to be serious all the time, especially when there was so much to be serious about.

And so she took a risk. "Merry Christmas, Mr. White."

He was examining the shelves. At her words, he turned toward her. His eyes slid from her waist up to her face, and Lavinia ducked her head and stared at the stack of pennies in front of her to hide her blush.

He didn't need to speak to make her giddy, not when he looked at her with that breathtaking intensity. For one scalding moment, she thought he was going to address her. He might even step toward her. Her hands curled around the edge of the desk in anticipation. But instead, he shook his head and turned back to the shelves.

A pity. Not today, then. Maybe not any day. And with Mr. William Q. White ignoring her again, it was time for Lavinia to set her fancies to one side and give herself over to seriousness. She counted the coins from the cash box and piled them into stacks of twelve, making sure to exactly align the pennies atop each other before starting a new pile.

Lavinia prided herself on her ability to get the take exactly right. Her longest stretch of perfection was thirty-seven days in a row, spanning the entirety of October. That run had been ruined by a penny's difference on November 4. She had no intention of letting October's record stand, however. It had been twenty-two days since her last error. Today would be number twenty-three.

She'd counted and double-counted every transaction. If she was so much as a ha'penny short, she'd eat Mr. William Q. White's extremely wet hat. Her hands flew as she placed dirty coins into careful piles. Four, six, eight, and with the loose coins, that made seven shillings, and four and one-half pence. Less than she'd imagined. She bit her lip in suspicion and glanced at the tally in the ledger.

Trepidation settled in an indigestible mass in Lavinia's belly. There, written in black and white in the daily ledger, was the final sum. Ten shillings, four and one-half pence.

She wasn't half a penny short. She was missing three full shillings.

Lavinia recounted the coins, but there was no error. Of course not; Lavinia did not make errors in accounting. Nobody would take her to task for the missing coins. Her father was too ill to examine the books, and her brother would never question Lavinia's jurisdiction over the shop.

Still, she did not like to question herself. How had she made such a stupendous error? She felt a touch of vertigo, as if the room were spinning in circles around the ledger.

She knew what she had to do. It hurt—oh, how it stung. Those three shillings could be the difference between a small goose and no goose at all. But with her father's creditors clamoring, and the cost of his medicines growing almost monthly, the family could not spare more than a handful of pennies' loss each day. Lavinia slid open the drawer to make up the difference from her precious Christmas hoard.

She always placed the bag in the same spot—precisely halfway back and flush against the left side. But her fingers met no velvet mass lumpy with coin. She groped wildly and found nothing but the smooth wood of the drawer from corner to corner. Lavinia held her breath and peered inside. There was nothing in the drawer but a cracked inkwell, and that—she checked—contained nothing but bluish smears.

"Hell." It was the worst curse word she could imagine. She whispered it; it was either that, or shriek.

She wasn't missing a few shillings. She was missing the full two pounds. All of Christmas had just disappeared—everything from the decorative holly down through her carefully planned menu.

"Vinny?" The words were a tremulous query behind her.

With those words, the rising tide of Lavinia's panic broke against an absolute certainty. She knew where her precious two pounds had gone.

Lavinia placed her hands on her hips. She forced herself to turn around slowly, rather than whirling as she wished. Her brother, still wrapped for the blustery weather outside, smiled weakly, holding out his hands in supplication. Water dripped from his coat and puddled on the floor.

James was four years younger than her, but Mama had always said to subtract ten years from a man's age when calculating his sense. James had never seen fit to prove Mama's formula wrong.

"Oh." He peered beyond her to the coins, stacked in grim military ranks along the edge of the counter and the ransacked drawer. His lip quirked. "I see you've, um, already tallied the cash."

"James Allen Spencer." Lavinia reached out and grabbed his ear.

He winced, but didn't dodge or protest—a sure sign of guilt.

"What," she demanded, "have you done with my two pounds?"

IT WAS WARM INSIDE the lending library, but William White still felt cold inside. His hand clenched around the solitary bank note in his pocket. The paper crumpled in his fist, cutting into his palm. It had been ten years since anyone had wished him a merry Christmas. Fitting, that it would happen on this day—and that Lavinia Spencer would be the one to do so.

Christmas was a luxury for the wealthy—or, perhaps, an illusion for the young and innocent. William had not been any of those since the winter evening a decade ago when he'd been cut off from the comfortable life he'd been living.

He stared past the books shelved in front of him, their titles blurring with the smooth leather of their bindings. The scene clouded into an indistinct, foggy mass.

Tonight, a solicitor had finally tracked him down. William had been leaving his master's counting house, having just finished another pitiful day of pitiful work, performed for the pitiful salary of four pounds ten a quarter. As soon as he'd set foot outside, he'd been set upon by an unctuous man.

For one second, when the lawyer had introduced himself, a flush of uncharacteristic optimism had swept through William. Mr. Sherrod had seen fit to remember the promise he'd made. William could come home. He could forget the menial work he did as a clerk. He could abandon the grim day-to-day existence of labor followed by sleep and bone-chilling want.

But no. It turned out Adam Sherrod was not generous. He was dead.

He'd remembered William in his will—to the tune of ten pounds. Ten pounds, when he'd been responsible for the loss of William's comfort, his childhood and, ultimately, William's father. Ten pounds, when he had promised most sincerely to take care of William, should it be necessary. It had become necessary ten Christmases ago, and Mr. Sherrod had not lifted a finger to help.

William had no real claim on Mr. Sherrod's money.

He had, in fact, nothing but the memory of a promise that the man had kicked to one side. But still, he'd remembered.

Thus dissipated one of the elaborate dreams he'd fashioned to motivate himself on the hardest days. He would never return to Leicester. He would never be able to rise above his father's errors; hell, he would never even rise above his fellow clerks. This evening, he'd been damned to live in the hell of poverty for the rest of his life. There would be no salvation.

That last legacy should have been no surprise. After all, it was only in fairy tales that Dick Whittington came to London as an impoverished lad and ended up Lord Mayor. In reality, a man counted himself lucky to earn eighteen pounds a year.

So yes, Christmas was for the young. It was for blue-eyed angels like Miss Lavinia Spencer, who would never be confronted with the true ugliness of life. It was for women who wished customers a merry Christmas without imagining the holiday could be anything other than happy. Christmas was not for men who'd had one of two fantasies shattered in one evening.

It was the second fantasy that had drawn William here.

Miss Spencer was slim and vivacious. She couldn't help but move her hands when she talked. She smiled far too much. She blushed far too easily. And her hair was forever falling out of its pins into unruly cinnamon waves that clung to her neck. She was one of those souls who remembered countless trivialities—names of customers, names of cats, the health of everyone's spouse.

If he'd received even a fraction of those ten thousand pounds, as promised... Well, that was a subject for many a cold and lonely night indeed. Because he'd have found a way to get her into his bed, over and over.

William paused, his hand on the spine of a book, and attempted to banish the image that heated thought conjured. Miss Lavinia Spencer, undoing the ties that fastened her cloak. The wool would fall to the floor in a swirl, and those cinnamon waves of hair would slip from their pins. He couldn't think of that. Not now. Not here. It was not, however, his strength of mind that sent the vision away. It was the sound of speech.

"Vinny, you have to understand." The recalcitrant whine of her brother was barely audible from where William stood, obscured by the shelves.

Over the past year, the elder Mr. Spencer had come into the shop less frequently. William had noted with some disapproval that it was Miss Spencer who'd taken his place downstairs. She'd greeted customers and accepted deliveries. Her brother, James, had been conspicuously absent from useful employment.

"It was just a temporary loan. He needed the money to pay the guards so he could get at his goods without his creditors finding out." James ended on a querulous note, as if his bald assertion yearned to become a question.

"*Bribe* the guards, you mean." That was Miss

Spencer—incorruptible, of course. She was speaking in an almost whisper, but the shop was quiet enough that William could hear every word, echoing amongst the books.

"But Mr. Cross promised me ten percent! And he even drew up a proper partnership agreement. Since you never let me help in here, I thought I could find a way to pay Papa's bills on my own. I was going to buy you a Christmas present. When's the last time you had a new dress, Vinny?"

"I'd rather have my two pounds. You *are* getting to the part where you took the money without asking me?"

"I thought I'd be able to slip it back in before you found out. After all, Mr. Cross's warehouse was supposed to contain three hundred bricks of tea, and several casks of indigo. Ten percent would have been a fortune."

There was a moment of disapproving silence. "I see. Since you do not seem to be weighed down by exorbitant shipping profits, I must conclude your foray into trade was unsuccessful."

A sullen scuffle of shoes followed. "After I gave him the two pounds, Cross told me we needed fifty more to pay the excise men."

"I see."

William had heard of similar tricks before. It was the sort of fraudulent promise made by ruffians who preyed on the greedy and the indolent—a pledge of fabulous wealth, soon, if only the mark in question handed over a tiny amount. It started with a few shillings. Next, the trickster would require three pounds for a bribe, followed by fifty for customs. The fraud only ended when the target was bled dry.

"Well, of course I saw through him *then*," the younger Spencer continued. "I called him a cheat. And then he told me he'd have me up in front of a magistrate for failing to deliver on my promissory note."

"Your *what?*"

"Uh." James drew the syllable out. His hesitance echoed among the books. "You recall that partnership agreement?"

"Yes…?" She did not sound the least bit encouraging.

"It turns out that paper I signed was actually a promissory note for ten pounds."

The inarticulate cry of protest Miss Spencer made was not angelic at all. William peeked around the corner. She was seated on her stool, her head in her hands. She rocked back and forth, the seat tipping precariously. Finally she spoke through her fingers. "You didn't *read* it when you signed it?"

"He looked honest."

Wood scraped against the slate floor as Miss Spencer pushed her stool back and stood. William pulled his head behind the shelves before she could spot him.

"Oh, my Lord," she swore, downright unrighteous in her wrath. "A man offered you a partnership predicated upon attempted bribery, and you didn't question his integrity?"

"Um. No?"

William did not dare breathe into the silence that followed. Then James spoke again. "Vinny, if I must appear before a magistrate, could we claim—"

"Be quiet," she snapped furiously. "I'm thinking."

So was William. Frauds and cheats, if they were any good, made excessively good barristers for themselves in court. The common person could not risk a loss at law. William would not want to stand in young James's shoes before a magistrate. He gave it even odds the boy would prevail.

"No," Miss Spencer said, almost as if she'd heard William's thoughts, and decided to correct him. "We'd win, but we'd have to pay a barrister. No magistrate."

"Vinny, do we have ten pounds? Can't we make him just go away?"

"Not if we want to pay the apothecary."

There was a bleak silence. Likely, Miss Spencer had forgotten William was in the room. If he were a gentleman, he'd have apologized minutes ago and taken his leave.

"We are not without options," Miss Spencer said.

Options. William had a fair idea just how many options Miss Spencer had. He suspected the number was equal to the population of single men who frequented the library—and perhaps included the married men. As the reading men of London were, by definition, neither blind nor completely idiotic, he knew there were many others who entertained charged fantasies about Miss Spencer. In fact, he rather suspected that old

Mr. Bellows, the wealthy butcher, would offer her marriage if she gave him the slightest encouragement. Ten pounds would be nothing to him—and the butcher was hardly alone in his lust.

William could not countenance the thought. He could not envision her beneath that fat, toothless man. And besides, the upright Miss Spencer chided her brother about bribery and petty theft. She would never stray from a husband, no matter how many teeth the man lost. If she married, William would never be able to pretend—not even on the darkest, loneliest nights— that he would one day have her.

He'd had enough dreams shattered today.

"I have a plan." There was steel in Miss Spencer's voice. "I'll take care of it."

"What must I do?" James asked instantly.

Miss Spencer was silent. "I think," she said quietly, "you've done enough for now. I'll take care of it for you. Just give me his direction."

Silence stretched, ungracious in its length. Finally her brother heaved a sigh. "Very well. Thank you, Vinny."

Like the foolish coward that he was, her brother complied. William could hear the scratch of pen against paper. James hadn't even asked her what her plan entailed, or insisted that he take care of the matter himself. He didn't care what she might have to sacrifice for him.

William's fists clenched around the bank note in his

pocket. If he were a gentleman, he'd hand Miss Spencer his ten pounds and solve all her problems.

Then again, William hadn't been a gentleman since he was fourteen.

No. His ten pounds—his last, minuscule legacy from childhood—would buy him the one fantasy he had left. If she had to sacrifice herself, it might as well be in his honor. She'd wished him a merry Christmas.

Well, she was going to give him one.

THE ADDRESS HER BROTHER had inked was still damp on the page when Lavinia's reverie was interrupted.

"He calls you Vinny?"

She looked up and felt her cheeks flush. It was Mr. William Q. White, leaning against the shelves. Of all the people to intrude at this moment. She'd thought the conversation had been quiet. She'd thought him safely ensconced back in the finance section, behind five shelves of books. Obviously she'd been wrong on both counts.

How much had he overheard? How embarrassed ought she to be at playing out that ridiculous drama in front of this serious man? Had she said anything stupid? And how absurd was it that, despite all that had transpired in the last half hour, her heart raced in pitter-patters because Mr. William Q. White had actually *started* a conversation with her?

As she always did when she was nervous, she began to babble. "Yes, he calls me Vinny. It's a pet name for—"

"I know your Christian name, Miss Spencer." His gaze did not move from hers. Instead, he walked across the room to her and stepped behind the counter. He stood too close. If she'd been sitting in a regular chair, she'd have had to crane her neck. Seated on a stool, her feet swinging well above the ground, she still had to lean her head back to look him in the eyes.

He smiled at her, a long, slow grin. In giddy excitement her stomach turned over. That dangerous curve of his lips was a new expression for him. *Assuredly* new. She would have remembered another one like it. Lavinia swallowed.

He set his hand deliberately atop hers.

Oh, she knew she should pull away. Pull away, and slap him for taking liberties with her person. But her brother had left her so cold—and his hand was so warm—and by all that was holy, after a year of encouraging Mr. William Q. White to do more than just look at her, she was not about to raise objections to a little liberty.

"I know what *Vinny* is short for. As it happens, I prefer *Lavinia.*" He leaned over her.

He said it as if he preferred *her,* not just her name. Lavinia's lungs seized. She could smell the starch of his cravat. *He's going to kiss me,* she thought. Her nipples pressed, painfully peaked, against her stays. His thumb ran along her wrist, down the curve of her fingers. Lavinia felt her lips part. She might even have arched up toward him, just a little. She focused on the pink of his mouth, so close to hers.

He's going to kiss me, and I am going to let him.

Instead, he released her hand. She could still feel the imprint of his fingers against hers as he stepped away.

"Miss Spencer, I do believe we'll talk tomorrow." He smiled. Before she could point out that tomorrow was Sunday, and the lending library would therefore be closed, he tipped his hat at her and set it on his head. "Come find me at one."

And then Mr. William Q. White strode away, the tails of his coat flapping at her. The bell jingled. The door shut. Lavinia raised her burning hand to her unkissed lips and looked down.

It was only then she realized he hadn't been angling for a kiss at all.

He'd taken the slip of foolscap containing the address of the man who'd cheated James.

CHAPTER TWO

LAVINIA WOKE TO A CLOUD of thick, choking smoke. Her first panicked thought was that the books downstairs had somehow caught fire, that their livelihood, half owned by creditors, was going up in flames. But then her conscious mind caught up to her racing fears and she correctly cataloged the smell.

It was the more mundane—and rather more unpleasant—scent of burning porridge.

Frowning, Lavinia pulled a wrapper over her nightdress and padded out into the front room.

James, his hands blackened with soot, was juggling a pot. The vessel let off billows of gray smoke, its sides streaked black.

"Ah," he said essaying a weak smile. "Lavinia! I made breakfast for you."

She didn't dare respond, not even with so little as a raised eyebrow.

He peered into the pot, frowning. "There's still some white bits in here. Isn't it odd that porridge turns *yellow* when it burns? I'd have thought it would go directly to black." He prodded the mass with a spoon, then shrugged and looked up. "Want some?"

Over fifteen years, Lavinia had become quite fluent in the foreign tongue known as Younger Brother. It was a tricky language, mostly because it employed words and phrases that sounded, deceptively, as if they were proper English.

For instance, the average woman off the street would have thought that James had just offered her burned porridge. Lavinia knew better. What James had *actually* said was, "Sorry I stole your money. I made you breakfast by way of apology. Forgive me?"

Lavinia sighed and waved her hand. "Give me a bowl."

That was Younger Brother for: "Your porridge is disgusting, but I love you nonetheless."

By unspoken consensus, as they prepared a tray to bring to their father in bed, James cut a slice of bread and Lavinia slipped it on a toasting fork. Ill as their father was, there was no need to punish him with either the details of James's transgression or an indigestible breakfast.

And perhaps, Lavinia thought as she choked down the nauseating glutinous mass, that was the essence of love. Love wasn't about reasons. It wasn't about admiring fine qualities. Love was a language all on its own, composed of gestures that seemed incomprehensible, perhaps even pointless, to the outside observer.

Speaking of the inarticulate language of love, what had Mr. William Q. White meant by his outrageous behavior last night? *Come find me,* he'd said. His words had seemed to come straight from her imagination.

But surely he hadn't meant for her to look up the address he'd given when he applied for a subscription? Surely he didn't mean she should pay him a visit? A woman who intended to keep her virtue did not visit a man, even if he did have lovely eyes and a voice that spoke of dark seduction. *Especially* if he had those features. Lavinia had gone nineteen years without making any errors at all on that front.

As it happens, I prefer Lavinia. *Come find me.*

She didn't need to remember the heat of his gaze as he looked at her to know he hadn't asked her to pay an innocent little morning call.

And yet what had her streak of perfection gotten her? Months and months of painstaking tallies had done her no good. Her coins were gone and the very thought of the barren holiday that awaited her family made her palms grow cold.

This somewhat dubious rationale brought Lavinia to the dark, imposing door of 12 Norwich Court. It was not quite an hour after noon, but a dark gray cloud hovered over the tall, bulky houses and blocked all hint of the feeble sun. A wild wind whipped down the street, carrying with it the last few tired leaves from some faraway square and the earthy scent of winter mold. Lavinia pulled her cloak about her in the gloom.

This residential street—little more than a dingy alley, really—was occupied at present only by an orange cat. The animal was a solitary spot of color against the gray-streaked buildings. In the next hour, Lavinia's life could change. Completely. Before she could reconsider, she rapped the knocker firmly against the door. She could feel the blood pounding in her wrists.

And then she waited. She'd almost convinced herself there was nothing unsafe or untoward about this visit. According to the subscription card, Mr. William Q. White had a room on the second floor of a house owned by Mrs. Jane Entwhistle—a cheerful, elderly widow who sometimes visited the lending library in search of gothic novels. Mrs. Entwhistle would doubtless be willing to play chaperone at Lavinia's request. She might even be kindhearted enough to look the other way.

The door opened.

"Oh, Mrs. Entwhistle," Lavinia started. And then she stopped.

It was not the bustling widow who'd opened the door, nor Mary Lee Evans, the scullery maid who was the object of Mrs. Entwhistle's complaints.

Behind the threshold, Mr. William Q. White stood in his shirtsleeves. He was in a shocking state of dishabille. Beneath that single layer of rough white linen, Lavinia could make out the broad line of his shoulders, and the sleek curve of muscles. His cuffs had been folded up, and she could see fine lines of hair at his wrist. She peeped behind him. Surely the respectable Mrs. Entwhistle wouldn't countenance such laxity of dress.

The widow was nowhere to be seen.

She glanced down the street. The cat sat, licking its paws, on a step three houses down.

"Mrs. Entwhistle is gone for the week to celebrate Christmas with her granddaughter." He raised his gaze to her. It ought to have been cold; his every word came out in a puff of white in the chilled air. But his eyes were hot, and suddenly, so was Lavinia.

"Mary Lee?" she asked in a squeak.

"Given the week off. Come in before you catch your death."

Her imagination gave those words a wicked quality—as if he'd asked her to catch something else instead. It was that accent again, that lilt in his voice that she just couldn't place. It made her think of unspeakable things, no matter how innocent his intentions.

But no, it was not just her imagination. It was a terribly wicked notion to enter a home alone with a young, attractive—very attractive—partially clothed man. Why, he might take liberties. He might take lots of them.

He smiled at her, a mischievous grin that unfolded across his face. Maybe it was her imagination again, but the smile didn't reach his eyes.

"I can't come in. It wouldn't be proper."

"I give you my word," he said carefully, "that I shall not do anything to you without your permission."

As reassurances went, this lacked some basic quality of…assurance.

"Your word as a gentleman?"

His lip curled slightly. "I'm hardly that."

Well, then. "What do you mean, without my permission? I could easily give permission to—"

She stopped herself before she could complete the sentence. Not only because she was embarrassed by her unintended admission, but because if she started cataloging the things she might let him do, given the proper persuasion, she would never stop with a mere peck on the cheek. He was a mere twelve inches from her, on the threshold. She could see him complete her sentence. His pupils dilated. His gaze slipped down her body, a caress that was almost palpable. His Adam's apple bobbed, once.

Still he didn't say anything. It was one thing to have him look the other way when she wished him a merry Christmas, or asked him what he'd thought of the Adam Smith he returned. It was quite another to admit she wanted a kiss, and to have him remain silent.

"Say something," Lavinia begged. "Say anything."

He moved closer. "Come inside with me." His voice enfolded her like warm velvet. And still he looked at her, those dark eyes boring into her, then settling against her lips like a caress.

No. She was past the point of fooling herself. Whatever Mr. William Q. White had done with the address, she had little doubt that if she followed him inside, she would likely be kissed quite thoroughly indeed. She'd known it all along. Perhaps, even, that

was why she'd come. And this time he'd said aloud
what she'd always imagined. *Come inside with me.*

He was going to kiss her. There was nobody about to
see her lapse. Even the cat had disappeared. It was nearly
Christmas, and Lavinia didn't suppose she would get any
other gift this year. She was cold, and his breath was
warm.

She untied her bonnet strings and followed him
inside.

The entry was cold and dark and empty, and Mr.
White didn't even stop to take her things. Instead, he
hustled her up two flights of stairs. The halls of the
second landing lacked the soft, feminine furnishings
that Mrs. Entwhistle employed downstairs. Instead,
they had a Spartan, military look. The walls were the
stark yellow of age-faded whitewash.

Mr. White glanced at her, his lips pressed together, and
then turned down a silent hall into a back room. The furniture was austere wood. From ceiling to baseboard,
there was not even a hint of color on the unadorned walls.
A white washstand bore a white pitcher and—a sign that
she was in territory that was undeniably masculine—a
black-handled razor. A single window looked out over a
desolate, gray yard. A solitary tree, stripped to its bare
branches by winter, huddled sullenly in the center.

And Lavinia was looking everywhere but in the
corner, where there was a bed. It was as cold and forbidding as the rest of the room, made perfectly, without
the smallest wrinkle in the white linens.

A bed. This visit was becoming most improper indeed.

Mr. White pulled up a chair—the lone chair in the room, a straight-backed wooden affair—for Lavinia. She sat.

He walked over to a small table and picked up a piece of paper.

"I've purchased your brother's promissory note," he said stiffly.

She hadn't quite known what to expect. "I hope you didn't pay the full ten pounds for it," she said. "Why would you do such a thing?"

He sat on the bed and fiddled with his rolled-up cuffs. She could see the blue lines of veins in his wrist. His fingers were quite long, and Lavinia could imagine them touching her cheek, a gentle tap-tap, in tune with the ditty he beat on his palm now. She wondered whether Mrs. Entwhistle often visited relatives, and if so, whether Mr. White regularly entertained women in his quarters.

But no. He was far too ill at ease. A practiced seducer would have plied her with brandy. He would have made her laugh. Certainly he would not have made her sit in this hard and uncomfortable chair. And he would not have said so little.

"Why do you suppose," he said, "I've asked to talk with you rather than your brother?"

"Because I'm more reasonable than him?"

"Because," he said uneasily, not quite meeting her eyes, "*you*—or rather, your body—is the only currency that can persuade me to part with that note."

It took her a second to unravel his meaning. He wasn't hoping for a kiss given out of gratitude. He wasn't even going to attempt a somewhat awkward seduction. Instead, he was trying to *coerce* her. There had been something magical about the looks he'd given her, occluded as they'd been with his two-word greetings. She'd felt as if they were uncovering a mutual secret—a world where Lavinia could forget the strain of trying to hold her family together. She could pretend for just one instant that nothing mattered but that she was a young woman, desired by an attractive young man.

But her own wishes were of no importance to him. If he was trying to force her in this ridiculous fashion, he saw nothing mutual at all about their desire. She had the sudden feeling of vertigo, as if the room were spinning about her, the floor very far away. As if she'd added all the lines in the ledger between them, and found that her tally did not match his coins.

Lavinia folded her arms about her for warmth.

"Mr. William Q. White," she said calmly. "You are a despicable blackguard."

WILLIAM KNEW HE WAS a despicable blackguard. Only the worst of fellows would have tried to claim a woman he could not marry. But he wanted her enough that he almost didn't care.

"I suppose you think I should forgive your brother's debt," William heard himself say.

"I do."

"And what would I stand to gain by that?"

She dropped her eyes. "He is not yet twenty-one, you see."

As if such a fact would have swayed him. Her brother was older than fourteen, and at that age William had first become responsible for his own care. Since then, he'd labored for every scrap of comfort. He'd had nothing handed to him—not a penny, not a kind word and certainly not a sister who shielded him from every discomfort.

"You will soon learn," he said, more harshly than he'd intended, "that everything has a cost." Coal and blankets in grim lodging houses cost pennies. The eye-straining labor of his apprenticeship had cost him his youth. For years, he'd spent his late nights reading business and agriculture by the dim red glow of the fire, not for pleasure or enjoyment, but to keep alive the futile dream that one day he would be asked to take his place managing funds that might have belonged to him. Mr. Sherrod's will had just stolen that dream from him, too. Oh, yes, William knew everything about cost.

Her color heightened. If he were the sort to engage in self-delusion, he'd imagine that the pink flush on her cheeks was desire. But the breaths that lifted her bosom had to be fear. Fear at his proximity. Fear that a man, intent and closeted alone with her, was looking down at her with such intensity.

But she did not shrink back, not even when he stood

and walked toward her. She didn't falter when he stopped inches from her. She did not quail when he towered over her and peered into the pure blue of her eyes.

Instead, she huffed. "You have not taken my meaning. It is surely in your best interests to collect on the debt owed over time. After all…"

Her voice was husky. Her breath whispered against his lips. He inhaled. Her scent coiled in his veins and joined the throbbing pulse of blood through his body.

"My interest?" His voice was quiet. "I assure you, my only interest is in your body."

Her eyes widened. Her lips parted. And that long, smooth column of throat contracted in a swallow.

And then, inexplicable woman that she was, Lavinia smiled. "You're not very good at this, are you? It works better if you give your villainy at least a thin veneer of pleasantry."

He might have been a blackguard, but he had no intention of being a liar. "Nothing really worth having is free. If the cost of having you is your hatred, I'll pay it."

She didn't shrink from him. Instead, she tilted her head, as if seeing him at an angle would change his requirements. The pulse in her throat beat rapidly—one, two, three, he counted, all the way up to twenty-two, before she raised her chin.

"Am I worth having, then? At this cost to yourself?"

"You're worth ten pounds." It was heresy to say those words, heresy to place so low a value on her. It was heresy even to think of someone as low as him touching a woman as incomparable as her. But he was going to be in hell all his life. He wanted one memory, one dream to keep with him in the years of drudgery that would surely follow. He'd have traded his soul to the devil to have her. A little heresy would hardly signify.

She stood. On her feet, she was mere inches from him. "You believe," she said, her voice unsteady, "that you must *purchase* the best things in life. With bank notes."

"I have no other currency to barter with."

She met his eyes. "Is there anything you want in addition to my body? That is—will once be enough, or will this turn into a…a regular occurrence?"

A regular occurrence. His body tensed at the thought. He wanted everything about her. Her smile, when she saw him; her sudden laughter, breaking like a sunrise in the night of his life. He wanted her, over and over, body and soul and spirit. But that was all well out of his price range. And so he asked for the one thing he thought he might get.

"I want one other thing," he said. "When I touch you, I want you not to flinch."

She frowned in puzzlement at this proclamation. As she bit her lip, she reached for the catch of her cloak. She fumbled with the ties, and then removed the wool from her shoulders, folding the cloth into a careful square. The dress underneath was a faded rose, the fabric old enough that it had shaped itself to the curves of her hips. He'd seen her in the gown before, but never while he stood close enough to touch.

She tugged on her left glove, loosening each finger before rolling the material down her arm. He noted, with some distraction, that there was a tiny hole in the index finger. Her fingers seemed impossibly slender.

"Very well," she said. "I agree."

He hadn't really believed it would happen. He had passed last night, after he'd retrieved her brother's note of promise, in a delirium of dazzled lust. But up until this moment, he'd expected her to walk away, snatched from him like all his other dreams. She removed her second glove, as slowly as she'd taken off the first, and aligned the two precisely before setting them atop her cloak. He swallowed. When she slid the pins from her hair, letting that coiled mass of cinnamon spill down her back, he realized he was really going to have her. Somehow, this impossible plan had worked.

If he were a gentleman, he'd stop now and send her on her way.

She turned her back to him—not, he realized, to hide her face. No, Lavinia didn't shrink from him. Instead, she lifted the mass of her hair so that he could unlace her dress.

The gesture gave him a perfect view of the back of her neck. It was slim and long. He could make out the delicate swells of her spine. Up until this point, nothing truly untoward had happened, except in William's mind. But once he touched her—once he unlaced that gown—it would be too late for them both. If he had any strength of character at all, he'd leave her untouched. But all his strength had turned into pounding blood, thundering through his veins. And if he had any will at all, it was directed toward this—this moment of heaven, stolen from the angel who had haunted his dreams for a year.

He would never find forgiveness if he took her, but then he'd been damned for a decade. All he would ever know of paradise was Lavinia. And so he laid his hands on her waist and claimed his damnation.

She was warm against his palms, and oh, it had been so long since he touched another human being. He leaned in and kissed the back of her neck. She tasted of lemon soap. His arms wrapped around her, drawing her against his body. She nestled against his erection, and by God, she did what he'd asked. She didn't flinch. Instead, she sighed and leaned back into his arms, as if she enjoyed the feel of his touch.

"Miss Spencer," he murmured in her ear.

"You'd better call me Lavinia."

His fingers found the ties of her dress and unraveled them carefully. Then he slid the dress off her shoulders. Long muslin sleeves fell away to reveal creamy shoulders, milk-white arms. When the gown hit the floor, she turned in his arms. She was wearing nothing but stays and a chemise. Her skin was warm against his hands and she arched up toward him. Her lips parted. Her eyes shone at him, as if he were her lover instead of the man who'd forced her into this. She'd looked at him that way, just last night in the library. Surely, then, she hadn't meant to invite a kiss.

He was not such a fool as to turn down that invitation twice. He kissed her, hard, savoring the feel of her lips against his. She tasted as sweet as a glass of water after a hard day's labor, felt as welcome as sunshine in the darkness of winter. He pulled her into his embrace roughly. She twitched in surprise when his tongue touched her lips, but she opened her mouth with an eagerness that made up for any apparent inexperience.

He had to remind himself that she'd not chosen this, that he'd ordered her not to flinch from his advances. It was not real, the way she nestled in his arms. It was not real, the way her hands pressed against his back, pulling his thighs against hers. It was not real, the way she opened up to him. It was all a fraud, obtained through coercion.

He was impoverished enough that he'd take her caresses anyway.

She pulled away from him, but only to unlace her stays. As she lifted her arms above her head, a stray shaft of light came through the window and illuminated the outline of her legs through her chemise. She let her stays drop to the ground. She didn't look up—no doubt suddenly ashamed, aware that William could make out the dusky purple of her areolae through her chemise. A shaft of heat rippled through William, and he could wait no longer.

Without thinking, he walked forward. His hands slid

up her waist. She was separated from him by the thinnest layer of cloth. She shivered as he drew her toward him. And then he leaned forward and closed his mouth around the dusky tip of her nipple. Even through her chemise, he could feel it contract, pebbling under his tongue.

"Oh!" Her hand clutched his arm spontaneously.

He licked that hard tip, as if somehow, her response would count as real acquiescence. Maybe, if he was good enough to her, if he brought her to the most trembling peak of pleasure, she would forgive him. Maybe he could give a hint of truth to this lie. He set his leg between hers as he tasted her body, and she ground her hips against him. She was either an incredible actress, determined not to flinch, or she truly wanted him.

He let one hand skim down her body to the edge of her chemise. He pulled it up, up, until his fingers slipped between her thighs.

She was not acting. She was silky wet. There was no space in his mind to encompass the wonder of her desire. He was lost, sliding his fingers through her curls until he found the spot that made her arch her back even more. He pinned her against the wall, pressing, tasting, touching, until she trembled, her breathing ragged. And then he sent her spinning over the edge.

She made a high, keening noise as she came.

A small sense of intelligence returned as she looked up at him. She was breathing heavily. Her skin glowed. Her chemise was rucked up to her waist. Her body pressed into his. He could feel her heart beat against his chest, feel her ribs expand with her every breath.

He was still dressed. His member was hard; his body screamed to sheathe himself deep inside her.

"William?"

No. He couldn't fool himself any longer. This was not some delicate virgin, submitting to his coarse lusts out of an excess of familial feeling. This was Lavinia. She was robust, and unbreakable. And for some unknown reason, she was not acting. She wanted him.

And he shouldn't take her. Not like this.

But when he pulled away, she followed. When he hesitated, she set her hands under his shirt. Her fingers slid up his abdomen, over his ribs. Any good intentions that might have entered his mind flared up in smoke, illuminating William's path to hell. He pulled off his shirt. The air was cold against his bare skin, but Lavinia was warm, and she was caressing him. Her hands slid to his waist. Her mouth found his again, and he could think of nothing but having her skin against his, her flesh pressed naked under his. He pulled his breeches off and pushed her onto the bed.

She landed and looked up at him. And then—time seemed so slow—she lifted off her chemise. Every fantasy he'd ever had compressed into this one moment. Lavinia Spencer was naked in his bed, lips parted, eyes shining. He spread her knees with his hands and leaned over her. He had a thousand fantasies, but only this one chance. He positioned his member against her hot, wet cleft.

He should not have been able to think of anything

except the pleasure to come, but she looked into his eyes. Her look was so clear, so devoid of guile, that he stopped, arrested on the edge of consummation.

You don't have to do this.

He didn't know where the thought came from— perhaps some long-atrophied sense of right and wrong had exerted itself. The tip of his penis was wet with her juices. Her nipples had contracted into hard, rose-colored nubs and she lay beneath him, legs spread.

The next step would be so easy.

It was not just her innocence he would take. Lavinia's beauty was not a mere accident that arose from the fall of hair against shoulder, the curves of her breasts, the petals of her sex. No, even now, spread before him like an offering, she glowed with an inner light. Her appeal had as much to do with the innate trust she placed in those around her, in the way she smiled and greeted everyone as if they were worthy of her attention. If he took her, like this, he'd shatter her trust in the world. He would show her that men were fiends at heart, that there was no forgiveness in the world for sins committed by others.

You don't have to do this.

But men were fiends. And there was no forgiveness. He had never been granted any forgiveness.

He didn't have to do it, but he did it anyway. He slid into her in one firm thrust, and it was every bit as awful—and as good—as he'd imagined. It was wonderful, because she was sweet and hot and tight about him.

It was wonderful, because she was his, now, in the most primal sense. But it was terrible, because he knew what he destroyed with that single thrust. Her hands came involuntarily between them, and he tensed and stopped.

"William." She touched his shoulders tentatively, as if he were the one who needed comfort. As if even his vile penetration could not shake her absurd trust in the world. And so he took her, thrusting into her. She clenched around him, the walls of her passage tight around his erection. She brought her hips up to his. And by God, that heat, that pulsing heat that wrapped around him, that cry she gave—it couldn't have been. She could not have come. But she had, and then he was pumping into her, loosing his seed into her womb and crying out himself, hoarsely.

As his orgasm faded and his mind cleared of lust, he realized what a despicable man he was. He'd taken her like an animal. Oh, she'd let him—but what choice had he left her? He should have stopped. He should have let her go. Instead, he'd been so intent on himself that he hadn't cared what she wanted at all. He was as sorry a specimen as had ever been seen.

He pulled out of her and sat on the edge of the bed, his back to her.

The mattress sagged as she rearranged her weight. "William," she said.

He could not bring himself to turn around and see what he'd done. Would her eyes reflect the betrayal of trust?

"William," she said. "You must look at me. I have something to tell you."

He knew already what a despicable blackguard he was. He'd taken her virginity, and damn, he'd enjoyed it. But everything had a price, and the price of William's physical enjoyment would be this: her cold censure, and a speech that he hoped would cut him to ribbons. He deserved worse. And so he turned.

There was no judgment in her eyes—just a quiet, unfathomable serenity.

"When I told you my brother was not yet one-and-twenty," she said, "I did not intend to engage your sympathies. I was trying to point out that he is legally an infant. He is incapable of forming a contract. That promissory note is unenforceable."

William's mind went blank. Instead of thoughts, his head seemed to fill with water from the bottom of a lake—chilled liquid, dwelling where light could not filter.

"You had nothing to coerce me with," she continued. "You could not have done. No magistrate would have compelled my brother to pay the debt."

Her words skipped like stones over the surface of his thoughts. Hadn't he coerced her? He was sure he'd forced her into his bed. He deserved her condemnation. Damn it, he *wanted* it.

Instead, he was as empty as the wick of a candle that had just been extinguished. "Oh," he said. That one bare word didn't seem enough, so he added another. "Well." Other thoughts flitted through his mind, but they were also single syllables, and rather the sort that could not be uttered in front of a member of the gentler sex. Even if he had treated her in a most ungentle manner.

There was a vital difference between lust and love. It had been lust—desperate lust for her body—that had brought him to this point. Lust did not care about the loss of a woman's virtue. Lust did not care if a woman's feelings were wounded. Lust howled, and it wanted slaking. It didn't give a fig as to how the deed was accomplished. Lust was a beast, and one he'd nurtured well with a decade of resentment.

William thought of his four pounds ten a quarter—eighteen pounds per year of drudgery—and of the many years ahead of him while he garnered the recognition and the recommendations he would need so that he could one day become a man who earned…what, twenty-three pounds a year? He thought of the hole in Lavinia's glove, and her brother asking when she'd last had a new dress.

"Lavinia," he said carefully, "I don't deserve such a gift."

"Nobody gets gifts because he *deserves* them." She stood up and shook out her wrinkled chemise. "You get gifts because the giver wants to give them."

She wasn't arguing. She wasn't throwing herself at him. She wasn't weeping and carrying on. If she had done any of those things, he could have borne it. But she exuded a calm, cool competence that lay entirely outside William's understanding.

"I can't support a wife," he continued. "And even if I could, I'm not the man for you, Lavinia."

She reached for her dress. "I knew that the minute you tried to coerce me into your bed."

He shifted and fixed his gaze past her on the blighted tree outside his narrow window. "Then why did you agree to it? You had no need."

She had not trembled when he'd threatened her, when he'd made his horrible proposition. She had not shivered, not even when he'd claimed her body. But her hands betrayed the tiniest of tremors as she fastened her dress and reached for her cloak.

"No need? You said that everything worthwhile had a price. You were wrong. You are absolutely and without question the most completely misinformed man in all of creation. Everything really worth having," she said, "is *free*."

"Free?"

"Given," she said, "without expectation of return." And she looked up at him, a fierce light in her eyes. "I wanted to show you."

That clear trust in her eyes was unbroken yet. He'd taken her virginity. How had she managed to keep her innocence?

"I have no notion what love is," he told her, almost in a panic. "None at all."

She picked up her cloak and shook it out. It flared about her shoulders and then fell, obscuring in thick wool the figure he had seen in such heartbreaking detail mere minutes before. "Well," she said. "Perhaps one day you'll figure it out."

And like that, she slipped past him. He listened, unmoving, as she stepped down the stairs and out of his life.

CHAPTER THREE

IT WAS LATE AFTERNOON when Lavinia slowly climbed the stairs to the family rooms above the lending library. She ached all over, a vital, restless throb that twinged in every muscle.

"Lavinia?" Her father's weak call came from across the way. "Is that you?"

"Yes, Papa." She took off her cloak and hung it on a peg by the door. Half boots followed. "I went out on a…constitutional after service. I'll freshen up and join you shortly."

She ducked into her own room.

As far as the basics went, her small chamber was not so different from William's. The walls were white-washed, the furniture plain and simple, and almost identical to his: washstand, bed, chair and a chest of drawers. Lavinia crossed to the other side of the room and poured water from a pitcher into the basin. As she washed, she examined her reflection in the mirror.

She knew what she was *supposed* to see. This was the face of a girl who'd been ruined. A woman of easy virtue.

The face that peeked back at her looked exactly the

same as the one she'd seen in the mirror this morning. There was no giant proclamation writ across her forehead, denouncing her as unchaste. Her eyes did not glow a diabolical red. They weren't even demonically pink. And her body still felt as though it belonged to her—sore, yes, and tingling in ways that she'd never before experienced—but still hers. Perhaps more so.

He didn't love her.

Well. So? The reckless infatuation she'd felt hours before had been transmuted into something far more complex and…and cobwebby. She wasn't sure if the emotion that lodged deep in her gut was love. It felt more like longing. Maybe it had always been longing. In the year since he'd first started coming to their library, he'd looked at her. Until recently, however, he'd always looked away.

It had been an unpleasant surprise when he'd put his proposition to her so baldly—and so badly. But it hadn't taken her long to understand why he'd chosen to approach her in such a fundamentally uncouth manner. She'd realized with an unbearable certainty that he was deeply unhappy.

In generalities, her room was not so different from William's. But the specifics… There were nineteen years of memories stored in this room. A blue knit shawl, a gift from her father, draped over one side of her chest of drawers. A lopsided painting of daisies, a present James had given her two years ago, hung next to the mirror. A pine box on her nightstand contained all of Lavinia's jewelry—a gold chain and her late mother's wedding ring. These were not mere things, of course; they were memories, physical embodiments of the nineteen years that Lavinia had lived. They were proof that people loved her. Her brother had similar items in his room—a stone he'd picked up years ago on the beach in Brighton, the pearl pendant he'd inherited from his mother, to one day give his wife, and the penknife Lavinia had scrimped to buy him.

Where did William keep his memories? There had been nothing—not so much as a pressed flower—in his quarters. Not a single physical item indicated that he passed through life in contact with others. He must hold his memories entirely inside him.

It seemed a dreadfully lonesome place to keep them.

Things had emotional heft. Lavinia did not imagine a man avoided all mementos because he had been blessed with an inordinate number of good memories. That William had felt compelled to resort to blackmail, when she'd been so giddily inclined to him, said rather more about the light in which he saw himself than how he saw her. For all the harshness of his words, he'd touched her as if he worshipped her. He'd caressed her and held her and brought her to a pleasure that still had her limbs trembling. He might claim to have had no notion of love, but he'd not approached her as if her touches were credits on a balance sheet.

"Vinny?" James swung her door open without so much as a knock.

Luckily, the same absorption that led James to ignore Lavinia's privacy meant he did not notice her dress was overwrinkled. He did not look in her eyes and see the telltale glow that lit them.

"Vinny," he said again, "have you taken care of my note yet? Because I could—I mean, I *should* help."

And how could she answer? *She* hadn't taken care of his note. But James wouldn't have to worry about the matter ever again. As for William…

Lavinia pasted a false smile across her lips. "You have nothing to worry about," she said. "It's all taken care of. He's all taken care of."

Or he will be, soon.

IT SEEMED INCONCEIVABLE to William that life should continue on as usual the morning after he'd damned himself. The night passed nonetheless. The London streets a few blocks over awoke and rumbled as a hundred sellers prepared for market. Not only did the clock continue on schedule, but—as if fate itself were laughing up its sleeve at him—they marched inexorably on to Monday morning.

Monday. After he'd betrayed all finer points of civilization, nothing so trivial as a Monday morning should have been allowed to exist. And yet Monday persisted.

When William stepped on the streets, he shrank into the shoulders of his coat and pulled his hat over his eyes. But as he walked down Peter Street, nobody raised the hue and cry. No cries of "Stop! Despoiler of women!" followed his steps. Yesterday he'd snared an innocent woman in his bed by the foulest of means. Today nobody even gave him a second glance.

Up until the moment when William arrived at the gray Portland stone building where he worked, just opposite Chancery Lane, the day seemed a Monday much like every other Monday that had come before: gray, dreary and unfortunately necessary. But as soon as William opened the door to the office, he knew that this was not going to be an ordinary Monday.

It was going to be worse. Everyone, from Mr. Dunning, the manager, to Jimmy, the courier boy, sat stiffly. There were no jokes, no exchanged conversations. David Holder, one of William's fellow clerks, inclined his head ever so slightly to the left.

There stood his employer. The elderly Marquess of Blakely was solid and ever so slightly stooped with age. If one were boasting in a tavern, the man might have seemed the most respectable master, the sort that any employee would feel proud to serve. When William had first arrived, he'd spun a fantasy in which his keen mind and meticulous work made him indispensable to the marquess. In his dreamworld, he'd been granted promotions, advances in wages. He'd won the respect of everyone around him.

That dream had been exceedingly short in duration. It had lasted a week from the day he was hired—until he'd met the man.

The old marquess was a tyrant. In his mind, he didn't employ servants; he grudgingly shelled out money for minions. The marquess didn't merely demand the obeisance and courtesy due his station, he required groveling. And, every so often, instead of raising a man up for skill and dedication, he chose an employee and delved into his work until he found an error—and no worker, however conscientious, was ever perfect—and then let the man loose. William and his fellow servants went to work every day swallowing fear for breakfast.

Fear did not sit well on a belly and heart as empty as William's was today. He stood frozen in the old marquess's gray-browed sights.

"Ah." Old as he was, the marquess's gaze did not waver, not in the slightest. It was William who dropped his eyes, of course, bobbing his head in hated obeisance. He fumbled hastily with his hat, pulling it from his head. For a long while the elderly lord simply stared at him. William wasn't sure if he should offer the insult of turning his back so he could hang up his hat, or if he must stand icebound in place, headgear uncomfortably clutched in his hands.

The marquess turned his head, looking at William side on. With that shock of graying hair, the pose reminded William of some dirty-white bird of prey. The image wouldn't have bothered him quite so much if William hadn't felt like so much worm to the other man's raptor.

His lordship glanced away, and William gulped air in

relief. But instead of moving his attention to another man, the marquess simply pulled a watch from his pocket.

"Whoever you are," he announced, "you're a minute late to your seat."

I wouldn't have been had you not glowered at me. But William held his tongue. He couldn't afford to lose his position. "I apologize, my lord. It won't happen again."

"No, it won't." The marquess gave the words a rather more sinister complexion. "Blight, is it?"

"Actually, it's White, my lord. William White."

He should not have offered correction. Lord Blakely's eyes narrowed.

"Ah, yes. Bill Blight."

He spoke as if William had not worked for him these three years. As if instead of names, his employees were possessed of empty pages, and the marquess could fill those bleak tablets with any syllables he found convenient.

"Come into the back office," the marquess said calmly. "And do bring the books you've worked on for the last two years."

An invitation to the back office was as good as a death sentence. It felt like an eternity that William stood, fixed in space. But what good would it to do to scream or shout? If he went quietly, Mr. Dunning might help him find another position when he was sacked.

How ironic, that he'd divested himself so unthinkingly of those ten pounds, when he might find them of such immediate use. No—not ironic. It was the opposite of ironic.

Perhaps it was appropriate that he'd been singled out. He wasn't fit for polite society, after all. Not after what he'd done to Lavinia. How could he ever make it up to her? Maybe this, finally, was the censure he'd been expecting all morning. He'd accept whatever came his way as his just due.

Once inside the back office, the marquess picked one of the books at random. He thumbed through it slowly, his fat fingers pausing every so often, before moving onward. William stared past him. The room's furnishings could well have been as old as the marquess. The wallpaper had long gone brown, and dry curls of paper at the edge of the baseboard were working their way off the wall.

Finally the lord lifted his head. "You seem to do good work," the old Lord Blakely said. Said by anyone else, it would be a compliment. But William's employer twisted the sentence in his mouth, giving a slight emphasis to the word *seem*. By the ugly glint in his eye, William knew he was adding his own caveat: *I am not fooled by your apparent competence.*

"Tell me," the marquess continued. "On September 16, 1821, you entered three transactions related to the home-farm in Kent. I'd like a few specifics."

Fifteen months ago. The man focused on transactions made fifteen bloody months ago? How could

William possibly recall the details of a transaction more than a year in age? One did not keep books so that one could browbeat the person who entered a transaction.

One didn't unless one happened to be the Marquess of Blakely.

"It is the first transaction, for two pounds six, that I—"

The door opened quietly behind them, interrupting his speech.

The old marquess looked up. His fists clenched the account book, and his eyes widened. He drew himself up, undoubtedly to castigate the fool who had the temerity to interrupt this ritual sacrifice. William drew his breath in, thinking he'd won a reprieve. If he had, the intruder would undoubtedly take on William's punishment. Whoever it was walked forward, steady, heavy footsteps crossing the room. A mixture of shame and relief flooded William. Perhaps he might keep his position—but it was a sorry man who hoped his carcass would be saved because a shark choked on another fish first. It was an even sorrier man who hoped so, knowing that of all the fellows in the office, he was most deserving of punishment.

But instead of one of William's fellow clerks or the estate manager, the young man who came abreast of William's chair was the one person the old marquess could not sack.

It was his eldest grandson. William had seen the man only once, and at a distance. But he'd been accounting for the details of the man's funds for three years. Gareth Carhart. Viscount Wyndleton, for now. The man was a few years younger than William. He had attended Harrow, then Cambridge. He had a substantial fortune, received a comfortable allowance from his grandfather, and he would inherit the marquessate. William almost felt as if he knew the fellow. He was certain he held the young, privileged lord in dislike.

The young viscount might have had a hundred servants available to do his bidding. But incongruously, the man was carrying his own valise. He set this luggage on the ground and placed his hands gently on his grandfather's desk.

No thumping, no shouting, no untoward drama of any sort. Had William not been a mere foot away, he would not even have detected the rigid tension in the muscles on the backs of his hands.

"Thank you very much." The viscount's words were quiet—not unemotional, William realized, but so suffused with emotion that only that flat, invariant tone could contain his disdain. "I appreciate your telling the carriage drivers not to take me to Hampshire. I applaud your decision to bribe—how many was it? It must have been every owner of a private conveyance in London, so that they would not take me, either. But it took real genius on your part to outright purchase the Hampshire coach lines in their entirety, five days before Christmas."

"Well." The old Lord Blakely preened and examined

his nails. Of course, the man did not find anything so uncouth as dirt near his fingers, but he nonetheless brushed away an imagined speck. "How lovely of you to admit my intelligence. Now do you believe that I was serious when I told you that if you did not give up your foolish scientific pursuits, you would not see that woman?"

William might have drowned in the sea of their exchanged sarcasm. Neither man seemed to care that he was in the room. He was invisible—a servant, a hired man. He might have been etched on the curling wallpaper, for all the attention that they paid him.

The young viscount lifted his chin. "That woman," he said carefully, "is my *mother.*"

William felt a twinge of satisfaction. He ought not to have reveled in the other man's pain, but it was delicious to know that even money could not buy freedom.

"I'm leaving," Lord Wyndleton continued.

"No, you are not. What you are doing is throwing a tantrum, like a child demanding a boiled sweet. It is long past time that you gave up that natural philosophy nonsense and learned to manage an estate like a lord."

"I can read a damned account book."

"Yes, but can you manage seventeen separate properties? Can you keep a host of useless and unmotivated servitors bent to their tasks?"

The young viscount's gaze cut briefly toward William. William felt himself analyzed, cataloged—and then, just as swiftly, dismissed, an obstacle as irrelevant and underwhelming as a dead black beetle lying in the middle of a thoroughfare.

"How difficult can it be?"

"Bill Blight, why don't you explain to my grandson what I had planned for you?"

"You were, I believe, going to look through my work until you found an error. My lord." *And then you were going to turn me off.*

"Blight, tell him what I really intended."

William pressed his lips together. "You were going to sack me to induce terror in your staff."

That sort of sentence—bald and unforgiving—ought to have gotten him tossed out on his ear.

Instead, the marquess smiled. "Precisely so. Wyndleton, how do you suppose I managed to thwart your ill-fated flight this morning? I assure you, I did not need to bribe every driver in London. I keep my staff in line—and that means they do as I say, what I say, no matter the cost."

The young viscount's nostrils flared.

"You think you can be a marquess? Like that?" The marquess snapped his fingers. "Get your valise. Spend these two days with me—do as I say—and you'll start to learn how it's done. Someday you might even get to thwart me. Or you would, if you had the money to do it."

Still Lord Wyndleton did not move. He stood next to William, his arms rigid, his fingers curving into the desk like claws.

"Come along," the marquess said. "I shouldn't have to spoon-feed you these lessons. If you'll listen to me, I'll have the carriage take you over late Christmas Eve." The old man stood up and walked to the door. He didn't look back.

After all, William thought bitterly, what else could mere mortals do but jump to perform his bidding? The thought almost put him in charity with the man standing nearby. The viscount slowly straightened.

"What I don't understand," William said quietly, "is why you don't buy your own carriage."

Lord Wyndleton turned to him. This close, William could see the golden brown of his eyes—predator's eyes, or at least, a predator in training. Like any wolf cub caught in a trap, he snapped in anger at anything that came near.

"He's holding the purse strings, you idiot." He straightened and wiped his hands on his sleeves. "My grandfather is sacking you, yes?"

"He'll get around to it."

Gareth Carhart, Viscount Wyndleton, picked up the valise. He nodded sharply. "Excellent," he said, and then he walked out of the room.

THE END OF THE DAY ARRIVED, but Lord Blakely and his grandson still had not returned. This meant that William had still not been sacked.

Winter struck directly through William's coat as he left his place of employment. Yes, he'd had a reprieve—

albeit a temporary one. He knew the marquess's tactics. Once he got a man in his sights, he did not let up. Today William survived. Tomorrow... It was going to be another damned cold night, one in a string of damned cold nights stretching from this moment until death.

"Mr. White."

William turned. There, in virulent yellow waistcoat, burgeoning over an ample belly, his locks pomaded to glossy slickness, stood Mr. Sherrod's solicitor. The corner of William's lip turned up in an involuntary snarl.

"Do you have another taunt to deliver on your late employer's behalf?" William pulled his coat around him and started walking away, brushing past the unctuous fellow. "As it is, I must be on my way."

The solicitor's hand shot out and grabbed his wrist. "Nonsense, Mr. White. I've come to a realization. A *profitable* realization. I wanted to...to share it with you."

William stared at the chubby fingers on his cuff, and then carefully picked them off his sleeve, one by one. The digits felt greasy even through his gloves.

"Adam Sherrod," the man said, "left the bulk of his fortune in his final testament to the serious little stick of a woman who served as his wife. Given the informal agreement he made with your father, you might contest the disposition of his estate. I had, in point of fact, hoped that you would. You accepted your fate with surprising grace the other day."

"Is there any chance of overturning the testament? I assume the document was valid and witnessed. And it was only an informal agreement between the two men, after all. I've heard that excuse often enough."

"Hmm." The man looked away and rubbed his lips. "To speak with perfect plainness, you could claim he was not in his right mind. You see, before he married, he actually had intended to keep his word. He'd left you half his fortune, five thousand pounds. It would be easy to argue that he did not see sense. After all, he did marry *her.* Overturn his latest version of the will, and you stand to win a great deal."

In William's experience, any time someone claimed to speak perfectly plainly, his words were rarely plain and never perfect. First, Adam Sherrod had been merely despicable, and not mad. Even setting aside this tiny detail of reality, the solicitor's suggestion felt as oily as his hair. It took William a moment to pinpoint why he was uneasy.

"You're his solicitor," he accused. "You're the trustee of the estate, are you not? This advice of yours cannot be in the estate's interest. Why are you giving it?"

The man licked his lips. "Mr. White. Must you ask? I don't like to see an upstanding young man deprived of what ought rightfully to be his. It doesn't sit well with my conscience."

The solicitor bounced on his toes and lifted his chin, unburdened by anything so heavy as a sense of right and wrong. William kept silent, staring at the man. The man rubbed the back of his neck uneasily. He shifted from foot to foot.

That dance of guilt was all too familiar to William. He'd felt that itch. The knowledge that he'd made an irretrievable error had nestled deep in his stomach all day. He'd *known* what he'd done to Lavinia had been wrong as he was doing it. He'd done it anyway.

"At what point in your legal apprenticeship did you acquire a conscience, then? And when did you first betray it?"

"Well. It's not so much a betrayal as…as a renegotiation, if you will. If you must know the truth, if you could tie up the estate in Chancery, the fees to the trustee from administration of her estate would be substantial. It's a profitable plan for us both. I'll protest, naturally, for form's sake. And you—you'll be able to strike an open blow at the man who had you put out on the streets when you were fourteen. You could have him declared mad, and destroy his reputation."

Greasy though the man was, he knew how to tempt William. There would be a delightful symmetry in ruining Mr. Sherrod's legacy just as William's father's had been ruined.

"And then what?" William demanded.

"Well, after a short, insignificant delay in the courts of Chancery—really nothing to speak of—you'll get his five thousand pounds."

"A short, insignificant delay," William said drily. "Naturally. Chancery being known for its alacrity. And you must mean, five thousand pounds minus the tiny fees for estate administration that would accrue over that infinitesimal delay."

The solicitor bowed. "Precisely so."

It would hardly be so smooth. The process might take years. Still, the money called out to him. Five thousand pounds. Five thousand pounds in the safe four-percent funds translated into a good two hundred a year.

As if sensing William's temptation, the solicitor continued. "Think on the money. You could buy your own home. You would not need to labor like a common man. You could buy yourself a new coat."

The solicitor reached out and flicked William's sleeve, where the fabric had become shiny with age. William recoiled.

"Mr. White, you would need never feel cold again."

The man misunderstood the nature of temptation. It wasn't himself he clothed in new finery. Instead, his breath caught, thinking what he could give Lavinia. She could have any dress she wanted. Every last penny she deserved. He could fashion himself into a gentleman. He could become a man she would respect, instead of one she gifted with her virginity out of pity.

He need never feel cold again.

But then, there was a catch. There was always a catch, and this one stuck in his skin like some barbed thing. He'd have to enter into a collusion with this unnatural creature. He would have to lie to the court. He'd have to cheat Adam Sherrod's widow—his *innocent* widow—and dispossess her of funds that she deserved.

What did a little thing like his honor signify? He'd toss his own grandmother to hellhounds if it meant he could have Lavinia.

He'd won a reprieve from the marquess. Now he'd gotten this offer. A little oil, a little grease. What was a little extra dishonor, atop the mountain he'd already constructed for himself?

The solicitor jogged William's shoulder. "Don't take too long. It took me weeks to track you down. The time for filing an appeal is disappearing. Stop by my office tomorrow morning to go over the details."

William opened his mouth to say he'd do it. The words filled his mouth, bitter as rancid lard, but they would not come out. *I'll do it,* he thought. *I'll do it.*

He conjured up the thought of Lavinia—but he could not imagine how she would forgive him, promise of money or no. And with the money…if he agreed to this scheme, he'd not be able to wash the stench of this bug of a solicitor from his skin. How could he beg for her absolution if he could not even face himself?

How could he have her at all, if he did not accept this desperate possibility?

What he finally said was, "Tomorrow. I'll decide tomorrow."

THE LIBRARY BUSTLED with customers that Monday evening—six of them, to be precise—and they kept

Lavinia very busy indeed, as none were willing to browse on his own. She was reaching up, up for the newest set of Byron's poetry when she heard the shop door open behind her.

A blast of cold air greeted this newest arrival. Yet it was not the temperature that had Lavinia's skin breaking out in gooseflesh. Without looking, she knew it was *him*. She froze, hand above her head. Her heart raced. But she could not react, not in this room, not with all these people here. And so she retrieved the leatherbound volume and handed it to Mr. Adrian Bellows before she allowed herself to turn.

Mr. William Q. White was as tall and taciturn as ever. This time, though, *he* caught her glance and ducked his head, coloring.

Oh, how the tables had turned. Two days ago she'd been the one to blush and turn away. Two days ago *she* had wondered, in her own giddy and foolish way, what he thought of her.

But then yesterday they'd come together, skin against skin. He'd had her; she'd had him.

Today the question on her mind was: What did *she* think of *him?*

It was not a query with an easy answer. He dawdled until the others trickled out, one by one. Even then he did not approach her. Instead, he studied a shelf of Greco-Roman histories so intently, she wondered if their spines contained the secrets of the universe. When she walked toward him, he turned his back to her. He bent, ever so slightly, as if he carried a great weight in his jacket.

Lavinia supposed he did.

"I am sorry," he said, still faced away from her. "I ought not to have come. If my presence distresses you, say so and I shall leave at once."

"I am not easily distressed." She kept her voice calm and even.

He turned toward her and looked in her face, as if to ascertain for himself whether she was telling the truth. "Are you well?" His voice was low, lilting in that accent that he had. "I could not sleep, thinking of what I had done to you."

She had not slept, either, reliving what he had done, touching herself where he had touched. But the expression on his face suggested that his evening had not been spent nearly so pleasurably.

"I am very well," she said. And then, because he looked away, his eyes tightening in obvious distress, she added, "Thank you for asking."

Politeness didn't seem enough after what had passed between them, but she was unsure of the etiquette for this occasion.

"Miss Spencer, I know I can never hope for forgiveness. I dishonored you—"

"Strange," Lavinia interjected, "that I do not feel dishonored."

He frowned as if puzzled, and then started again. "I ruined you—"

"Ruined me for what? I am still capable of working in this shop, as you see. I do not believe I shall turn toward prostitution as a result of one afternoon's pleasure. And as for marriage—William, do you truly think that any man worth having would put me aside for one indiscretion?"

"Put you aside?" His gaze skittered down her breasts to her waist, and then traveled slowly up. "No. He would take you any way he could have you."

She was not one bit sorry that she'd given herself to this man, however foolish and impulsive the gift had been.

"As I see it," Lavinia said carefully, "you are feeling guilty because you attempted to coerce me into your bed. Then, believing I was forced, you took me anyway."

He flinched, looking away again. "Yes. And for that, I ought to be—"

"I was not forced, and so you did not dishonor me."

"But—"

"But," Lavinia said, holding up one finger, "you believed I was, and thus you dishonored yourself."

His expression froze. His eyes shut and he put his hand over his face. A shaky breath whispered through his fingers. "Ah." It was not a sound of understanding or agreement, but one of despair. "You are very astute."

There was nothing to say beyond that, but he looked so unbearably alone that she reached out and placed her hand atop his.

He shut his eyes. "Don't." His hand bunched into a fist underneath hers, but he did not pull away. Apparently, "don't" was William Q. White for "keep touching me." Lavinia pressed her hand against the heat of his knuckles.

"Tell me," he said presently, "the other evening when you told the young Mr. Spencer that you had a plan, why did you not tell him immediately he could not be held accountable?"

It took Lavinia a few seconds to remember what he was talking about—the moment when James had first presented her with his idiocy.

"Why would I have told him? I would have taken care of it. He didn't need to know any details. It was simply a matter of deciding upon an approach."

"You would have done everything yourself? Without assistance?"

Since her mother had died this year past, Lavinia had assisted everyone else. She had assisted in the library, until her father's illness destroyed all pretense that she was a mere assistant. She had assisted with housekeeping; she had assisted her younger brother in his lessons, and bailed him out of the sort of scrapes that younger brothers occasionally got into. She had never begrudged them the time she spent; she did it because she loved her family.

She wasn't sure she knew how to let someone help her instead.

She tightened her hand about his, letting his warmth seep into her. "Of course I'd have done it alone."

"Tell me." His voice dropped even lower, and she leaned in to listen. "If I had offered that evening—would you have let me assist you?"

She looked up into his eyes. He watched her with that expression in his eyes—desire, she realized, and dark despair that ran so deeply, it was almost outside detection. He wasn't asking out of an idle desire to know.

"But you didn't. You didn't offer."

He shut his eyes.

And then the door burst open, and William snatched his fingers from hers. She pulled her hands away and tucked them behind her back with alacrity and jumped away.

James darted through the entry, his face a picture of excitement. But even he was sufficiently observant to see she'd sprung from William like a guilty child. It was easy to think of him as her younger brother, as a child. But when he looked from Lavinia to William, his lips thinning, she realized he was not as young as he'd once been.

"We're closed," he said, in a chilly tone of voice. "And you—whoever you are—you're leaving."

Before Lavinia could protest, William had pulled away and was walking out the door.

James looked her over, his gaze resting first on her flushed cheeks and then on the telltale way she put her hands behind her back. Then he cast a glance of pure scorn at William's back. "I'm leaving, too," he announced, and he followed William out the door, into the cold.

CHAPTER FOUR

LAVINIA'S BROTHER, William thought wryly, was a thin spike of a boy. Attach a sufficient quantity of straw to his head, and he'd have made a passable broom. In polite society, he might have served as a chaperone, a place-holder designed to do little more than observe. But James Spencer, this pale wraith of a child, apparently believed he could *protect* his sister from someone who threatened her virtue. He had been alarmingly misled. Standing outside Spencer's on the freezing pavement, James folded his arms—a posture that only emphasized the sharp skin-and-bone of his shoulders.

There was a saying, William supposed, about guarding the cows after the wolves had already come a-ravening. The adage seemed rather inappropriate as cows could only be eaten once. He'd promised himself he'd not importune her again, but one touch of her hand and he'd been ready to go a-ravening all over again.

James tapped his toe, frowning. "Did you kiss her?"

Oh, the barren and virtuous imagination of callow youth.

"Yes," William said. It was easier than resorting to explanation.

James peered dubiously at William, as if trying to ascertain whether there truly was a patch on his coat. "And what are your prospects?"

"Too dismal to take a wife. Even if I chose to do so, which—at present—I do not."

Lavinia's brother gasped. If the boy thought kissing a woman without wanting to marry her constituted open devilry, God forbid he ever learn what had really transpired.

"If you're not going to marry her," he said, shocked, "then why'd you kiss her?"

William had long suspected it, but now he was certain. Lavinia's younger brother was an idiot.

"Mr. Spencer." William spoke slowly, searching for small words that were nonetheless sharp enough to penetrate her brother's dim cogitation. "Kissing is a pleasant activity. It is considerably more pleasant when the woman one is kissing is more than passably pretty. Your sister happens to be the loveliest lady in all of London. Why do you suppose I kissed her?"

"My sister?"

"You needn't pull such a face. It's not something to admit in polite company, but we're both men here." At least, James would be one day. "You know it's the truth."

"No," James said incredulously, screwing up his eyes. "You want to kiss my *sister?* I never thought—"

"Well, you'd better start thinking about it, you little fool. *Everyone* wants to kiss your sister. And what are you doing to protect her? Nothing."

"I'm protecting her now!"

"You leave her in that shop with nobody to call for if she needs help except your father, who is too ill to respond. You send her out to capture your vowels from known ruffians who live near docks where sailors cavort. Don't tell me you protect your sister. How many times have I found her alone in the library? Do you have any idea what I could have done to her?"

He was angry, William realized. Furious that he'd been allowed to take from her the most precious thing she could give, and angrier still that nobody—least of all Lavinia—was willing to castigate him for it.

"I could have taken a great deal more than a kiss," he said. "Easily."

James's face paled. "You wouldn't. You couldn't."

He had. He *would*. He wanted to do it again.

It felt good to admit what a blackguard he was, even if he was hiding his confession behind safely conditional statements. "Lock the door and anything becomes possible," William said. "I could have had—"

James punched him in the stomach. For a skinny fellow, he struck hard. The blow knocked the wind out of William's lungs and he doubled over. That punch was the first real punishment he'd suffered since he'd had Lavinia. Thank God. He deserved worse.

When he regained his breath and his balance, he

looked up. "Don't tell me you protect your sister. You put everything on her—the burden of caring for your entire family—and give her nothing in exchange. I've seen her. I know what you do."

James stood over him. "If you're such a blackguard, why are you telling me this?"

"Because I'll go to the devil before Lavinia kisses a scoundrel worse than me."

James stopped and cocked his head. In that instant William saw in the boy's posture something of Lavinia— a chance similarity, perhaps, in the way his eyes seemed to penetrate through William's skin. William felt suddenly translucent, as if all of his foolish wants, his wistful longing for Lavinia, were laid out in neat rows for this boy's examination. He didn't want to see those feelings himself. He surely didn't want this child sitting in judgment over affections that could never be.

William shook his head. "No."

Her brother had not said a word, but still William felt he must deny what had gone unspoken. "Don't look at me like that. I can't care for her, you idiot, so you'd better start."

James could not have accrued any substance to his frame in these few minutes. Still, when he lifted his chin, he looked taller. "Don't worry," he said quietly. "I will."

LAVINIA HEARD her brother's footsteps fall heavily on the stairs that led to their living quarters. James had seen her embracing a strange man. Half an hour ago he'd followed William outside. Now he was coming back, and she didn't have answers for any of the questions he might put to her. She didn't want to defend her virtue tonight. Instead she stared at the account books in front of her. Industriousness would ward off any hard questions.

She forced herself to concentrate on the numbers in front of her. *Five plus six plus thirteen made four-and-twenty....*

The door squeaked behind James, and then closed.

Four-and-twenty plus twelve plus seventeen was fifty-three.

He crossed the room and stood behind her. She could hear the quiet rush of a resigned exhalation. Still, Lavinia pretended she couldn't hear him. Yes, that was it. She was so engrossed in the books that she didn't even notice he was breathing down her neck.

Fifty-three and fifteen made sixty-eight.

"Vinny," James said quietly. "I don't think you should always be the one to slave away over these books. Isn't it about time I began to take over?"

No accusations. It would have been easier if she'd been able to lie to him. Lavinia carefully laid her pen down and turned to her brother. His eyes were large, not with accusation, but with the weight of responsibility. She'd wanted to save him from that.

"Oh, James." Lavinia arranged the lapels of his damp coat into some semblance of order. "That's very sweet of you."

"I'm not being sweet. It's necessary. I need to be able to manage without you."

Why? I can do it better.

She caught the words before they came out of her mouth. How many times had James offered to help, in his awkward way? How many times had she refused him? She couldn't even count.

"After all," he continued, his voice slow, "you might marry."

"I'm not getting married." Her denial came too fast; her light tone sounded too forced. He'd *seen* her with William. And even though he hadn't actually caught them kissing, they'd been clasping hands in easy intimacy. How was she supposed to explain to her younger brother she had engaged in such conduct with a man she was not marrying? Best to talk of something else.

But before she could offer up even the most ham-handed change of subject, James let out a slow breath. "Still. Should I not help?"

What had William said about them? Oh God. Had he told James the embarrassing details? Lavinia's hand shook, ever so slightly, where it rested on her brother's coat. "You're right. Maybe I can assign you some task—something small."

He frowned and folded his arms. "I should have thought you would be happy to step down."

Step down? Step down! That would ruin *everything*. Her brother had no notion how to argue with creditors for a favorable repayment schedule; he'd not learned how to account precisely for the location of every volume in the library. If she left the shop to him, he'd lose a ha'penny here, a ha'penny there, until the flow of cash dried up. The library would falter and then fail. Everything she'd worked for would fall to pieces.

James didn't seem aware he'd just proposed complete disaster. He continued on, as if he were a reasonable person. "I think I should be able to handle the work very well. I *am* almost sixteen years of age."

"James." In her ears, her voice sounded flat and emotionless. "I can't step down. There are too many things to remember."

"So you can tell me what to do at first."

"I can't tell you everything! Would you think to save pennies each day, so we might have a Christmas celebration? Would you think to bargain with the apothecary, giving him priority on the new volumes in exchange for a discount on medicines?"

She could see his fine plans crumbling, his desire to do more faltering. He drew his brows down. "Would it be so awful, then, if I made a mistake or two? I just want to do my part."

Lavinia shut the account book in front of her. "If it weren't for your mistakes," she said, her voice shaking, "we'd be having a real celebration on Christmas, just like Mother gave us. It would be as if she were not gone. Now we're having nothing. Why do you suppose I'm staring at the accounts, if not to conjure up the coins you lost?"

His face flushed with embarrassment and anger. "I

said I was sorry already. What more do you want from me? You're not my mother. Stop acting as if you are."

"That's not fair. I'm just trying to make you happy." She wasn't sure when her voice had started to rise, when she had begun to clench her hands.

Her brother shook his head. "You're doing a bang-up job of that, then. So far, all you've managed to do is make me miserable." He stomped away. He couldn't get far; the flat was simply too small. He paused on the edge of his chamber, and then turned. "I despise you," he said. A second later the door to his chamber slammed. The walls rattled.

Lavinia curled her arms around herself. He didn't hate her. He wasn't miserable. He was just…momentarily upset?

"One day," she said softly, "you will understand how idyllic your childhood has been. You have nothing to worry about. That's what I've saved you from."

She clenched her hands around the account book, the leather binding biting into her palms. Then she opened the book carefully and found the spot where she'd left off adding columns.

Fifty-three and fifteen made sixty-six….

EVERY TIME LAVINIA AWOKE that night, tossing and turning in her narrow bed, she remembered her words to William. *You thought you had forced me, and thus you dishonored yourself.* She could call to mind the precise curl of his mouth as he'd realized what he'd done, the exact shape of his hands as he grasped the dimensions of his dishonor.

She had wanted to lessen his hurt, but she'd made it worse.

All you have managed to do is make me miserable. Not William's words, but they seemed to apply all the same.

No, no, no. Lavinia stood and walked to her window. Thick, choking fog filled her vision. It was past midnight, and thus it was now Christmas Eve. But it was not yet near morning. The night fog was so thick it would swallow an entire troupe of players juggling torches. It could easily hide one nineteen-year-old woman who didn't want to be seen. She *would* make William feel better. She had to.

Silently she opened her bedroom door. She crept out into the main room and removed her cloak from its peg. She found her boots with her toe, and then bent to pick them up. Slowly she crept down the not-quite-creaking stairs, and across the lending library. And then she was outside, the fog enshrouding her in its cold embrace.

Lavinia lifted her chin, put on her boots and walked. In the few nights before Christmas, a musicians' company sent men on the streets to play through the darkness of night. There were no players anywhere near her house, of course, but in these quiet hours before dawn, the haunting sound of twin recorders came to her in tiny snatches. The sound wafted through the fog like fairy music. She'd catch a bar, but before the melody resolved itself into a recognizable tune, it slipped away, melting into the fog like the shadow of a Christmas that had not yet come.

As she walked through the engulfing mist, those enchanted notes grew fainter and fainter. By the time she reached Norwich Court, they had disappeared altogether.

When she arrived at his home, she realized she had no key to unlock his door. Surely, his chamber was too distant for him to hear her knock.

A little thing like impossibility had never stopped Lavinia.

She was systematically testing the windows when the creak of a door opening sounded behind her.

"Lavinia?" His voice.

She turned, her stomach churning in anticipation at the sound of her name on his lips. He stood, four feet away from her, his form barely visible through the fog. She jumped down from her uncomfortable perch on the windowsill, and would have run into his arms—but he'd crossed them in a most forbidding manner. Instead, she walked slowly toward him, her heart pounding.

"You must be freezing." His words reeked of disapproval. "Thank God I couldn't sleep again. Thank God you didn't meet anyone on your way over. If you were my—"

She had come close enough that she saw the scowl flit over his face at that. He shut his mouth and turned away, walking into the house.

She followed. "If I were your *wife*," she threw at his retreating back, "I wouldn't need to risk all this fog just to see you on a morning."

He didn't respond. But he left the door open, and she went after him. This time, he had not climbed the stairs to his bedchamber. He was headed down a narrow cramped hall into the back of the house. Lavinia sighed and closed the door behind her.

She was not his wife. She was not even anything to him so clean and uncomplicated as his sweetheart. She was the woman who'd made his life miserable. Still, she followed him down the hall. The narrow passage gave way to a tiny kitchen in the back of the house. Without looking at her, he pulled a chair out from under a narrow, wooden table and placed it directly by the hearth. She sat; he stoked the fire and then placed a kettle on the grate.

For a long while he only stared into the orange ribbons that arched away from the flames. The dancing light painted his profile in glimmering yellow. His lips pressed together. His eyes were hooded. Then he shook his head and stabbed the coals with a poker. Bright sparks flew.

"If you were my wife," he finally said, "this moment would be a luxury—enough coal of a morning to heat the room."

He shook his head, set the poker down and turned away. William moved about the tiny room with the efficiency of a man used to dealing for himself. He set out a pot and cups, and then turned back to her. "If you were my wife, you'd take your bread without butter. You would mend your gloves three, four, five times over, until the material became more darn than fabric. And when the babes came, we'd have to remove from even these tiny and insupportable quarters into a part of London that is even less safe than this address. We'd have no other way to support a family."

"When the babes came?" Those words sent a happy thrill through her.

He turned to contemplate the fire again. "I am not such a fool as to imagine they wouldn't. Lavinia, if you were my wife, the babes would come. And come. And come. I couldn't keep my hands off you. I pray one is not already on the way."

It was not her fog-dampened cloak that left her chilled. He spoke of putting his hands on her as if she were one more bitter sip from a cup that was already starkly devoid of happiness.

"It would be worth it," she said quietly. "The gloves. The bread. It would be worth it to me for the touch of your hands alone."

"Is that why you came here this morning?" He spoke in tones equally low to hers. "Did you come here so that I would touch you?"

Yes. Or she'd come to touch him—to see if she could salvage the moment when he'd thought himself dishonored. He'd said once he had no notion of love. She'd wanted to show him.

"Did you come thinking I would kiss your lips? That I would undo the ties of your cloak and let my hands slide down your skin?"

Her body heard, and it answered. The heat of the fire flickered against her neck; she imagined its warm touch was his hands. She imagined his hands tracing down her cheek; his hands cupping the curve of her bodice and warming her breasts; his hands coaxing her nipples into hard points. She ached in tune with his every word. Her breath grew fast.

He knelt on the floor in front of her, one knee on the ground. With that frozen, almost supercilious expression on his face, his posture seemed a gross parody of a proposal of marriage.

"In the year since I first saw you," he said, "I have imagined your giving yourself to me a thousand times. If these were my wildest dreams, I'd have you now. On that chair. I would spread your legs and nibble my way from your thigh to your sex. I'd slip inside you. And when I'd had my way with you, I would thank the Lord for the bruises on my knees."

As he spoke, her legs parted. Her sex tingled. His breath quickened to match hers. *Do it. Yes, do it.*

He reached out one hand and laid it on her knee. It was the first time he'd touched her all morning, and her whole body thrilled in wicked recognition of his. She leaned forward. For one eternal second, she could taste his breath, hot and masculine, on the tip of her tongue. She stretched to meet him. But before her lips found his, he stood.

"Lavinia." His words sounded like a reproach. "I can't have you in dishonor. I can't have you in poverty. And so I will not be marrying you."

She stared up into his eyes. Those dark mahogany orbs seemed so far away, so implacable. She *had* to fix this. But before she could speak, a hissing, sputtering noise intruded from her left, and he turned away from her.

It was the kettle, boiling with inappropriate merriment over the fire. He found a cloth. For a few minutes, he busied himself with the kettle and teapot, his back to her.

When he finally turned back, he held a cup in his hands.

"Here," he said. "The very nectar of poverty. Five washings of the leaves. I believe the liquid still has some flavor." He handed it to her. "There's no sugar. There's never any sugar."

She took the cup. He pulled his hand away quickly, before she could clasp it against the clay. In her hands, the warm mug radiated heat. Tiny black dots, the dust of broken tea leaves, swirled in the beverage.

"You don't speak like a poor man." She darted a gaze up at him. "You don't *read* like a poor man, either. Malthus. Smith. Craig. *The Annals of Agriculture.*"

He turned away from her to pour his own cup of tea. He did not drink it. "When I was fourteen, my father, a tradesman who aspired to be more, engaged in some rather risky speculation. A friend of his had lured him in. He promised to see me through my schooling, and to settle some significant amount on me should the investment fail."

William lifted the mug to his mouth. But he barely wet his lips with the liquid. "The investment did fail—quite spectacularly. My father shot himself. And his *friend*—" he drew that last word out, a curl to his lip "—thought that a promise made to a man who killed himself was no promise at all. What little property remained was forfeit when he was adjudged a suicide. And so down I went to London, to try and make shift for myself."

"Where did all this take place?"

"Leicester. I still have the edge of their speech on my tongue. I've tried to eradicate it, but…"

He looked down, moving his cup in gentle circles. Perhaps he was trying to read his own tea leaves. More likely, Lavinia thought, he was avoiding her gaze.

"So you see, I am in fact the lowest of the low. I am the son of a suicide. I make a bare eighteen pounds a year. I was once a member of that unfortunate class that your lovely books label the deserving poor. After I had you—after I took to my bed a woman I could not afford to marry—I don't qualify as deserving any longer. Even if I had the coin to take you as my wife, I don't think I'd have the temerity."

Lavinia stood, the better to knock sense into his head.

But already he was setting down his tea, stepping away from her.

"It's getting on toward morning," he said. "I'd best get you home." And then he turned toward the hall and left her.

CHAPTER FIVE

WILLIAM WALKED DOWN the hall. He had made the matter as plain as he dared to her. She'd wanted to argue—he'd seen it in her eyes. Her words could have tied him in knots. And having to watch her deliver those arguments—having to hold his distance from her when every fiber in his being yearned toward her—had been almost impossible. But she had no way to debate straightforward gestures. He hid behind those unarguable motions now. He got his coat. He walked to the door. He opened it, and stood there in silence until she came from the kitchen.

Even then she stopped by his arm and looked up at him. Her blue eyes seemed to see right through to the contents of his soul. So what if she took the measure of that sorry item? After all, he'd set it out for her to see, a tattered standard past the point of all repair.

He walked outside, into the chill of early morning. She followed, her eyes liquid, her skin seeming to light with an incandescent glow against that mass of white fog. He wasn't sure he could bear another fifteen minutes in her presence—but whatever depths he'd plumbed, he had not sunk so far as to send a woman alone into the maw of that dampening mist. Least of all Lavinia.

Outside, Norwich Court was a silent sea of mist. Tendrils of white curled around the gaslight on the corner and combed long, thin fingers through the tangled branches of the trees. Lavinia came up behind him. He could feel the warmth of her body radiating through the fog. She was mere inches away from his embrace. She'd never felt so distant.

"I rather think," she said, "that *I* should be the one to decide if you're deserving."

He hunched his shoulders deeper and drew his coat about him. "I don't wish to speak about this at present."

"Not at present? Very well."

He was surprised—and perhaps a touch disappointed—at the grace with which she accepted his pronouncement. Silence enfolded them. They walked in darkness. William counted to thirty slowly, one number for every two steps, and then she spoke again.

"How about now, then?"

He was staring straight ahead as they walked, the better to ignore her. But there wasn't much to see on an early, foggy morning. A bakery had just come to life, the light from its windows diffusing gold through the mist. As they passed, the smell of the first baking of cinnamon-and-spice bread wafted out.

But the scent of those warm ovens was soon left behind, and there was nothing else he could focus on in the swirling fog. He felt a muscle twitch in his jaw.

"Very well," Lavinia said. "You don't need to say anything."

That muscle twitched, harder.

"I shall supply both halves of the conversation. I'm rather good at that, you know."

He had to admit, her proclamation came as no great surprise.

"Besides," she said slyly, "you're very handsome when you're taciturn."

Oh, he was not going to feel pleased. He was not going to look toward her. But damn it, he was delighted. And his head twisted toward her—until he caught himself and converted the motion into a shake of his head.

"*That* gesture," Lavinia said, "must be William Q. White for 'Dear Lord, she's given me a rabid compliment! Run away before it bites me!'"

He ruthlessly suppressed a traitorous grin.

"I shall imagine," she said, "that what you really meant to say was, 'Thank you, Lavinia.'"

William lifted his chin. He set his jaw and looked ahead.

"And that impassive, stony look," Lavinia continued, "is William Q. White for 'I must not smile, or she'll figure out precisely what I am not saying.' Really, William, is this silence the best you have to offer me on the way home? You've said all there is to say, and you have not one question to put to me?"

They were almost to her home now. William stopped walking and turned to her. He looked into her eyes—a dire mistake, as she smiled at him, and then his blood refused to do anything so sensible as flow demurely through his veins. It thundered instead, insistent and demanding. He wanted to learn the curve of her jaw, every lash on her lids. He wanted to run his hand down her cheek until he'd committed the feel of her skin to memory.

"I do have one question, Miss Spencer."

He should not have spoken. Her eyes lit with such hope. If he'd remained silent, perhaps she'd have realized he had nothing to give her—nothing but his eighteen pounds a year. And even that was subject to the arbitrary and rather capricious whims of Lord Blakely.

But instead, her lips curled upward in anticipation. "Ask. Oh, do ask."

He ought not. He should not dare. But he did.

"Why do you call me William Q. White?"

Her eyes widened. Her mouth opened in discomfited surprise. Clearly, she'd not been imagining anything along those lines. "Oh," she said on an inrush of breath. "I know it's too familiar. You've never actually given me permission. I ought to call you Mr. White. But I thought, perhaps, after—you know—the formality seemed somehow wrong, after we—after we—after we—" She paused, took a deep breath as if for courage, and then said the words aloud. "After we shared a bed."

Good God. She thought he was objecting to the use of his Christian name? "Don't be ridiculous."

"Oh," she said. "I know I sound mad. Completely *mad*. I can't help but be a little mad when you're looking down at me. You make me feel foolish, right to the bottom of my toes."

William ruthlessly suppressed the thrill that ran through him at her words.

"It is not the familiarity I object to," he said slowly. "I am rather more curious as to why you persist in placing a *Q* in the middle."

"Because I don't know what the *Q* stands for. Quincy?"

He must have looked as baffled as he felt, because she forged bravely onward.

"Quackenbush? Quintus? Come, you must tell me."

Finally he managed to put words to his befuddlement. "What *Q?*"

"Your middle initial. What other *Q* would possibly come between William and White?"

He blinked at her in continued bewilderment. "But I don't have a middle initial."

"Yes, you do. When you first applied for a subscription, I asked your name, and you told me, William Q. White. I may be a little giddy, and perhaps I might lose my head when you look at me, but I could not have manufactured such a thing out of whole cloth."

A memory asserted itself. He'd saved two years to make the initial fee for the subscription. When he'd walked into Spencer's library on High Holborn, he'd thought of nothing but books and self-improvement.

And then he'd seen her, lush and lovely and briskly competent. He had suddenly known—he would be reading a great deal more than he had imagined. He'd been quite stupid that day.

Well. He'd never really stopped.

"Ah. I had forgotten. *That* Q." He smiled, faintly, and looked away.

"No, no. You cannot keep silent. You must tell me about the *Q*. I am all ears."

He glanced back at her. "All ears? No. You're a good proportion mouth." The grin he gave her slid so easily onto his face. "When I first applied for a subscription you asked my name. And I said, 'William White.'"

"No, you—"

He held up a hand. "Yes, I did. And *you* didn't even look up at me. You sat there, nib to paper, and you said, 'William White. Is that all?'" He folded his arms and gave her a firm nod.

Now it was her turn to frown in perplexity, as if his explanation were somehow insufficient.

"So you made up a middle initial rather than simply saying yes." Lavinia frowned. "The only thing I gather is that I am not mad. You are."

"Absolutely." His voice was low. "Have you any idea what a declaration of war those words are? You're a lovely woman. You can't just look at a man and ask, 'Is that all?' Any man worth his salt can give only one answer. 'Is that all?' 'No, damn it. There's more. There's *much* more.'"

She laughed with delight. "Mr. William Q. White," she said, wagging a finger, "you sly devil. I've been wanting to know the more ever since."

They were almost to her home, and William could not help but wish he could tease that laughter out of her every day. He held up his hands as if he could ward off their shared happiness.

"But, Lavinia," he said, "there will be no more. I can never make it up to you, this debt that lies between us. You have already given me more than I can repay."

The smile on her face faded into nothingness. "Is that how you see matters between us, then? As some sort of grim commerce, where the transactions are ones of personal worth and desert?"

"I took your virginity," he said baldly. "I took it, believing you had no choice—"

"Oh!" She reared back and kicked him in the leg.

He barely felt it—she'd not been aiming to hurt him—but she hopped briefly on one foot as if her own toes stung with the blow.

"No choice? Even if the promissory note had been real and enforceable, I had a choice. I could have pawned my mother's wedding ring for the funds. I could have let James take his chances with the magistrate and debtor's prison. I could have married another man—I've had offers, you know, from well-to-do gentlemen who wouldn't blink at paying ten pounds in pin money. Do not think me such a poor creature as to be confined so easily without choice. I chose you, and I would choose you again and again and again."

It was sheer torture to hear those words, to look into those blazing eyes and not take her in his arms.

"And, as we are speaking of debts," she said grimly, "what of *my* debt to *you?*"

"What debt?

"Ten pounds. You paid *ten pounds* to save me from having to choose between those unpalatable options. And do not tell me you did it to force me into your bed—because you and I both know that if I had said no, you would never have enforced the note. I am deeply in your debt."

"You're talking nonsense. It's nothing."

"Nothing? Bread with no butter? Tea, persuaded to give up its flavor seven or eight times? Don't tell me ten pounds means nothing to you, William. I know you better than that. Tell me—with all the uses to which you could have put that windfall, did you even hesitate to dedicate it to my service?"

"It certainly doesn't signify," he continued. "Mere money, in comparison with what you've given me."

"So it's nonsense, what I owe you. But what you owe me is a tremendous burden, one that can never be repaid? Love is not about accounting. It's not lines on a ledger. You cannot store up credit and redeem yourself at some later date, not with gifts or deeds or any number of coins, no matter how carefully you bestow them. You repay love with love, William."

She watched him expectantly. All he had to do was move forward, into the space she claimed. His hands would find hers; her lips would naturally lift to his. And she would be his. His partner—but in this game of better or worse, and sickness or health, all he could offer her was poorer and poorer and yet poorer again.

If she'd built an unstable house around the two of them out of romantic notions, it was best to kick it to twigs quickly.

"It's nonsense," he said. "It's nonsense because I don't love you." He forced himself to look in her eyes, to take in the hurt spread across her face. Her pain, her rejection of him, would be his just reward. But better to hurt her once than to drag her into joint misery with him.

But she did not flinch away. Her eyes did not cloud with tears. Instead, she shook her head, very slowly. A shiver ran down William's spine. She stretched up on tiptoes and set her hands on his forearms. Her warm mouth pursed a finger's breadth from his. It would take her only an instant to place those soft lips against his. And if she did—if she kissed him now—she'd recognize his words for the obvious lies they were.

"William," she said softly. Her breath was the sweetest cinnamon against his lips. "Do you think me such a goose as to believe your idiotic assertions, after all this?"

"Oh?" The word was all he could manage—one syllable, trying to breathe a world of distance between them.

"Oh," she said with great finality. "You are hopelessly in love with me."

He'd tried to run. He'd tried to keep himself from that realization. But she pronounced sentence upon him as a matter of fact, as if she were reading the price of cotton from the morning paper. And she was right. He could not admit it, not aloud. Instead, he leaned down and rested his forehead against hers in tacit acknowledgment. *Yes. I am hopelessly in love with you.*

It didn't change anything.

She stepped back and let go of his arms. He felt her departure like a palpable blow to his gut.

"As it turns out," she said quietly, "I haven't any use for hopelessness."

He couldn't have her. Still, her rejection felt as if she'd kicked him not on the leg, but rather higher.

"Lavinia, I dare not—"

"Dare," she said, her voice shaking. "That's a command, William. *Dare.* Hope. If you won't accept my gift, I won't accept yours. And you really, *really,* do not want to know what I shall have to do to come up with ten pounds."

And with that, she turned and walked into her family's circulating library.

EVEN THOUGH IT FELT as if three days had passed, it was still early morning when Lavinia came quietly up the stairs. She came as she'd left, her quilted half boots in her hand. But when she reached the top landing, she discovered she was not alone. James sat, awake and dressed, at the kitchen table. He watched her come into the room, watched as she hung her cloak on a peg and set her footgear on the floor. He didn't ask where she'd been. He did not accuse her of anything. He didn't need to; she accused herself.

She felt adrift. Her gaze skittered across the room and fell on the books where she'd kept the family accounts. How many times had she stared at those figures? How many times had she wanted to make them right, hoped that if they were correct, that everything would be right?

She'd imagined herself saving enough pennies so she could pick out a scarf for James—something soft and warm. She'd wanted to swaddle him up and keep him safe. But she'd held him so tightly he'd never learned to do for himself.

Instead of giving him safety, she'd handed him powerlessness. Instead of gifting him with stability, she'd robbed him of the capacity to survive in rough seas. She'd smothered him with competent, loving efficiency.

Lavinia swallowed a lump in her throat and walked across the room, away from James. She'd left the account books open on the desk last night. Careful entries on the page looked up at her. Hadn't she just said it?

Love is not lines on a ledger. You repay love with love.

She shut the books gently and placed the smaller atop the larger. Even now, it bothered her that the two ledgers were of slightly different sizes, and so could not be aligned properly. She gathered them in her arms, uneven though the stack was, and walked across the room to where James sat.

He didn't say anything. She sat down next to him and placed the heavy volumes on the table.

Still he didn't open his mouth.

Finally, Lavinia let go of the doubts bedeviling her heart and pushed the books across the table toward him. "Here," she said abruptly.

It turned out, her brother was not the only one who spoke a foreign tongue. A stranger off the street might have thought she was giving her brother so much bound paper. But she knew without even asking that James had understood precisely what she'd just said.

I was wrong. You were right. I'm sorry. I trust you.

She'd once heard a Scotsman boast that up north, they had a hundred words for rain. Mizzle clung to coats in wet, foggy mists; rain dribbled down. On dismal, dreich days water fell in plowtery showers. When liquid falling from the sky was all the weather you had, you manufactured a lot of words to capture its nuance.

Maybe there was no language of Younger Brother or Older Sister. There was only a language of families, a tongue woven from a lifetime of shared experiences. Its vocabulary consisted of gestures and curt sentences, incomprehensible to all outsiders. Inside, it wasn't difficult to translate at all.

I love you.

James didn't say a word in response. Instead, he put his arm around her and pulled her close. She ruffled his hair. A hundred awkward and unwieldy words, all coming down to the same thing after all: *I love you.*

WILLIAM HAD THOUGHT he'd made up his mind to refuse Mr. Sherrod's solicitor. But Lavinia had dared him to hope. If she was willing to forgive a black stain on his honor, ought he not be prepared to swallow a little oiliness in exchange?

He'd met the man at first light, early on Christmas Eve. They'd had an appointment in a dingy upstairs office, just off Fleet Street. The solicitor had dressed for their morning appointment with sartorial stupidity. He wore a ghastly waistcoat of red-striped purple—or was it purple-striped red?—paired with a jacket and trousers in a cheap, shiny blue fabric. An ostentatious gold-headed cane leaned against his chair.

"Right," the solicitor said, shuffling a pile of papers on his desk. His tone was all brisk business. "I assume we've come to an understanding, then. You'll file for relief in Chancery, contesting Mr. Sherrod's will on the grounds of insanity. I will protest, saying that the foibles of his mind were precisely what one might expect in a man of his age."

"And then I'll get the money?" Two weeks ago, five

thousand pounds might have meant surcease from drudgery, an escape from his cold world. It would have meant hot fires and fresh meat and large, comfortable rooms. Today, he could think of only one thing he wanted. Five thousand pounds meant Lavinia. It meant he could ask her to marry him, selfish idiot that he was. He could lift his eyes to her face. He could offer her everything she deserved—riches and wealth, without any hint of privation. She would have everything of the best.

No. Not everything. The man that came with it would not be up to her standards.

"Well," the solicitor hedged, "you might not get the money *immediately.* You might have to wait until after Chancery has sorted matters out, after it has conducted a hearing or…or two on the matter. But surely then, you'll have his fortune."

She would want him to grasp at any chance for her. Wouldn't she? Wouldn't she want a man who was able to hope?

William swallowed the bitter taste in his mouth. "What would I have to tell the courts?"

"Simple. Tell them Mr. Sherrod was mad. Manufacture stories, explaining that he saw things that were not present, that he spoke to pixies. Find folk who would attest to such tales. It would be a simple matter, if you paid—ahem, I mean, if you found enough of them."

"You expect me to lie, then."

"Goodness. I would never suborn perjury. I want

you to tell the truth." This supercilious speech was
somewhat weakened by a wink. "The truth, and nothing
but the truth. A hint of embroidery, though, would not
be amiss. Think of a court case like a woman's frock—
you hide the parts of the figure that are not so flatter-
ing, and frame the bosom so that everyone can look at
the enticing bits." The solicitor made a gesture in the
direction of his own chest. "Just enough embellishment
to convince the court of your claim, hmm?"

No matter what this greasy lawyer told him,
William was fairly certain he had nothing but a tiny
chance at success. He might not find people to testify.
The court might not believe them. Sherrod's widow
would undoubtedly claim otherwise. Still, a tiny
chance was a chance nonetheless.

Was this hope that he felt, this grim determination
to see the task through? Was it hope that wrapped
around his throat, choking him like a noose? Was that
morass, sinking like a stone in his stomach as he gritted
his teeth and prepared to do business with this oily
man, what he needed to accept?

Yes.

He opened his mouth to give his assent.

But as he did, he heard that voice again.

You don't have to do this.

The voice was wrong. He did have to do this. Today,
when he went in to work, he might lose everything. He
might have no position, and Lavinia could be pregnant.
He *had* to accept any chance, no matter how small, that
could help.

No, you don't. You don't have to do this.

This time, he recognized the words for what they were. They didn't come from some outside agency. He was the speaker. Even if he denied it—even as he betrayed himself—he'd always retained some semblance of his honor. It had not disappeared. It had simply been here, waiting for him to follow.

For so long, he'd simply believed he had sunk so low in society that he did not dare to lift his face. Oh, yes, he'd dishonored himself. But he couldn't find honor by seeking forgiveness. He could not wait for Lavinia or anyone else to absolve him of his sins.

If William ever hoped to have some measure of honor, he had to be an honorable man.

The solicitor must have seen his hesitation.

"Think," he said, "on the *revenge* you could take on the man who destroyed your father."

He'd dwelled on that dark thought for a decade. But how could he expect forgiveness for his own sins, if he could not grant absolution to the man who'd wronged him?

He would have to give up any chance at those five thousand pounds. That meant he would give up any chance at having Lavinia—but then, when Lavinia had told him to hope, she hadn't meant that he should hope for her.

She'd wanted him to hope for himself.

"No," he said. It felt good in every way to know that he could choose to be honorable, even knowing the cost.

Confusion lit the solicitor's face. "No? What could you possibly mean by no?"

"No, I won't embellish the truth past recognition. No, I won't tell lies. No, I won't seek revenge to keep you in Chancery fees. I'm not that kind of man." He had been, once, but he was no longer.

"Who will ever know that you lied?"

William shrugged. "Me?"

"You?" The solicitor laughed in scorn. "Well, trust in yourself, then. You'll not deliver yourself from poverty."

William stood. He'd thought his soul had depreciated until it was worth less than nothing. Strange he'd not realized: it always had precisely the value he chose to give it.

As he left, the man called out after him. "I hope you take great pleasure in yourself. Likely it's all you'll ever have."

The words no longer sounded like the curse they once would have been.

ON CHRISTMAS EVE MORNING, Lavinia shared the responsibility of running the shop with her brother. The two of them, even in that small downstairs room, should not have made the room feel so close. Yes, there were nearly fifteen hundred volumes packed into a tiny space. The shelves stretched head height and above. But Lavinia had never found the two tiny rooms confining before, not even with a surfeit of customers. But today the books seemed to tower over her, choking her with memories.

She would look up from her desk and remember the first time she'd seen William, standing so ill at ease in front of her, asking for a subscription. She would place a volume back on the shelf and remember the sight of him in that very spot, searching for a title. He would run his finger carefully down a leather binding. In those days, she'd envied the books. But now, he'd touched her with greater reverence.

He'd not been able to hide the meaning of those gestures. Over and over, he'd told her he loved her. He loved her, and so he made her wretchedly watered-down tea. He loved her and he longed to touch her, but instead he warned her she'd have no butter with her bread. He loved her.

And yet she'd brought him hopelessness rather than happiness. Together, they'd managed to share a fine portion of guilt. She might gladly have suffered deprivation for him, but he was not the kind of man who could watch the woman he loved be deprived.

Over at the small table near the door, Lavinia watched as James entered a book loan in the ledger. He slipped two pennies in the cash box and then wrapped a book and waved farewell to Mr. Bellow. As he recorded the transaction, he avoided her gaze. She came up to the table anyway, approaching it from the front, as if she were a customer instead of a fellow laborer. Still, he winced.

"I did it exactly as you instructed," he whispered. "Did I do it wrong? Oh God, I did it so completely backward you can tell it's wrong without even reading what I've entered." He put his head in his hands.

"You're doing very well." She resisted the urge to turn the book upside down to check. "Perfect, even." No, she was not going to even glance down. "You're doing so well, in fact, that I am going upstairs to rest."

He lifted his face. His eyes shone in pleasure. "I'll take care of everything." Then he paused. "But perhaps an hour or two before we close up the shop, would you be willing to take over again? There is one thing I should like to take care of this evening."

She patted her brother's hand. "Of course," she said with a smile.

She headed upstairs. She would not have minded deprivation for herself. But William… If her gloves had holes, William's hands would freeze in sympathy. If she ate brown, unbuttered bread, the bitter taste would linger on his palate.

She'd given him hopelessness. She'd made him miserable. If she truly loved him, perhaps she needed to let him go.

CHAPTER SIX

TWENTY-FOUR HOURS EARLIER, William had cowered in the office where he worked, for fear of losing his position. Today when he walked in, he felt not even a hint of disquietude.

Why had he been so afraid? He was young. He was competent. And even if he were turned off, he would find something else. Losing a position where he was regularly treated like the grimiest gutter refuse was not something to fear. It was something to celebrate.

When the door to the office opened just after nine and in walked Lord Blakely followed by his glowering grandson, William felt triumph.

When he was let go, it would be a financial setback. It might take weeks to find work again; his wages might even be reduced. He ought to have been terrified. But this was not a punishment, to be allowed to walk out of this dark and dismal place. It was an opportunity.

The two lords stepped into the back office. After a few minutes Mr. Dunning walked up to William and whispered that he'd been asked to enter the room. They were unlikely to be inviting him to a picnic lunch. Just before he stood, Mr. Dunning laid his hand on William's shoulder—an empty gesture of pointless support.

William smiled and stood, calm. *Let them sack me. Please.*

He'd expected the back office to appear precisely as he'd left it yesterday.

But when he arrived, there had been one tiny alteration. Lord Blakely still peered at him from beneath white, bushy eyebrows, examining him as if he were some strange insect. But the marquess had not seated himself in his throne behind the desk. Instead, he'd ensconced his grandson in the position of power. Lord Wyndleton sat, ill at ease. He smoldered with a repressed anger so fierce that William thought he would leave scorch marks where he tapped his fingers against the desk.

Three account books, a small portion of the work William had done over his years of employment, made a small pile on the edge of the desk.

The old marquess picked up one negligently and thumbed through the pages. "Sometime between the months of January and—" a pause, and a last glance at the end of the third book "—April, Bill Blight here made a mistake."

William did not mind being stripped of his position and his wages. He no longer fancied losing his dignity alongside. "My lord, my name is William White."

Naturally, Lord Blakely took no notice of the interjection. "Bill Blight made an error. Find it and then sack him. When you can lay the mistake before me, I shall allow you to leave."

Lord Wyndleton sighed heavily, but reached for a book. He opened it and stared intently at the first page. His grandfather watched, silent, for a few minutes as the young lord scanned the entries. Finally he shook his head and walked out, leaving the two younger men together. William heard the front door to the building rattle shut; shortly after, the jingle of his carriage sounded.

As soon as they were alone, the young lord looked up. "Did you make a mistake between the months of January and April?"

William rolled his eyes. "Yes."

"Well, tell me what it was. I haven't got all day."

"I don't know. Between the months of January and April, I must have accounted for upward of four thousand transactions. Of course there was a mistake somewhere in the lot—it's impossible not to make one. If your grandfather were even halfway rational, he wouldn't sack his employees for minor imperfections."

William had thought the insult to the marquess would be enough to have him sent on his way.

"Hmm," Lord Wyndleton said. "Four thousand transactions." He glanced up at William, and then shook his head as if it were somehow William's fault he'd been so efficient. "What a bloody nuisance."

With that, the man turned his head down to the

books. Minutes passed. His eyes moved slowly down column after column. He turned one page, then another. At the turn of the tenth page, William sighed and sat down without permission.

The old marquess might have turned him off for that offense in an instant, too; his grandson didn't even appear to notice.

At the twentieth page, William began to wish he hadn't been so meticulous in his accounting. If he'd missed a shilling on the first page, at least he would have been able to leave.

At the twenty-sixth page, Lord Wyndleton sighed loudly. "I bloody hate this," he muttered.

How sweet. They had something in common. It was time to escalate his plan to get sacked.

William was already bored. And he had nothing to lose. "I hear you are interested in scientific pursuit."

Lord Wyndleton's eyes moved only to glance down the page of numbers in front of him. He turned his hand over. It might have been an unconscious gesture. It might have been the barest acknowledgment of William's uttered words.

William decided to take it as acknowledgment. "Well, then. I should think you'd enjoy numbers."

Lord Wyndleton shrugged but still did not look up. He flipped to the front of the book, then back to page twenty-six. For a long while William thought the man was going to ignore him.

But the viscount finally spoke without lifting his

eyes from the page. "I do like numbers. I like numbers when they are attached to little *t* and double-dot-*x*. Maybe a calculation of probability." He spoke in swift, clipped tones, his voice unemotional and unvarying. "I dislike arithmetic. Finance bores me. It has no rules to discover. Just opportunity for error."

"Ah," William said. "You prefer calculus?"

Lord Wyndleton sighed and turned to page twenty-seven. Then he looked up—although he didn't look directly at William. Instead, he leaned his head back and fixed his gaze on the ceiling. "Let me tell you what I *dislike*. I dislike servants who make obscure mistakes, forcing me to spend Christmas Eve morn studying dusty accounting tomes. My dislike accelerates when said servant attempts to distract me from my duty by yammering on. That means, *Bill,* I dislike you."

"That," said William, "makes us a pair. I despise men who let their vast fortunes go to waste. You're so helpless, you can't even get thirty miles on a Christmas Eve. You're spending your morning glowering at books instead of going to Tattersall's and purchasing a very swift horse."

"If my grandfather did not control my fortune, I would have done precisely that."

The viscount was angry. He was, also, William realized, entirely serious.

William stared at him for a few moments, his own pique dissipating. "You really don't like finance," he finally said. "Your grandfather doesn't control your fortune."

"Ha." Lord Wyndleton undoubtedly intended that single syllable to be a dismissal.

"It wasn't I who made the mistake. It was the marquess."

"Do be quiet."

"He ought never have left you alone with me."

Lord Wyndleton slammed his pen down. "Oh, Lord almighty," he muttered to the desktop. "What are you going to do to me? Annoy me to death?"

"You see," William continued, "I've recorded the accounting for your trust every month since I started here. Those funds became yours, free and clear, upon your majority."

Viscount Wyndleton cocked his head and turned it. It was a gesture reminiscent of his grandfather—and yet on him, it seemed attentive rather than predatory. His eyes were steady and almost golden-brown. For a few seconds he stared at William, his lips parted.

William knew precisely what that look meant. He was entertaining hopes. Then he let out a breath and shook his head. "No. When the trust was established, the money would have become mine on my majority. But six years ago I came to an agreement with my grandfather. I signed over control of my funds after my majority. In exchange he let me—well, never mind that. Your information is wrong."

He paused, tapping his pen against his wrist. "Next time, if you have something to say, come out and say it. I don't hold with talking in such a roundabout fashion, as if you're a cat circling your prey. Pounce already and be done with it."

For a second William thought the young lord intended to leave his words at a rebuke. But then Lord Wyndleton looked up again. "But thank you," he said. "It was well-meant."

So the grandson was not the grandfather, however alike they might have seemed at first. What had started as resentment on William's part had turned into something—something more. He wasn't sure what it was yet.

William stood. "I've seen the statements. I've recorded the accounts. I know every detail, and they're in your own name."

"Couldn't be. There must be some legal nicety you're missing. Blakely is too meticulous. I signed a contract, and I have no doubt the matter it covered was executed immediately. *He* wouldn't miss the opportunity to keep me under his thumb."

"This contract—you signed it six years ago?" The hackles on William's neck rose. His calm dissipated. A great and sudden weight tensed on his shoulders. "You're two-and-twenty now?"

Lord Wyndleton waved his hand and turned back to the books, dismissing William. "This isn't getting me any closer to my mother's home."

William strode forward and slapped his hand over the page Lord Wyndleton was reading. "I'm pouncing. The agreement wasn't executed because it couldn't have been. Legally you were an infant. The contract was a nullity. It's the rankest abuse of power for your guardian to have required you to give away what was rightfully yours in exchange for…for something else that is rightfully yours."

Lord Wyndleton let out his breath, slowly. "Are you sure?"

"I can prove it," William said. "Tell them you need to verify my figures against another set of books. They won't deny you."

A curt nod, and William left the room. Forty-five minutes later, with the books spread out in front of him, Lord Wyndleton believed. He looked up.

"Aren't you some kind of lowly clerk or some such? How do you know arcane details about the legalities of contracts?"

William smiled faintly. *I made love to a beautiful woman* hardly seemed to be an answer that would keep him in his lordship's good graces. "I read," he finally said. It was true. Just not the whole truth. "I've been training myself to take over an estate."

"Expectations?"

"No, my lord. None. Just…" William nodded once. "Just hopes, really."

Lord Wyndleton drummed his fingers against the desk. "If I had my way," he said quietly, "I'd leave England entirely. I've wanted to explore the Americas—but lacking funds, of course, it's never been an option. It is now. But I need someone here. He would have to be someone who could be trusted to make sure my funds arrived wherever I had need of them. Someone who could not be suborned by my grandfather. Someone competent and efficient—perhaps even someone who likes finance—even if he does make the occasional mistake sometime between the months of January and April. Now—" Lord Wyndleton leaned back and looked at the ceiling "—if only I knew someone like that."

The viscount was curt, rude and demanding. But he was not a tyrant like his grandfather. And he was fundamentally fair in a way that the marquess had not been. William shrugged. "And here I thought you didn't like roundaboutation."

"Well," Lord Wyndleton said, "are you in need of a position?"

"As it happens, yes. Although I regret to inform you, my previous employer is not likely to speak highly of my character, as I helped his grandson uncover the secret of his financial independence. It was a shocking lapse of judgment on my part."

Lord Wyndleton pursed his lips and nodded. "A shocking lapse. Can I trust you, Mr. White?"

"Of course you can," William said, holding his breath. "You're going to pay me seventy-five pounds a year."

The viscount leaned back in his chair. "I am?"

William had chosen the salary to be deliberately, obscenely high. He'd had no doubts his lordship would argue him down to a reasonable thirty—perhaps forty—pounds. Forty pounds. On forty pounds, a man might rent decent quarters for himself and a wife. He might have children without worrying about whether he could provide for them. Forty pounds a year meant Lavinia. He was about to open his mouth to lower his demand when the young lord spoke again.

"Seventy-five pounds a year." Lord Wyndleton sounded distinctly amused. "Is that supposed to be a lot of money?"

"You're joking. God, yes."

His lordship waved a hand negligently. "My mother and sister live in Aldershot. If you are good enough to get me out of London before my grandfather notices," he said quietly, "I'll treble that."

He stood as William stared after him in shock.

"Come along," he said. "I believe you have your resignation to tender."

BY TWO IN THE AFTERNOON, William and his new employer had barred the old marquess from his grandson's personal finances. The viscount's first purchase had been a coach and four. They'd obtained money for changes, and his new employer had been on his way. William went to Spencer's circulating library.

He made it there by three. The building was lit with a dim glow; the door, when he tried it, was unlocked. Good. She hadn't yet closed the shop for Christmas Eve.

He opened the door. She was sitting at her stool again, winding a strand of hair through her fingers. Up. Down. Soon those would be his fingers there, stroking her hair. Rubbing her cheek. There was a thread of melancholy to her movements.

She glanced up and saw him, but her face did not light. Instead, it shuttered in on itself. Lavinia, the woman who smiled at everyone who entered her shop, pressed her lips together and looked away. It was not the best of beginnings.

William advanced on her.

She spoke first. "I have a Christmas gift for you." Still she kept her eyes on the desk in front of her. Her hands lay on the table—pressed flat against that solid surface, not relaxed and curved. Her fingertips were white.

"I don't want a gift, Lavinia."

Still she didn't look at him. Instead she pulled open a drawer—the quiet protest of wood against wood sounded—and she rummaged inside. When she found whatever it was she was looking for, she lobbed it in his direction. As she still hadn't looked at him, her aim was poor. He stretched to catch what she'd thrown. It was a pouch barely the size of his hand. The container was light. It might well have been empty.

"I told you," she said quietly, her eyes still on her hands. "I told you, you wouldn't want to know what I would have to do to pay back your ten pounds." Her voice was small.

His heart stopped. "I don't want ten pounds from you."

Finally she lifted her chin to look in his eyes. "I know," she whispered. "But I want you to have it."

There was the faintest tinge of red at the corner of her eyes. His hand contracted around the fabric. She'd had options. But William's original ten pounds had disappeared. That left... No. She couldn't have agreed to marry another man. She wouldn't have.

Would she? She sat, pale and stricken. She looked miserable.

"Don't do it, Lavinia," he warned. "Choose me. I came here to tell you—you wanted me to find hope. I've found another position, a better one. I can afford you now."

She jerked back as if she'd been slapped. "You can *afford* me, William? You coerce me to your bed. You lie to me and say you don't love me. And you think I was waiting for you to gather the coin to purchase me?"

William bit his lip. If he'd been a better man—if he'd been worthy of her from the start—if he hadn't coerced her into intercourse, and then hurt her to drive her away from him not once, but *twice*—perhaps he might have had her. He'd as good as told her to give up hope this morning. Now she had.

"I'm sorry," he said simply.

She raised her chin. "I never wanted your apology."

"I know," William said. "It's all I have."

She didn't say anything. Instead, she bit her lip and looked away. Once, he'd tried to steal her choice back from her. He'd not do it a second time. He let out a deep breath.

"Merry Christmas, Lavinia," he whispered.

Somehow he managed to find the door. Somehow he

managed to wrest it open and walk through it with some semblance of grace. He even managed to stumble down the street. Halfway to the crossroads he realized he was still holding that damned bag she'd thrown at him, with its ten bloody pounds. He balled it up in his hand and squeezed in frustration—and stood still.

If he had bothered to think about such a thing, he would have supposed that the sack felt light and deflated because it contained a single bank note, folded into quarters. But instead of the crisp, malleable shape of a paper rectangle he felt a single circle press against his palm.

A circle? There was no such thing as a ten-pound coin. Besides, he realized as he ran his hands over the cloth, coins were not hollow in the middle. And this one was barely the diameter of a sixpence, but three times as thick.

Breath held, he opened the pouch and pulled out the object inside. It was a plain, round circle of gold—a ring too dainty to ever be intended for a man's finger. He stared at it in frozen wonder. She'd had other choices besides marrying another man. *I could have pawned my mother's wedding ring.*

But she hadn't pawned it. She'd given it to him.

LAVINIA WATCHED THE DOOR where William had left.

Her choices were few. Should she humiliate herself and run after him? Should she at least wait a decent amount of time before hunting him down and making him pay in kisses? Or should she kick the desk in frustration and give up on Mr. William Q. White ever figuring out how to express the concept of love without reference to funds?

Lavinia sat down at her desk and put her head in her hands. She didn't dare cry—not now, not when she needed to head upstairs to see her father. It was Christmas Eve and tonight the family needed to laugh. She needed to pretend Christmas had come without mulling wine or roasting goose. What she didn't need to do was cry for the man's sheer perversity.

The bell rang.

The door opened.

Lavinia lifted her head from her hands. Her heart turned over. William stood, framed by the doorway against the dark of the night. Little wisps of snow covered his collar and kissed the brim of his hat. He took off his coat, folding it and setting it on the low table to his right. Then he turned and shut the door. She heard the snick of a key turning in the lock, and she swallowed. He did not say anything, but he drank her in, top to bottom, his eyes running languidly down her form.

"Does that door behind you lock, as well?"

She shook her head.

"Pity." He lifted a chair off the floor and strode past her.

"What are you doing?"

"I'm rearranging your furniture." He tilted the chair at an angle and wedged it under the door handle.

"There. This time we shan't be bothered by intruding little brothers." He turned to her. She was still seated on her stool. Her toes curled in her slippers as he walked forward. He towered before her. Then he bent and picked her up. His arms around her were warm and strong.

The doors were barred, so nobody could save her. For that matter, with the books piled in front of the one tiny window, nobody could see her. Thank God. She melted into his arms.

He straightened. But she had only a few bare seconds of his warm embrace before he set her on the desk. He did not move away from her. Her thighs parted, and he stepped between her legs. She was still looking into his eyes. He rested his forehead against hers, and she shut her eyes.

"I collect," William said, his hand reaching up to cup her cheek, "that you want me to give your ring back."

She opened her mouth to answer, but all that came from her vocal cords was a pointless squeak. Instead she nodded.

"You can't have it." His eyes bored into her. His fingers whispered down the line of her jaw, to rest against her chin. He tipped her head back.

"You can't have it," he repeated, "unless you wear it for me."

She nodded again.

"I also collect," he said, "that when I came in, I should have said something rather more like—"

He leaned forward.

"Like?" she prodded.

His lips touched hers.

He tasted like cinnamon and cloves, like the Christmas she no longer dreaded facing. His lips roamed over hers, tasting, testing. His hands slid from her jaw down to her waist. And she was touching him, his shoulders pulling the hard length of his body against hers. She was catching fire, yearning to consume him. Her hands ran through his silky hair, pulling his head toward hers. But however intimate the touch of his tongue against hers, however insistent the press of his hard erection through the layers of her skirts, his hands remained virtuously clasped on her waist.

He pulled away from her. She'd rearranged his hair into a tangled and adorable mess.

"Well," he murmured, smiling at her.

"Mr. William Q. White," Lavinia said, "I should like to know your intentions."

"I intend to love you as you deserve."

"That is a good start. I should like to be loved more, however."

He leaned in and kissed her again, a sweet touch of his lips, when she wanted heat.

"But you asked for my intentions. You must know I intend to ask your father's permission to call the banns."

Close to him as she was, his hands still on her waist, she felt a subtle tension fill his body, as if he were wary of her response. As if *she* had not asked him to marry her already.

Lavinia clucked and shook her head. That wariness grew, and he pulled away from her ever so subtly. She reached up to touch his cheek. His skin was rough with evening stubble. "Do not tell me you barred the door just so that you could steal a mere kiss. Really, William. Is that all?"

A slow smile spread across his face. His hands pressed against her waist and then slid lower, the heat of his palms burning into her hips.

"Is that all?" he echoed. "No, damn it." His hands inched down to her thighs. "There's more. There's *much* more."

And then his lips fell on hers again. This time, he exercised no restraint. His body pressed hers. His hands pulled her against him. He kissed down her neck; she threw back her head and let his tongue trail fire along her skin. She felt his warm lips trace her collarbone. He breathed heat against the neckline of her dress. And then he was rearranging her bodice, tugging, persuading, until he caught her breast in his mouth.

A sharp swirl of excitement filled her. But his touch didn't satisfy her. Instead, it only whetted her hunger. His other hand was on her ankle now, lifting her legs to one side, pushing her skirts up. His fingers fluttered against her damp sex.

Pleasure twined with want.

She desired—she needed—she *required*. And what she needed she couldn't have said, except more, damn it, more. But he knew. His body was hard against hers.

He fumbled with his breeches—and then he filled her, hard and thick and long.

His hands braced against the desk; her legs wrapped around his waist. And then she could think of nothing but the heat of his skin against hers, the thrust of his body inside hers, his hand on her breast, his lips on her mouth. And then even these thoughts were ripped away from her as she gave herself up to him.

Afterward, her body still throbbing with delicious satiety, his hair slightly damp and spiking from his exertions, he held her close. His breath was warm against her cheek.

"I am," he said in her ear, "completely, utterly and devotedly yours. If you will have me."

She leaned her forehead against his chest. "I suppose I shall." His arms were around her shoulders now, his hands caressing her. She inhaled. He smelled of starch, of salt, and of…of burning cloves?

Lavinia pulled back and sniffed the air in puzzlement. A complex, bitter scent had wound its way into the room. It had just the faintest hint of sulfur to it. But the disturbing smell did not waft from William. Instead, it was coming from upstairs.

Lavinia disentangled herself from his embrace. She jumped off the table and patted her gown into place. Quickly she bounded across the room and yanked the chair from its spot under the door handle. She was running up the stairs, her footfalls heavy, before she could even imagine what was going on.

Her brother stood by the hob, his hands full of heavy cloth. He held a pot that emitted clouds of dark steam.

"Ah," James said with a smile. "Lavinia. I'm mulling wine."

"Wine? Where did you get wine? How did you purchase the spices?" And then, seeing what sat on the table, Lavinia gave a little shriek. "A goose? However did you obtain a goose?"

James shrugged. "I sold mother's pearl pendant. She gave it to me, and I thought…well, I thought she would want us to have this." He shrugged, and then continued brightly. "Besides, what with my making mistakes in the shop, and your getting married, we could use a little extra money now."

Behind her, Lavinia could her William's footsteps as he ascended the stairs.

"How did you know I was getting married? *I* just found out."

James fixed Lavinia with his most serious look. "Next time," he said, "if you are trying to keep secrets, you might consider writing something other than 'Mrs. William Q. White' in the margin of the account books when you test your pen."

She stared at her brother, her cheeks burning in embarrassment. "James—please—he's coming up the stairs now. I haven't done that in almost a year. Don't tell him."

Her brother shook his head in gleeful amusement. William reached the upstairs landing and hesitated, as if not quite sure whether he would be welcomed into the family.

James cast one pointed glance over his shoulder to the desk where the books lay, pages spread open, telltale margin scribbles and all. But instead of teasing Lavinia further, he gestured with the pot he held in his hands. "Did you know," he asked William conversationally, "that wine can *burn?* I hadn't thought it possible, as it's a liquid—but look at this. The pot is completely scorched."

EPILOGUE

London, precisely thirteen years later.

"Mr. White."

William looked up from his desk. He had served Gareth Carhart for many years now. First he'd served the Viscount Wyndleton. But in the past year the man had taken on the mantle of Lord Blakely. And William's duties had been correspondingly increased.

"A year ago," the new marquess said, "you told me you could assist with the management of the marquessate. I allowed you the chance to temporarily prove yourself."

William knew better than to interject his own commentary into the brief pause that followed. Lord Blakely disliked being interrupted, and the thread of the conversation would resume at his leisure.

"You have. Congratulations. You may consider the position, and the salary, permanent."

"Thank you, my lord." It was hardly a surprise. He'd served Lord Blakely well, and curt as the man was, he was always fair.

Another awkward pause ensued. Finally his lordship glanced at a clock. "Well?" The time showed seven past three. "Isn't it past time for you to be on your way tonight?"

In the thirteen years that William had worked for the man, he'd learned to interpret these curious pronouncements. Bad news Lord Blakely announced directly. Good news he cloaked in disdain. Outright gifts—like dismissing his man of business a full three hours early on Christmas Eve—he hid in…roundaboutation.

White stood and reached for his things. "My lord." He walked to the door. On the threshold, he paused. "My lord, if I may—"

"No," interrupted Lord Blakely. "You may not. I've no desire to hear your insincere wishes for the happiness of my Christmas."

White inclined his head. "As you wish. My lord."

Unlike his predecessor, who had descended on the hapless clerks in the Chancery Lane office like a one-man plague of locusts, the current Lord Blakely preferred that William White—his manager, man of business and otherwise facilitator of marquesslike behavior—present his reports in his Mayfair town home. He was harsh, demanding—and eminently fair. It also meant that at the end of the day, William's walk back home—now a tall town house in a respectable part of town—was substantially shortened.

As soon as he opened the door, he smelled cinnamon and citrus wafting in the air, tangled with a hint of bitter wine. But something was missing. It took him a moment to ascertain what was wrong. The house was *quiet*. It was astonishingly quiet.

He found Lavinia, sitting in a chair, twisting a lock of her hair around one finger as she read. *Not* a novel— a finance circular. A shawl, woven through with gold thread, covered her shoulders. For a long minute he watched her read. Her eyes darted intelligently across the page. Her tongue darted out to touch her finger, and she turned a page. She was, he thought, the most beautiful woman he'd ever seen.

She looked up. She did not jump or evince the least surprise that he'd arrived hours before he was expected.

"Let me guess," she said. "You conveyed my invitation to Christmas dinner to the marquess and he sacked you for the effrontery. Ah, well. It doesn't matter." She smiled at him, so he would know she was not serious. "In any event, I made more money last quarter than you, so we shall make do."

Lavinia may have been the only woman in all Christendom to invest the excess from the household accounts in railways. He walked over to stand by her.

"You also spent more money last quarter than I did," he said, laying a hand on the imported silk of her shawl. He took the excuse to stroke her shoulder.

"This? Oh, no. This was quite inexpensive. Now, tell me—am I going to have a marquess appearing at dinner tomorrow?"

"No, thank God. I did intend to ask him—truly I

did—but he stopped me before I dared. It was probably for the best."

"He is the most dreadfully lonely man." She shrugged. "But I suppose it is his choice."

"Speaking of lonely. Or what is far more interesting to me, let us speak of being alone. I notice that something—or rather, some *ones* are missing."

"James has the boys. He shut the shop early today and he's taken them all out to see the Italian players."

That would explain the unearthly quiet.

"Mrs. Evans is in the kitchens. And I've sent the maids to the market. I don't believe anyone will come into the sitting room. Not for hours."

William smiled and extended his hand. "Mrs. White," he said slyly, "I think that your very expensive shawl would look far lovelier and more expensive on this floor."

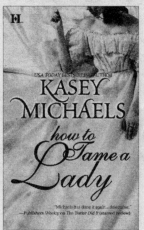

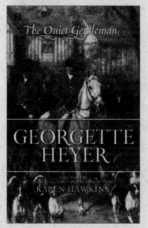

HARLEQUIN® HISTORICAL:
Where love is timeless

The Winter Queen
AMANDA McCABE

Lady-in-waiting to Queen Elizabeth,
Lady Rosamund Ramsay lives at the heart
of glittering court life. Charming Dutch
merchant Anton Gustavson is a great favorite
among the English ladies—but only Rosamund
has captured his interest! Anton knows just
how to woo Rosamund, and it will be a
Christmas season she will never forget....

Available November 2009
wherever books are sold.

REQUEST YOUR FREE BOOKS!

2 FREE NOVELS
FROM THE ROMANCE/SUSPENSE
COLLECTION PLUS 2 FREE GIFTS!

YES! Please send me 2 FREE novels from the Romance/Suspense Collection and my 2 FREE gifts (gifts are worth about $10). After receiving them, if I don't wish to receive any more books, I can return the shipping statement marked "cancel." If I don't cancel, I will receive 4 brand-new novels every month and be billed just $5.74 per book in the U.S. or $6.24 per book in Canada. That's a savings of at least 28% off the cover price. It's quite a bargain! Shipping and handling is just 50¢ per book.* I understand that accepting the 2 free books and gifts places me under no obligation to buy anything. I can always return a shipment and cancel at any time. Even if I never buy another book from the Reader Service, the two free books and gifts are mine to keep forever.

185 MDN EYNQ 385 MDN EYN2

Name	(PLEASE PRINT)	
Address		Apt. #
City	State/Prov.	Zip/Postal Code

Signature (if under 18, a parent or guardian must sign)

Mail to **The Reader Service:**
IN U.S.A.: P.O. Box 1867, Buffalo, NY 14240-1867
IN CANADA: P.O. Box 609, Fort Erie, Ontario L2A 5X3

Not valid to current subscribers of the Romance Collection,
the Suspense Collection or the Romance/Suspense Collection.

Want to try two free books from another line?
Call 1-800-873-8635 or visit www.morefreebooks.com.

* Terms and prices subject to change without notice. Prices do not include applicable taxes. Sales tax applicable in N.Y. Canadian residents will be charged applicable provincial taxes and GST. Offer not valid in Quebec. This offer is limited to one order per household. All orders subject to approval. Credit or debit balances in a customer's account(s) may be offset by any other outstanding balance owed by or to the customer. Please allow 4 to 6 weeks for delivery. Offer available while quantities last.

Your Privacy: Harlequin is committed to protecting your privacy. Our Privacy Policy is available online at www.eHarlequin.com or upon request from the Reader Service. From time to time we make our lists of customers available to reputable third parties who may have a product or service of interest to you. If you would prefer we not share your name and address, please check here. ☐

BOB09

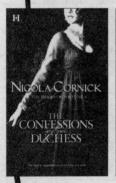